BUT NOT FOR FAME

A CLINT WOLF NOVEL
(BOOK 29)

BY

BJ BOURG

WWW.BJBOURG.COM

TITLES BY BJ BOURG

LONDON CARTER MYSTERY SERIES

CLINT WOLF MYSTERY SERIES

BUT NOT FOR FAME
A Clint Wolf Novel by BJ Bourg

This book is a work of fiction.
All names, characters, locations, and incidents are products of the
author's imagination, or have been used fictitiously.
Any resemblance to actual persons living or dead, locales, or events
is entirely coincidental.

Cover design by Christine Savoie of Bayou Cover Designs

PUBLISHED IN THE UNITED STATES OF AMERICA

CHAPTER 1

Monday, May 15

"How do you like life in the mosquito-infested swamps?" asked Carrie Young. "I can't believe he dragged you all the way out there in the middle of nowhere."

"You know Thad," Ann said, dropping to the gliding rocker on her front porch. "He needs to be where his characters live. That's why he's so good at what he does."

"I understand visiting the area for research, but uprooting his entire family just for money?" Carrie scoffed on the other end of the phone. "That's just selfish of him."

"Girl, you know me better than that. If I didn't want to move, we wouldn't be here."

Carrie gasped. "You told me you didn't want to leave Plain Ridge!"

"No, hon, I said I didn't want to leave my bestie," Ann corrected. "And I didn't, but Thad's Cajun books have gotten really popular and he needs to be close to the swamps to write with authenticity."

"Your husband becomes a famous author and all of a sudden you're using them big words," Carrie complained playfully. "Don't forget, I know the real you."

Ann laughed and repeated something she and Carrie used to say when they were young and in school. "You can take the girl out of the hills, but you can't take the billy out of her."

It was Carrie's turn to laugh. "I haven't heard that one since we were little."

There was a long pause as the laughter died off, and it was Carrie who spoke next.

"At least you got to escape." There was a hint of bitterness to her tone. "You married a famous author and bought a giant brick house in a fancy neighborhood. Your kid goes to private school, you drive a Lexus, and you get your asshole waxed. Me? I married the local mechanic. We're lucky if we can put food on the table, thanks to this shitty economy. Have you seen the price of eggs lately?"

"He doesn't go to a private school," Ann said with a frown. "It's a good school, but it's public."

Ann wanted to tell Carrie that Thad hadn't always been famous, that he'd been a struggling writer who couldn't even get a short story published when she'd first met him. She wanted to explain how they had been forced to skip more than one meal in order to pay the rent, and how she had sold her mom's wedding ring so they could afford that first trip to Louisiana for Thad to do some research on the new series he had been planning for a while. But her friend already knew all of it…and more.

Thad's first mystery series, which was about a big city detective that was set in Atlanta, had been a flop. He had spent the better part of three years driving back and forth from Plain Ridge to Atlanta researching and writing the first six books, while she had worked two jobs in town to help make ends meet and to support her man. It had all been for nothing, and Thad had been about to throw in the towel and take a job with the railroad when he saw a popular show on TV about alligator hunting.

"You know," he had said over dinner that night, "I bet a series about alligators attacking people would be a big hit. I could write something like Jaws, but with alligators, and my main protagonist could be a Cajun deputy who works on the water. He would be from a small Louisiana town. Some place rich with culture."

Ann remembered that night quite vividly. They had eaten Ramen noodles—that was all they could afford at the time—and had put Wess to bed early. She also remembered Thad's excitement growing as he talked, and so had hers. She had pushed her chair next to his when he had begun looking up small Cajun towns on the Internet. He had begun by searching "Cajun Country" and then drifting as far south as he could go.

"You can't get farther south than Terrebonne and Lafourche," he had said, butchering the names of the parishes. "They're practically in the ocean."

Neither of them had known how bad he had butchered the names at the time, and they hadn't realized the large body of water they were seeing on the map was actually the Gulf of Mexico, and not the ocean. Once they'd been in the Deep South for about five minutes, though, they had learned the error of their ways.

After selling Ann's mom's ring, they had loaded up the old Ford Ranger she'd gotten from her dad and they'd headed south. Once they had reached Lafourche Parish, they'd headed down LA Highway 1 and visited Galliano, Golden Meadow, Leeville, and Port Fourchon. They had slept in a tent on the beach for one week, using it as their base camp. She had spent most of her time soaking up the sun while Thad had driven up and down Bayou Lafourche, interviewing locals and going on boat rides throughout the marsh and swamps. He had even talked a charter fisherman into taking them far out into the Gulf of Mexico on his boat, in exchange for using the captain as a character in the upcoming Gator Haven series.

Sunday of the following week, they had driven along a desolate road called the Bourg-Larose Highway that connected Lafourche and Terrebonne Parishes. It had been late in the evening and it had been an eerie ride. However, Thad had insisted on stopping multiple times to take in the sights, sounds, and aroma of the area.

After a short stop in the town of Bourg to fuel up, they had made it to Pointe-aux-Chene, where they would spend their second week. During their exploring, they had spent a lot of time in Chauvin doing research at a local library there. They had also driven as far south as they could to visit the Louisiana Universities Marine Consortium in a place called Cocodrie. A scientist there named Grace had taken them for a boat ride all over the marsh. Thad had filled up an entire notebook on the information he'd learned from Grace, and he'd promised to make her a prominent character in his books.

Finally, they had returned home for him to get to work. He had been so inspired that he'd finished the first book in eight weeks. He self-published it the following month, and it had become an instant success. From the moment they had received that first royalty check, they were never hungry again. And after the release of the second book, Thad had purchased her a Lexus. With the third book came the biggest house that Thad could find at the end of Tiger Plantation Boulevard in Mechant Loup, Louisiana. With that purchase, they had left their old lives and friends behind.

That had been two months earlier. Although she had wanted to wait until the end of the school year to move Wess away from his friends, Thad had insisted on leaving right away. He'd wanted to do more research on a giant alligator that had plagued the waters of Mechant Loup for years, and he said it was pivotal to the plot of his latest book.

"Besides," he had said, "I've already sent press releases to all the newspapers, radio stations, and television networks in Louisiana to announce our move. They're expecting us there any day now."

"Holy moly," she had said, still unsure how she felt about all the fame and fortune that had come with her husband's success. She would've been perfectly happy with Thad writing on the side while working the railroad, but it seemed as though God had had other plans for their lives. And who was she to question Him?

Once Thad had started getting a little media attention in Plain Ridge, people had begun begging autographs off of him everywhere he went. They would stop him at the grocery store, on the streets, in car line at Wess' school, and even at the doctor's office. Although he had remained humble, she could tell that it made him feel good to hear from his readers, and she was glad he was finally receiving the recognition she knew he deserved.

"They're eating this shit up," he had said. "I've already got six interviews lined up in Louisiana."

Ann and Wess had gone with Thad on a few of the interviews, but she had felt uneasy about all the attention that had been put on Wess, so the two of them had remained home for the subsequent media appearances.

"What are you doing?" Carrie asked, her voice turning slightly heated. "Are you ignoring me?"

Ann jerked at the suddenness of Carrie's voice and shook her head to clear it. "No, I was just thinking back to how it all happened," she said, still feeling guilty for leaving her childhood friend behind. "I wish we could've taken you with us. You and I would rule this little town."

"Are there any single men around?" Carrie wanted to know. "Maybe I can divorce Jim and move out there with you."

"Don't say that!"

Carrie grunted. "Why not? When he leaves the garage he heads straight for the bar. His friends see him more than me and the kids do. Hell, I don't even think he would miss us if we left. Find me a good Cajun man who wants to raise Jim's kids and I'll leave tonight."

Ann was about to respond, but stopped when she thought she heard a door close. She looked toward the garage. When Thad had gone to bed last night, he had warned her that today would be a long one, because he was having problems with a particular scene in his book. Thus, she hadn't expected him out of his office so early.

One of the many things she loved about Thad was his work ethic. When he entered his "nest"—as he called his office—he never left until he met his word count for the day. It didn't matter how late it got or how much he had left to do, he forced himself to stay in the saddle until the job was done. With a grunt, she remembered a few weeks earlier when he didn't leave his office for two days, scaring her nearly to death.

When they'd first moved into their new home, they had built a kitchenette and bathroom into his office so he would never have to leave for any reason. While she knew this, and he often joked about staying in there for a week at a time, she began to worry when she woke up the next morning and didn't see him beside her in bed. She downright panicked when nighttime rolled around and he still hadn't descended the stairs. She was so convinced he had died behind his keyboard that she had called 9-1-1. Thad had laughed so hard when he saw the medics and the police officer in his office that he'd started crying. Ann had been embarrassed, but Thad assured her that it showed how much she loved him.

"I think I have to go," Ann said, still looking toward the garage. "I think Thad's finished for the day. He's been working really hard lately, so I want to spend some time with him if he's finished."

"How's he doing?" Carrie asked, as though Ann hadn't said she had to go. "His mom misses him. I saw her in the grocery store the other day. She said she was worried about him overworking himself."

Before Ann could respond, she heard an engine fire up from the garage. It was Thad, after all. She figured he must need to go for a ride to scout a scene or to interview someone. He did that from time to time when he was working on a book. Although he tried to scout the scene locations and conduct his interviews before the book was written, he oftentimes had to fill in some holes in his research.

"Call me tomorrow," Ann said. "It sounds like Thad's about to drive off, so I want to see if he needs anything."

"Okay," Carrie said, a sense of sadness obviously creeping into her voice. "I love you, Bestie."

"Love you, too."

After ending the call, Ann shoved her cell phone into the loose pocket of her shorts. She then stepped off the porch and began walking along the wrap-around sidewalk. When she reached the driveway in front of the garage, the large door began to rise. As it grew higher and higher, the brake lights on her Lexus came into view. Thad's truck was parked in the bay right next to hers, so she wondered why he wasn't taking his own vehicle. He never drove her car.

She was about to step to the side in case Thad didn't see her, but it was too late. The engine revved loudly and the rear tires screamed. Without much warning, the Lexus shot out of the parking bay, barely clearing the partially open garage door. Unable to react in time, the rear bumper hit her in the waist, causing her upper torso to pitch forward. She felt as though she were being folded in half. Before she could even process the pain she was feeling, the driver's rear tire passed over her left foot and sucked her under the car like a shredder pulling a stack of pages into its grinding teeth.

Ann Griffin felt the smothering weight of the car's tire burning up her leg, across her torso, over her face, and up onto her head. In one split—and horrifying—moment, there was a loud popping sound from inside her ears, and her skull caved in beneath the weight of the tire. It was the last thing she would ever remember.

CHAPTER 2

Mechant Loup Boat Launch

Homer Verdin pulled his boat up to the pier and killed the engine. He sat for a long moment staring straight ahead, listening to the bayou water lapping against the aluminum hull and wondering if he was making the correct decision. Things were moving too fast for him. He had turned eighteen the previous month and was set to graduate high school in two days. He wasn't ready to leave the land he shared with his family and other members of the Chateau Band of the Biloxi-Chitimacha-Choctaw Tribe. He wasn't ready to step into adulthood.

A car turned into the Mechant Loup Boat Launch and Homer looked up to see a marked patrol cruiser heading toward him across the massive shell parking lot. He sighed and secured his boat to one of the cleats attached to the pier. Grabbing his backpack, he hopped lithely from the hull and waited for Officer Baylor Rice to reach him.

Baylor pulled up beside the pier and buzzed his window down. He flashed an easy smile.

"How's it going, Homer?"

Homer returned the smile. "Good."

"Great, jump in and let's get started."

Homer hesitated. He glanced back at his boat and thought about getting in it and riding right back into the jungles of the Dark Swamps. Things were simpler back there. For the past eight or nine years, he had made the same boat ride to the same boat launch and had taken a bus to school. He had always made good grades, but that had been a mystery to him. The entire time he was in school, he would sit at his desk and watch the clock, waiting for the final bell to ring. That had been the sound of freedom. It meant it was time to head back to the swamps…the place he felt the most comfortable.

While there were a million things that could kill a body in the swamps—and Homer had encountered most of them in his short lifetime—he had never been more scared than two weeks earlier, when he had been asked to attend an awards ceremony in town. It had been held at the fire department and the giant room had been crowded. He had nearly passed out when Mayor Pauline Cain read a big old speech about how he had saved one of the best police snipers around named London Carter, and how he had ended a murderous attack that had claimed the lives of six innocent people from the Raymond clan.

Homer could vividly remember feeling lightheaded as he'd walked to the front of the room to receive the award. London Carter was there, and so was Chief Susan Wolf, Chief of Detectives Clint Wolf, Lieutenant Melvin Saltzman, and everyone else who worked for the police department. He couldn't remember all of their names, but he remembered that they were all nice to him. His own family was there, as were other members of his tribe, and their presence had given him the strength to endure the embarrassing ordeal. Sure, he was extremely grateful to the ones responsible for giving him the award, but he didn't think he deserved it. He wasn't special. He had done exactly what anyone in his tribe would've done—well, maybe not *exactly*.

Homer didn't know what had possessed him to scalp the man who had killed his friend, Jenny. If asked, he could only say that something otherworldly had come over him. There had been no thought process. No pre-planning. It had just happened. One second he was fighting for his life, and the next second the man's hair was dangling from his bloody hand.

He was surprised the cops hadn't asked a single question about it. So surprised was he, in fact, that he began to think he had imagined the whole thing. Surely, someone would've said something about it, and he would've definitely gotten in trouble for doing it—right? However, nary a word had been spoken. *One day,* he mused, *I might return to the place where it happened to see if the scalp's still hanging there. Then I'll know for sure.*

He had displayed it as a warning to anyone else who might venture onto their land with bad intentions.

"It'll be fun," Baylor called cheerfully from his patrol car, breaking through Homer's thoughts. "We'll head to the station to check in and you can get your uniform on. Then we'll hit the road."

Homer nodded and rounded the hood to get in on the passenger's side. The weeks since the ceremony had been a blur. Chief Susan Wolf had offered him a job right there in front of his mom, dad, and siblings. His younger siblings had bounced around gleefully, saying that their big brother was going to be a policeman. Tears had welled up in his mom's eyes, and she had squeezed him so tight that he thought she would hurt herself. As for his dad, the elder Verdin had gazed upon him with such a sense of pride that Homer couldn't turn down the offer.

Next, he had met with the chief at the police department to fill out some paperwork, get sworn in, and get fitted for uniforms. Afterward, he had met one of the police academy instructors for the Magnolia Parish Sheriff's Office and became certified to carry a handgun. Chief Wolf had told him that he'd have to wait until August to attend the academy, but that he could go to work immediately. He would begin by riding along with other officers for on-the-job training, and when they felt he was ready, he would begin patrolling on his own.

It had all been very exciting and surreal, and things had progressed at lightning speed. Now, though, he was wondering if he could even do the job. He knew it was hard work. He would have to learn hundreds of laws and procedures, he would have to apply them correctly in situations where he would be making split-second decisions, and he had to maintain discipline at all times. There were also strict rules he would have to follow. He couldn't just go around scalping people and stabbing them in the chock. And he had to talk a certain way—in a professional manner. He had never filtered anything he ever said—except in front of his mom—so, how was he supposed to start now?

"Say, Officer Rice, how do you keep from slipping up and saying bad words?" Homer suddenly asked. "Like, when you're talking to people in the public?"

"First off, call me Baylor. Secondly, do you curse in front of your mom and dad?"

"No way!" Homer shook his head for emphasis. "I'm eighteen, but my mom would still throw me over her knee and whip me with a leather belt if I cursed in front of her."

"Well, when you're out there in the public doing your job," Baylor said, "pretend your mom's standing right next to you."

Homer smiled wryly. "Huh, that's a good idea."

CHAPTER 3

Homer didn't say much on the drive to the police department. Baylor took the time to talk about the ten-codes they used for communicating over the radio. He even gave Homer a sheet with all the codes and complaint signals listed on it. They read like a whole different language, and Homer decided he would memorize that sheet before his next ride-along.

It was a little before five o'clock in the evening when they arrived at the police department and Baylor parked under the massive building. Although he had been there before, Homer still stood in awe at how strong the building looked. It was situated high off the ground on thick pilings, and the entire building seemed to be constructed of solid concrete. He was certain that no hurricane that had ever formed in the Atlantic could shake the building, and he figured it could withstand the force of most tornados.

When they entered through the back entrance, Baylor showed Homer where he could change, and then said they would meet in the dispatcher's station afterward. With a nod, Homer entered one of the interview rooms and quickly slipped into his green and tans. After throwing the gun belt around his hips, he cinched it in place and pulled his pistol from his bag. It was a Beretta 92 FS 9mm like the one that Clint Wolf carried. The veteran detective had recommended it as a sidearm, and who was Homer to question him?

Homer slipped a round into the chamber and released the slide. He then de-cocked the pistol with his thumb, flipped the safety off, inserted a fully loaded magazine, and holstered it. The loaded handgun felt heavy on his hip, and he wondered how fast he could run with all the gear and the new combat boots that pinched his toes. He was accustomed to running around in shorts and no shoes, so he definitely felt weighted down.

After he was done, he took one last look in the two-way mirror to make sure his badge and buttons were in the proper position. He had never imagined himself in uniform, but he had to admit the tan shirt accentuated his dark hair, dark eyes, and olive complexion. His mom had teared up the first time he'd tried it on for her, and it had made him feel good to see the pride in her eyes when she looked at him. He just hoped he wouldn't disappoint her.

When Homer reached the dispatcher's station, he saw that Lindsey Savoie was still working. He remembered her from when he'd been sworn in. He had sat in the office with her while waiting on Chief Wolf, and she had taught him a lot in the short time he'd visited with her. She was smart and nice. He liked her.

"Welcome back, Homer," Lindsey said, flashing a pretty smile. "You're gonna learn a lot from Baylor."

"Thanks," he said. "I learned a lot from you the other day. Things are starting to make sense to me."

Lindsey gave him a wink that made him blush.

One of the first things that Chief Wolf had taught him was the importance of the dispatcher's job.

"Lindsey and our other dispatchers have some of the most important roles in law enforcement," she had explained on the day he'd gotten sworn in. "Not only are they the link between the public and our officers, but they also serve as safety managers. If you do a building check at three in the morning, you're not out there alone— they're right there with you. They pay close attention to the clock, and if they don't hear from you in a reasonable amount of time, they'll radio you to make sure that you're Code Four. If they don't get a response, they'll have backup running code to check on you."

"Code Four—that means everything's cool, right?" Homer had asked.

Susan, as she preferred to be called, had smiled. "That's correct. And when you're running code to a hot call, the dispatcher on duty will be riding along. She'll experience the same emotions as you, and probably more. While you'll be distracted thinking about what you'll find at the scene and what kind of action you might have to take, her number one priority will be your safety. If you get hurt, she'll feel the pain, too, and question what she could've done differently to keep you safe. The job is stressful, demanding, and often thankless, and it's not for the faint of heart. They're our unsung heroes, but we sing their praises every chance we get."

Homer's only experience with law enforcement had been limited to the few times he'd encountered police officers and sheriff's deputies around town or at school, so the information was all new to him. After listening to the way Chief Wolf talked about Lindsey and the other dispatchers, he had an immediate respect for them and the job that they did.

"They're the lifeline between you and your backup, and they're the main reason we can outrun criminals."

Homer had frowned, not sure he understood, and Susan had recognized his expression.

"If you're chasing a suspect and he gets away from you," she had explained, "all you have to do is let Lindsey know his description, vehicle information, and direction of travel, and she'll call ahead to your fellow officers down the road, so they can snatch him up." She had paused to smile. "I've yet to meet a man or woman who could outrun radio waves."

That had made sense to Homer, and he had said, "Their job seems really important."

"So important, in fact," Susan had continued, "that they're the first thing a terrorist will take out. If you can't communicate with headquarters, it makes it extremely difficult to do your job—"

Right then, Clint Wolf entered the room, and they all looked over at him. He was the chief of detectives, but he joked that he was the chief of one, and that one detective—Amy Cooke Rice, Baylor's wife—was pregnant and on light duty at the moment.

"Hi, Detective Wolf." Homer stuck out his hand. "It's good to see you again."

"This is the last time I'm gonna say it...call me Clint."

Homer blushed. "Yes, sir."

"And I'm not your sir," Clint said. "I'm much too young for that shit."

Homer chuckled and nodded his head.

Clint was the first person Homer had met from the police department, and it was Clint who had interviewed Homer after the incident with the killer sniper two months earlier. That situation had served as an excellent example of how a lack of communication could interfere with law enforcement work. At the hospital after the incident, he had overheard a large man with a cowboy hat say they were trying to get more radio towers up in the swamps, but that it would be years before it would happen. He was pretty sure the man was Sheriff Buck Turner, and he remembered being afraid that the man would ask about Spider's scalp. Strangely, the sheriff had also seemed uninterested in that small detail.

Clint opened his mouth to say something, but a phone rang and interrupted him. It sounded different than a regular phone, and everyone jerked their heads around to look in the direction of the ring. Lindsey wasted no time in whirling around and snatching it up.

"It's the emergency line," Baylor explained, as he and Clint stepped closer to Lindsey. "It's from the 9-1-1 call center."

As soon as she answered, Lindsey's shoulders stiffened and her tone became serious. She spoke quickly with someone on the other end of the line.

Homer didn't know what was about to happen, but he could feel the tension in the air—could see the focus on Clint and Baylor's faces. His heart began to pound with anticipation. He could feel his muscles tighten. His breath was coming faster. He tried to imagine what was being said on the other end of the phone, and what they might find when they arrived at the scene—if, indeed, they were being called to it.

"Okay, give me her number and I'll try to get her back on the line," Lindsey said quickly, and then turned to Baylor and Homer. "Get to the last house on Tiger Plantation ASAP. A man found his wife dead in their driveway. It looks like she's been run over. I'll try to reach the complainant and get more. She hung up on the 9-1-1 operator before she could find out who was dead, if it was an accident, a vehicle description, or anything else."

Without wasting a second, Baylor darted for the door they'd just entered, while Clint and Susan headed for the front. Lindsey snatched up a phone and began trying to make contact with the original complainant.

As Homer raced after Baylor, he thought about how everyone looked like they knew what they were doing. There was no hesitation, no questions, no doubt in their movement. They all just jumped immediately into action, each of them doing a particular job, and doing it calmly.

Homer took the stairs two at a time during his pursuit of Baylor, who also navigated the stairway like he was born to do it. Within seconds, Homer was in the passenger seat of Baylor's marked police cruiser and the tires were screeching as they sped out from under the shadows of the building. Baylor had his left hand on the steering wheel, so he used his right one to flip the switch on his lights and siren.

As they whisked past the front of the building, Homer saw Clint and Susan sprinting across the front sidewalk toward Clint's black Tahoe.

The speed, the sound, the rushing bodies, the sense of urgency—it all had an effect on Homer. Excitement surged through his blood stream like a raging river. It was like nothing he had ever felt before. While it was similar to the excitement he felt right before jumping on an alligator's back, it was much more intense.

Homer didn't realize it at the time, but it was right at that moment that he became addicted to police work.

CHAPTER 4

I had been standing in the dispatcher's station telling Homer Verdin—Susan's newest patrol officer—not to call me sir when the emergency phone rang, and Lindsey received a call about a woman being run over by her own vehicle. I was parked in front of the building and I should've made it to my unmarked Tahoe before Baylor and Homer made it to the parking area under the building, but the younger men somehow beat me and were speeding from the building just as I was firing up my SUV.

Even my wife had made it to my Tahoe before me, and I had gotten out of the police department before her. I cursed my healing leg—I had taken a bullet to the left one two months earlier—and also cursed my advanced age, and then drove out of my parking space. I drove faster than usual—albeit within reasonable limits—up a crowded Washington Avenue, but then I let the horses run when we turned onto Main and headed north. My Tahoe nearly went airborne when I raced across the Mechant Loup Bridge, but I maintained control and increased my speed on the other side.

Tiger Plantation Boulevard was about a mile and a half north of the bridge. As part of the town's newly incorporated boundaries, it was within our jurisdiction. As our population had soared over the years, so had our areas of responsibility. Since the command center for the sheriff's office was so far away and their officers were stretched thinly throughout the entire parish, the developers of the new subdivision had petitioned the town and parish councils to include their property within Mechant Loup's jurisdiction. There had been little pushback from anyone in town, but it was becoming evident that we would soon need to increase our manpower, especially during the summer months when tourism reached its peak.

We were still considered a small town, but it wasn't as small as when I'd first blown into the area nearly ten years earlier, and it was no longer the hidden gem I'd known it to be. A recent fight with out-of-state developers shined a light on how lucrative the tourism business in Southeast Louisiana could be, and to what lengths grubby land moguls would go to in order to take advantage of small towns around the country for their own gain.

I was right behind Baylor when he turned down the boulevard. Since we were entering a residential area, we both slowed to the speed limit and shut off our sirens. School had ended for the day, so kids would be home and probably playing outside. Even if they were inside, a blaring siren usually meant that Santa Claus was coming through their neighborhood on a fire truck to hand out candy, so they would probably rush eagerly outside at the sound of our sirens. It wouldn't matter to them that Christmas was still seven months away. While we wanted to get to the scene as quickly as we could, we didn't want to kill or injure any children in the process.

There was a small group of people at the end of the street when we arrived on the scene, and I saw one man down on his hands and knees next to a mailbox at the end of a cul-de-sac. I figured him to be the husband, because he was visibly distraught. Due to a line of trees shielding the home from the rest of the neighborhood, I didn't see the twisted body in the driveway until we were right up on them.

"Shit, Sue!" I muttered as I put my Tahoe in park. "Someone should've gotten the husband out of here!"

I tucked some latex gloves and my portable radio in my back pocket, and handed Susan some gloves on our way out of my unmarked SUV. Baylor and Homer began securing the scene while Susan headed for the victim. I went straight for the husband.

A man and woman were standing over him, and they made room when I approached. I squatted on the smooth concrete in front of him. He wore pajama pants, a wrinkled shirt, and he was bare-footed. His face was buried in his hands and he was crying. He didn't look up when I touched his shoulder.

I glanced inquiringly at the couple who stood above me. The woman got the hint and immediately said, "His name's Thad…Thad Griffin."

"Mr. Griffin," I said soothingly, turning my attention back to the grieving husband. "I'm Clint Wolf. I'm a detective with the Mechant Loup Police Department. Can you tell me what happened?"

Through his sobs, he said, "I...I don't know what happened! I...she was just there...she was on the ground when I went outside!"

I shot a glance toward Susan. I could tell by her demeanor that the woman was truly deceased. Even if she wasn't, she would probably have wanted to be, because her body was twisted in ways that should've been illegal. I cursed under my breath. There was no worse way to start a Monday morning than with a homicide. Whether it was a murder or a tragic accident had yet to be determined, but it was certainly a homicide, as there was no way she could've done it to herself.

"Do you know who did this?" I asked, not ready to rule him out just yet. Hell, I couldn't rule out anyone at that point. We knew nothing except for what Lindsey had learned from the 9-1-1 operator, and that hadn't been much, thanks to the initial caller hanging up. "We need a description to put out over the radio."

He looked up for the first time, and I saw that his hair was disheveled and his eyes were swollen from crying. He seemed confused.

"*Who* did this?" he asked, repeating my question.

"Yes, sir." I waited a second for him to think it over. "Do you know who did this to your wife?"

It was as though the idea clicked in his mind for the first time. "Someone *did* this to her? Are you saying someone actually *murdered* my wife? But...but how can you know that? You just got here."

I took a patient breath. I wanted to tell him it would've been next to impossible for her to do it to herself, but I refrained. "Yes, sir, someone did this to her. We still don't know if she was murdered or if she was accidentally run over, but it would help if you could tell me who was at your house today."

"Um...no one was here. I was alone. We were alone." He shook his head. "We didn't have company. I was upstairs in my office and she was downstairs. We didn't have any visitors."

I scowled. Was it really a run-over homicide? Or had the woman been beaten? From my vantage point, the woman's position looked consistent with having been run over by a vehicle, but it was also possible that someone could've beaten her into that shape. It was also possible she could've fallen from the sky, but that was highly unlikely. She was too far up the driveway to have jumped from the top of the house, and there were no large trees hanging over the scene.

I wanted to get more information from the husband before

moving on to where Susan was squatting beside the body, so I asked if he had any idea who might want to hurt his wife.

"Nobody," he said. "No one even knows her. We've only been here a couple of months. I mean, everyone knows me, but they don't know her. If they wanted anybody dead, it would be me."

CHAPTER 5

I blinked, confused at Thad Griffin's last statement. Other than just learning his name, I had no clue who he was. I had lived in Mechant Loup for almost ten years—longer than the neighborhood had been alive—so I should have heard of him if he was someone important. And I was certainly curious as to why he would think someone might want him dead. Did it have anything to do with his supposed popularity?

I glanced up at the couple again, and the woman mouthed, "He's the author of the Gator Haven Mystery Series. He's famous."

"Gator Haven Mystery Series?" I mouthed back.

Her face seemed to light up as she nodded her head. "It's really good," she said out loud, unable to contain her excitement.

"What's good?" asked Thad Griffin, looking up. There was a wistfulness in his expression, and he glanced toward where Susan was still leaning over his wife. "Is it Ann? Is she okay?"

"No, I'm sorry," the woman said. "I was just telling the detective that Gator Haven is a good series."

Thad groaned and his shoulders slumped. He lowered his head without responding. At least he seemed too concerned over his wife to worry about how well-liked his series might or might not be. That was a good sign.

And while I hadn't heard of him or his series, that didn't mean much. I didn't get to read as much as I liked to, so I was out of touch with the latest and greatest books. Lindsey, on the other hand, would probably know all about him. She was never without a book in her hands, and she read enough to know what was good and what was not.

"You said if they wanted anybody dead, it would be you," I began. "Are you talking about someone in particular, or just speaking in general?"

"In general," he mumbled, not lifting his head to look at me. "No one wants us dead. We're good people. I have no idea who would want to do this to her."

I had noticed that the garage door was open and the bay area on the left side was empty. It was directly in front of that area, and about twenty feet from the garage door, that the woman lay dead. As I looked at the situation, there were two options. Someone had entered the driveway from the cul-de-sac and run her down, or the vehicle had come from the garage.

"You said you didn't have visitors and that you don't know who did this," I began slowly, making sure he would be able to process what I was about to ask through his grief, "but you were upstairs in your office and she was downstairs, right?"

He nodded halfheartedly.

"Is it possible someone came over to visit, but you didn't know about it?"

He seemed to consider the possibility.

"I guess so," he finally muttered.

I didn't want to draw his attention to the garage, because I didn't want him to look in that direction and see his wife again, but I asked if there was supposed to be another vehicle in there along with the truck.

"Yeah," he said. "My wife's car is supposed to be inside, but it's gone. I…I don't know what happened to it. When I went in the garage to look for her, I saw it gone and thought she had left. That's when I opened the overhead door and saw her lying there. It…it was so horrible. I've written about this kind of thing and I've imagined what it might look like in real life, but I never guessed it would look that bad. I…I can't imagine what she went through. The pain…it…it had to be so unbearable!"

He broke down crying again, but I didn't give him any more time to grieve. I had just gotten the biggest clue since arriving at the scene, and it was that a car had been taken. Suspects always left something behind at crime scenes, just like they always took something with them. In most cases, what they would leave behind would be invisible, like DNA and fingerprints, and what they'd take would be small and sometimes microscopic, like a speck of dirt on the sole of their shoe. Even if they stole expensive jewelry and guns, they would usually have to do something with those items before we would be alerted—like pawn them or try to sell them around town. But taking a vehicle was golden for us, as that would be the easiest thing to locate.

"What kind of vehicle does she have?" I asked, quickly reaching for my portable radio.

"It's a Lexus."

"What color and model?"

"It's black and has tinted windows all around." He took a wailing breath and scrubbed at his eyes. "Um, it's an ES with the V-6 engine."

"Do you know the license plate number?" I asked, not thinking he would.

He shook his head.

"Was it registered in your name or hers?"

"Mine."

"Did you register it in Louisiana yet?" I asked, considering he had recently moved to Louisiana and knowing most people put that kind of thing off until the last minute.

"No," he said, "it's still registered in Plain Ridge, Georgia."

I nodded and, after getting his date of birth, called Lindsey over my radio to have her run a registration check for the Lexus.

"When you get the info, please put out a BOLO to all of the surrounding states," I said. "The driver is wanted for questioning in a homicide, and the vehicle was possibly used as the weapon, so we'll want it confiscated and held for processing. Also, pull everything you have from this address."

I turned back to Thad Griffin when I finished relaying the traffic. "Where was the Lexus parked when you woke up this morning?"

"I mean, I guess it was in the garage. I didn't go outside and look, but that's where she usually keeps it." He seemed to have gotten better control of his faculties, and I could understand him more clearly.

I straightened and asked the couple still standing there if we could use their house to continue the interview. They nodded in unison and I asked Mr. Griffin if he wanted to walk with me. He nodded and stood shakily to his feet. I thought I might have to help him walk, but he managed to cross the street and take a seat on a wicker chair on their front porch.

Baylor and Homer had strung some crime scene tape across the entrance to the Griffin driveway, and they were standing by in case their assistance would be needed. The scene was organized and would've been easy for Susan and me to control on our own, but it would be nice to have them around when we began searching the house and property. Before that could be done, I would need a search warrant, so I sent a text message to Amy giving her a quick rundown of the evidence we had, and asking her to begin preparing the affidavit.

When that was done, I joined Thad and the couple on their porch. I remained standing as I continued questioning the despondent husband.

"You mentioned being upstairs today," I said, wanting to pin down his activities and whereabouts during the homicide. "What were you doing up there?"

"What I always do," he said tiredly. "I was writing my next book. I get up every morning and lock myself in there until I've reached my goal for the day."

"What time do you get in your office in the morning?" I asked.

"Usually five."

I needed him to be more specific, so I asked, "What time did you get there *this* morning?"

"Five o'clock."

"And what time did you leave your office?"

He was thoughtful. "What time is it now?"

I pulled out my cell phone and glanced at the time displayed on the screen. "It's five-thirty-seven."

"Well, it must've been thirty minutes ago when I finished for the day," he said. "I went downstairs and started looking for—"

He abruptly stopped talking and jumped to his feet. His eyes were wild and his mouth was open. "Wait—did you say *five*-thirty? In the afternoon?"

I nodded. "That's right."

"Where's Wess?" he cried frantically, jumping out of the wicker chair. "Where in the hell's Wess?"

"Who's Wess?" I asked, stepping forward to grab him in case that was necessary.

The woman gasped. "Oh, my God, you don't think—?"

"Wess is my son!" Thad bellowed, his mouth beginning to tremble violently. He was turning his gaze frantically from the front of the street to his house, and back again. "Ann was supposed to pick him up from the bus stop at three o'clock! Where in the hell is my son?"

CHAPTER 6

I glanced toward the crime scene. We were about 130 yards away, but I could plainly see the victim still sprawled out on the driveway. Susan hadn't said anything about the presence of a second victim, and there didn't seem to be a second blotch anywhere else on the driveway or along the private lane that led to the cul-de-sac, so I figured it was safe to assume that Thad's son hadn't been hit by the car.

"How old's your son?" I asked, speaking loud enough to break through the emotional tornado that must've been ripping through his brain. His mouth was moving, but no words were coming out. I needed to keep him on task, or it seemed he would have a break down. If that happened, he would be of no use to us, and we needed him alert and talking.

When he still didn't answer me, I clapped my hands together in front of his face. "Thad! I need your help to find Wess."

He blinked out of his trance when my hands came together in front of his face.

"Huh?" he asked.

"How old is Wess?"

"Um…eight…Wess is eight years old." He spoke in a robotic tone. "He…he goes to the Mechant Loup Elementary School. He gets off the bus around three o'clock every day. Ann…um, my wife is always there to pick him up."

"Do you know if she picked him up today?"

Based on what he'd said earlier and the way he'd reacted when he'd learned what time it was, I was thinking he wouldn't know the answer to that question, but I couldn't assume anything. I needed to hear him say it.

"I...I have no idea."

"Is it possible he's in the house?" I asked, shooting a glance toward where Baylor and Homer were waiting near the entrance to the driveway. "Is it possible Ann picked him up and brought him home before she was run over?"

"I don't know." Thad seemed to sway on his feet, so I directed him to his chair. He sagged back into it and sat there with his shoulders slumped. After a long moment, he said, "What am I supposed to do now? How do I find him? Where do I even begin to look?"

"You don't need to do anything except answer our questions," I explained softly. "We'll do all the work. Okay?"

He nodded blankly.

"Now, do you know what bus Wess rides?"

"Shit, what is it again?" Thad squeezed his eyes shut and slapped his forehead several times. "Um, I think the driver's name is Emily. Bus...fifty-seven, I believe?"

It was my turn to nod. I knew Emily Baker. I had interviewed her five years earlier about a kidnapping that had occurred south of town. She had only been twenty-two or twenty-three at the time, and had been the youngest bus driver I'd ever met up to that point, or ever. I said a silent prayer that we weren't dealing with a situation similar to that one and asked Thad if we could search his residence. I wanted a search warrant before we started looking for evidence, but I needed to know if Wess was inside.

"For what?" he asked.

"For Wess," I explained. "Before we go any further, I want to make sure he's not in the house."

"Sure." He seemed hesitant. "I hollered for Ann as I walked all through the house, but I didn't get an answer from him or her, so I don't think he's in there. If anything, the bus driver probably brought him back to the school when Ann didn't show up to get him off the bus. That's happened once or twice before when we lived in Plain Ridge. The principal would just call Ann and tell her to go pick him up at the school."

I didn't want to tell him that they would have simply let an eight-year-old walk to the back of the street, because that might've sent his thoughts spiraling in a bad direction. Instead, I thanked him and asked him to stay with his neighbors while we searched for Wess.

As I hurried toward Baylor and Homer, I called Lindsey to see if she'd gotten anywhere with the registration.

"I did," she said, a hint of curiosity in her voice. "His name sounds familiar. I know I've heard it somewhere. Is he in law enforcement or something?"

"He's some kind of famous writer," I said. "His neighbor said he writes the Gator Haven Mysteries, or something."

"Oh, yeah," she said, growing excited. "I remember seeing an article about him moving here. It was right about the time you and Melvin were lost in the Forbidden Swamps."

At the very mention of the incident that had occurred two months earlier, the old wound in my leg began to throb. It suddenly made sense why I hadn't heard about some author moving to our area. We had all been a bit preoccupied during those days.

"I've seen his books advertised online," Lindsey continued. "They show up at the top of nearly every search page for mysteries and thrillers. I've never tried one. I guess they're pretty popular. I might have to read them now."

"What about the Lexus?"

"Yeah, I put out a BOLO for the car like you asked, and added a note that it would be driven by an unknown suspect." She paused for a quick breath. "I also called Melvin and Takecia, and they've gone ten-eight to search for the car."

Ten-eight was code for *in service*, and it was just like Melvin and Takecia Gayle to readily go to work during an emergency, even when they were off duty or had worked the night shift.

"Let them know we've got an eight-year-old boy who's unaccounted for," I said, trying to keep the apprehension from my voice. "I don't know if he's in that Lexus or not, but we need to let everyone know that he might be in that vehicle. They need to know to approach the car with caution if they find it."

"Oh, no," she said. "Was he kidnapped?"

"I'm not sure," I admitted. "We're about to search the house. I'll let you know if we find him."

"Ten-four."

I could hear her typing furiously in the background, and I knew she was updating the information on the NCIC computer.

"Were you able to pull all the complaints from this address?" I asked.

"Yep, but we've only had one," she said. "The wife called 9-1-1 to say that her husband hadn't come out of his office in two days. She thought he'd died behind his keyboard. Takecia responded with an ambulance, but they found him sitting behind his desk writing."

I laughed out loud, but quickly stifled it. "Was he mad?"

"According to Takecia's report, he took it in good humor," she explained. "He said he was stuck on one particular scene and he wouldn't leave his computer until he had fixed it."

"Anything else?"

"Nope. I ran them for wants and warrants, but they're clean. I also ran a nationwide check on them, but nothing came back. They seem clean."

Although she couldn't see me, I nodded and was about to end the call when I thought of something else.

"Hey, Lindsey, do you read from those electronic devices?" I asked, trying to remember the names of them. "Kindles or something?"

"Oh, God no," she said, her fingers pausing for a second. I could hear the defiance in her voice when she went on. "I would never. I only read paperbacks or hardcovers. I want something I can bend and smell. Reading a digital book is as cold as having a digital boyfriend. What's the point if you can't cuddle up with it?"

I wasn't about to touch that comment, so I mentioned that I'd heard the electronic readers were popular, and that a lot of people used them.

"To each his own," she said, resuming the furious typing in the background.

"I was hoping you might delve into his books and see if there's anything useful in them," I explained. "You're the fastest reader I know, so you're the only person for the job. But unless you can find some at the library, it might be useless. It would take too long to buy his print books online and wait for them to come in. We need to know everything we can find out about him as quickly as we can, so the digital books would be the way to go."

"What kind of information are you looking for?"

"I'm not sure," I admitted. "Maybe he wrote a book that was controversial, or he might've tackled a subject that set off some deranged individual. Hell, if you call someone by the wrong name nowadays you're liable to end up in a fight to the death."

Lindsey was quiet, and I could almost hear her brain working. "There was this one author who wrote a book so controversial that a bounty was put on his head. He was even stabbed on stage in New York a year or so ago. Is that what you're talking about?"

I didn't know what she was referencing, but I didn't have time to hear about it, so I said, "We just need to figure out if he wrote anything that might've pissed off a person or group of people to the point of them wanting him dead. It'll probably be something that a reasonable person wouldn't think twice about, so you would have to read it like it was your job to be offended by something."

"You really think this is why they killed his wife?"

"I don't know what to think, Lindsey," I admitted. "If he didn't orchestrate this whole thing, then someone killed his wife and possibly took his son, and I don't think it was a random attack by some local. They haven't been here long enough for his wife to have made enemies, so it either has to do with something he wrote, or someone from his past got wind that he settled here and they tracked him down."

"Don't underestimate the soccer moms around this town." Lindsey chuckled. "You cut one off in car line, and they'll hunt you down and kill you. It could also be a jealous author. I hear things can get pretty competitive among those trying to make bestseller lists. It's not impossible to think one author might off him to keep him from stealing the top spot from them."

I chuckled at her joke, and gave serious thought to her last comment. It was definitely something to consider.

"How about it?" I finally asked. "Can you take one for the team? I can buy you a Kindle, or whatever they're called."

She sighed. "I can download eBooks on my cell phone. I'll see what I can find out."

"Grab the credit card from the top drawer in my desk." I had reached Baylor and Homer, so I was talking faster. "This is considered research, and you're doing it at my request, so it shouldn't cost you anything."

She squealed. "In all my life, I never thought I'd see the day that I'd get to make a living off of reading books!"

CHAPTER 7

"Can y'all grab a camera and follow me?" I asked Baylor and Homer when I'd ended the call with Lindsey.

I didn't need to tell them twice. They sprang into action as I headed for Susan. She was still photographing the crime scene. I noticed what appeared to be vomitus on the concrete next to the body. It wasn't near the victim's face, so I figured it had come from the husband's stomach.

When Baylor and Homer caught up to me, I told them about the missing boy. I asked them to search the interior of the home.

"While y'all are looking for the boy," I explained, "take pictures of everything that's in plain view. We don't know much right now, so anything and everything should be considered evidence. Amy's typing up a search warrant as we speak. We'll be able to conduct a more thorough search once the judge signs it, but time is money, and we need to collect whatever information we can as quickly as we can. For all we know, Thad killed his wife and stashed the boy somewhere."

They both nodded and headed straight for the house.

When they were gone, Susan pointed to the victim's head. "The tire went up her leg, across her torso, and directly over her head," she said. "It crushed her skull. She was alive when it happened, so she felt the weight of that car pushing the life out of her."

I winced and shook my head. I'd investigated a number of rollover deaths in my many years working law enforcement, and I couldn't imagine the extreme pain the victims had been forced to endure for the short moments before they expired. It was much different than being hit by a truck going 100 miles per hour. While that type of scene was more gruesome to behold, death usually came much quicker for the victims, thus they suffered less. I didn't know how fast the Lexus had been driving as it exited the garage, but it would've been going much too slow to show mercy to our victim.

"Do we have a name yet?" Susan asked.

I nodded. "Ann Griffin. The missing boy is Wess."

I watched for another minute while Susan finished photographing the scene, and then I heard Baylor call my handle on the radio. When I told him to go ahead with his traffic, he said initial indications showed that the house was clear.

"We're doing a more thorough search now in case he's hiding somewhere, but there's no signs of him or anyone else so far," he continued. "And the house is in pristine shape. If there was a fight or some kind of struggle, there are no obvious signs of it."

"Shit!" After thanking him, I pulled out my cell phone and searched for the number to the elementary school. When I found it, I pressed the number to call it. It was late in the afternoon, so I wasn't very optimistic that I'd get an answer. I was wrong.

"This is Clint Wolf," I said to the woman who answered. "I'm a detective with the—"

"I know who you are, Clint," said the woman. "This is Trish Boudreaux, the principal here."

"Ah, yes," I said, remembering her. "How are you?"

She had contacted me the previous year and asked me to attend career day. I had readily accepted, and it had been a lot of fun. Someday, Grace would attend that same school, and I hoped to be able to speak to the student body when she was going there.

"I'm well," she said. "You just caught me walking out. What can I do for you?"

"I need to know if Emily Baker was driving her bus today," I began, "and I need to know if she dropped off Wess Griffin on his street."

"Wess is a recent transfer student, if I remember correctly," she said. I could hear her pecking away at her keyboard in the background. Finally, she spoke again. "Give me one second. I'll get Emily on the phone."

While she connected the call on her end, I watched my wife work. Susan was the most beautiful woman I had ever seen, and I couldn't believe how lucky I'd been when she'd accepted my marriage proposal. She was also one of the smartest women I knew. Although I had been a homicide detective for many years in La Mort and I had taught her a lot about the job, she was as insightful as anyone I'd ever met. I was glad she was working this case with me. We were in the infancy stages of the investigation, but it was already shaping up to be a complicated and urgent one.

Trish apologized for taking so long. Although I was in a hurry, I told her to take her time.

She was still trying to get a hold of Emily when Baylor and Homer exited the Griffin home and announced that the residence was clear.

"His room's surprisingly clean for a kid," Baylor said when I covered the mouthpiece of my cell phone. "We checked every room, every closet, and every cabinet—anywhere big enough for a small kid to hide—but he's nowhere to be found."

"We even checked the attic, but it's empty except for some boxes and crates," Homer said. "There was a kid's bowl with a little milk and a few pieces of Lucky Charms in the sink, so it looks like he was here for breakfast."

I scowled, not liking it one bit. There was nothing more frightening than a case involving a missing child, and the murder of his mother certainly compounded things and raised the level of angst in my chest.

"Did you see a schoolbag in his room?" I asked. "Or a nametag lying around?"

Baylor shook his head. "There was nothing you'd expect to see from a kid who'd just gotten back from school."

"Can y'all hit the road and search for the Lexus?" I asked. "We've got deputies looking to the north, so maybe y'all can search the town in case the suspect headed that way."

They nodded in unison and hurried off. I was still scowling when I turned to see Susan shifting Ann's head. I muttered a curse under my breath when I saw how Ann's face caved in under the soft pressure of Susan's hands.

I cursed again when the principal responded to my first mutterings, asking if everything was okay.

CHAPTER 8

I apologized profusely for cursing in the principal's ear, but she laughed and assured me that she had heard a lot worse—and from her students, no less.

After another minute or two of waiting, she told me that she had Emily Baker on the line.

"I'll sign off and let y'all talk in private," she said.

I heard a click, and began talking.

"Hey, Emily, how are you?" I asked, trying to sound pleasant. Most people would naturally be apprehensive upon first being contacted by a detective, and rightly so. We never called with good news. "It's Clint Wolf, with the police department."

"I'm good," she said in a pleasant, yet cautious, tone. "Aren't you the same detective who worked that kidnapping a while back?"

"I am."

"Oh, I remember you," she said, sounding a little relieved. "Mrs. Boudreaux said you had a question about a drop-off."

"Yeah, I was wondering if you know Wess Griffin, and if you remember dropping him off today?"

"I do know him, and I did drop him off today. His dad's an author and they moved here from somewhere in Georgia. The mountains, I think? He's got a really cool country accent. The boys tease him for it, but the girls love it. He's an adorable kid." She paused, and then asked, "Is something wrong?"

"What time did you drop him off?"

"Um, it would've been around three, maybe three-fifteen. That's usually the time I get to Tiger Plantation."

"Was anyone waiting for him at the bus stop?" I asked.

"Oh, yeah, his mom."

I scowled. If his mom had picked him up at three or three-fifteen, she would've been killed after bringing him back home. If that was true, then the boy should be home. Unless, of course, he had been taken from the house.

As soon as the thought entered my mind, another one jockeyed for position and took hold. What if Thad was leaving with Wess, and Ann didn't want him to go? Lindsey hadn't turned up a history of domestic violence at the Griffin home, but they hadn't been in town long enough to get comfortable. If he were an abusive spouse, it was quite possible he had hit Ann for the last time and she had threatened to leave. She might've tried to leave in her Lexus and take Wess with her, but Thad might've stopped her.

If that was how things had played out, it wouldn't be the first time a couple had argued or struggled over custody of a child. It also wouldn't be the first time a father had refused to let an abused wife remove a child from the home. It occurred to me that Thad might've jerked Ann from the car and tried to leave with Wess himself. At that point, she might've tried to stop him by standing behind the car, and that would've been when he had run her over. However, the thing that puzzled me about that scenario was the child's whereabouts. If they were new to town, where would Thad have taken the kid?

My heart sank as I thought of what Thad might've done to his kid in a fit of rage and after having run the boy's mom over. Wess would've been hysterical after witnessing that, and he might've tried to jump out of the car or fight with his dad. I didn't know Thad, so I didn't know if he was prone to anger, but I'd seen some terrible things during my career, and nothing surprised me.

"Emily, are you sure his mom was there to pick him up?" I asked after I'd been silent for too long mulling over the possibilities.

"I mean, her car was parked at the front of the street like it always is," she said, a hint of doubt starting to creep into her voice. "I didn't actually see her, because her windows are tinted, but Wess walked right to the car and got into the front passenger door like he always does."

I turned and approached the cul-de-sac, where I could look toward the front of the street. "Did he seem surprised or hesitant before he got in the car?"

"I...I don't know," Emily said. "I just watched until he reached the car, and I closed my door and drove off. I figured his mom had him from that point on, so I drove away. Is...did I do something wrong?"

"Oh, no," I said quickly. "Not at all. I'm just trying to figure some things out."

"Did something happen?" Emily's voice had changed to one of sheer worry. "Did something bad happen to Wess?"

I didn't want to lie to her, but I didn't want to broadcast details of our case, so I said, "Oh, I'm sure Wess is fine. I just wanted to see if you noticed anything out of the ordinary during your drop-off. So, did you?"

"No, sir. Like I said, he just got in the car like normal."

"Did any other kids get off the bus with Wess?" I asked, squinting to see toward the front of the street.

"No, sir, he's the only one who gets off the bus there," she explained, "and he's my last stop."

"Did you see any other vehicles in the area when you dropped him off?"

"No, sir."

"Did you see what the car did when you drove off?"

Emily hesitated. "Um, well, I glanced once in my rearview mirror and saw them heading toward town."

Had I been one of my dogs, my ears would've perked up. "The car headed toward Mechant Loup?"

"Yeah, it did. It seemed like they were going kind of fast, too, like they were in a hurry." Emily took a breath. "I remember thinking Wess might be late for something. I know his dad is a famous author and he's got an event planned at the library soon, so I thought it might be something like that."

"Did you notice anything else?" I pressed, hoping for more. "Like, was there another car following her? Did she stop or turn around at any point that you saw?"

"I was heading in the opposite direction, so I wouldn't have seen if she turned around," Emily said. "And I don't remember seeing any other cars in the area. It's usually kind of quiet on this side of town during that hour. It's not until around five that it starts getting busy with people leaving or returning from work."

She was right about that, but I didn't acknowledge her comment. I kept pressing her for more information, hoping to trigger some memory, but it was no use. She knew what she knew, and that was all.

Finally, I thanked her, ended the call, and dialed Lindsey again. When she answered, I gave her the new information.

"It doesn't mean they're still in town," I cautioned, "but we've got a place to start. Can you call Sheriff Turner and have him send a dozen or so deputies down here to help flood the streets?"

"Will do," she said quickly, and then signed off.

I met briefly with Susan to let her know what I'd learned, and then told her I was heading to the front of the street. I hurried to my Tahoe. I shot a glance toward where Thad was still sitting on the front porch of his neighbors' house, and I frowned when I saw the man hunched over with his face in his hands. Everyone reacted differently to tragedy, but he seemed to be acting how a reasonable person would—unless he was actually acting.

Before going about my work, I sauntered over and asked him if he needed anything from me. He looked up with bloodshot eyes.

"Where's Wess?" When he asked the question, spittle sprayed from his mouth. "Where's my son?"

"We don't know," I said, wanting to tell him as much as I could without jeopardizing the investigation. "He was dropped off at the bus stop, but he's not in the house."

"You need to find him!" He lunged to his feet and grabbed the front of my shirt, which brought a gasp from his neighbors. I made no move to stop him. Through gritted teeth, he said, "Get my boy back!"

I frowned heavily. I had never been in the business of making promises I couldn't keep, and I wasn't about to start. I gently pulled his hands away from my shirt and guided him back to the wicker chair.

"We've got people all over Louisiana and the neighboring states looking for your wife's car," I said. "If your son's in it, we'll find him. Have you been able to think of anyone who might want to do this?"

He shook his head in despair. "I don't know anyone sick enough to murder an innocent woman and kidnap a child."

I knew a number of people who fit that description, but none of them had anything to do with the present case, so I kept that information to myself.

"I'll do everything I can to get him back."

He only nodded and sank into the backrest.

CHAPTER 9

I made my way slowly to the front of Tiger Plantation Boulevard, scanning the fronts of every house as I drove by. Not one of them had a surveillance system that I could see, and I wasn't surprised. It was a nice neighborhood with nice houses, and some people didn't like to deface their homes with cameras and other preventative devices.

When I reached the front, I stopped my Tahoe in the street and stepped out. Before ending the call with Emily, I had asked her where the Lexus had been parked on that particular day, and she said it had been where it always was—on the southern shoulder of the right lane, mostly in the grass, and facing the highway.

The first lot along the southern side of Tiger Plantation was empty, except for several trees—three oaks, three pines, and a smattering of small Dogwoods. To the north, there was a modest home, but it appeared empty. There was a *For Sale* sign in the front yard, so I knew my chances of getting answers there were minuscule. The bayou side across the highway was also empty for about a mile, with only a line of trees to bear witness to what had happened at the front of the boulevard.

I cursed my luck and walked to the spot where Emily said she had seen the car parked. I carefully searched the ground for the slightest clue, even getting on my hands and knees, but it was apparent the killer had left nothing behind. If what Emily had said was true, he wouldn't have left anything behind anyway, because he never exited the vehicle.

My phone began to ring, so I straightened and took the call. It was Sheriff Turner.

"Hey, Clint, I've got some deputies heading down there right now to help y'all search for the missing kid," he said. "If there's anything else you need, just let me know."

An idea came to me. "As a matter of fact," I said, "can you send someone from victim's assistance to stay with the husband? If he is a victim, he'll need all the help he can get. If he's a suspect, I'll need someone to keep tabs on him while we try to find his son."

"Consider it done."

I thanked him and ended the call. I was about to head to the back of the street when I heard a vehicle approaching at a high rate of speed. I looked toward the sound and saw Amy's unmarked Charger coming from the south. She slowed rapidly, turned onto Tiger, and stopped on the opposite side of the boulevard.

"I've got the search warrant," she said as she slipped out of her car. At nineteen weeks pregnant, she was showing a bump and had taken to wearing her shirts untucked, but she moved around as well as ever. "Do you need me up here or at the scene?"

I took one last look at the ground where the car had been parked, and shrugged. Some sod had been kicked up when the car sped off, but the ground wasn't wet enough for tire impressions to have been left behind.

"If you want to work the scene with Susan, I'll head to town and help them look for the car," I offered after filling her in on everything we knew up to that point.

In Amy's present condition, it was better for her to stay off the streets, but she was fine to work a crime scene. And an extra pair of eyes could go a long way toward finding the boy before it was too late, so my time would better be spent driving around town.

After nodding, Amy frowned wistfully. "I love being pregnant, but I can't wait to have this little tiger. Not only do I want to meet the kid, but I want to get back to doing what I love."

"Well, if it means anything, I appreciate everything you've been able to do while carrying that little kangaroo around in your pouch," I began, "but I sure miss having you out in the field."

She flashed a smile and tossed her blonde hair back. "I already knew that."

CHAPTER 10

Home of Thad Griffin

Susan looked up when Amy's unmarked cruiser approached the cul-de-sac. Clint had left earlier to search the front of the street. She'd heard him call out on the radio to say he was heading south to search for the Lexus, and she was happy that Amy had arrived.

Since losing Regan Steed, an officer who had recently been killed in the line of duty, and finding out that Amy was pregnant, Susan had been understaffed. Everyone had been overworked, but such was the nature of the law enforcement profession. All of our officers had taken it in stride and tackled the extra work with dogged determination and good humor.

Well, except for Amy. She had grumbled a lot about not being able to carry her weight. Although everyone told her not to worry about it, she was constantly writing IOUs when Clint had to cover her call weeks, and she promised to pay her debt with interest.

"If that's the case," Clint had joked the previous week, "I won't have to catch another call week until I'm forty."

Amy had immediately feigned surprise and retorted, "I thought you hit that landmark three years ago!"

Susan, herself, had been working double duty to fill Regan's vacant shift. Clint tried to take a number of her shifts, but she refused to let him. Patrol was her responsibility and the detective work fell to him, so she wouldn't let him sacrifice his work for hers. Things were about to change, though, now that she had hired Homer Verdin. Soon, she would be able to go back to straight days, and she would be able to spend more time with Clint, Grace, and Isaiah.

Susan straightened and called the coroner's office while waiting for Amy to approach with her crime scene box. She let the woman who answered know that they had a pick-up, and that she would be ready for them within the hour. Amy had reached her by the time she'd ended the call.

"I need to measure the body before I turn her over," Susan said. "I heard a phone chirp, and I think it's in one of the pockets of her shorts. I want to see if she received a call before she died."

Amy nodded and dug through her box for a measuring device. "Doesn't it seem odd that she would've been standing in the middle of the driveway, and behind her car?" she asked when she found a 100-foot tape. "And what's the deal with her picking up the kid from the bus stop and then heading to town? Do you think she took him somewhere else because she was fighting with her husband? And then came back just to be run over by the prick?"

"It's hard to say." Susan didn't look up from where she was drawing a rough sketch of the scene. "The killer could've run her over and then taken the car to the bus stop. From what the husband said, the windows are tinted, so it's possible the kid didn't realize someone else was in the car until it was too late."

"Or he wasn't afraid because it was his dad," Amy countered. "I looked good at that supposed author when I drove by his neighbor's house. He looks like a wife beater."

That got Susan's attention. She shot a glance in the direction of Thad Griffin. She hadn't picked up any weird vibes from him, but she also hadn't paid much attention to him when she'd first arrived. Her main concern had been for the victim. Unfortunately, there was nothing anyone could've done for the lady when they arrived. She was already dead.

"You think he's a beater?" she asked Amy, trying to see Thad's face as he sat bent over with his neighbors. He was more than 100 yards away, so it was hard to make out his facial expressions.

"He's got it written all over him," Amy said with a nod. "Wait until you get close to him and see."

Susan grunted curiously. She turned back to the task at hand and quickly made the sketch while Amy set out to establish reference lines. The scene was controlled and compact, so it didn't take them long to document it with measurements. When they were done, she packed up her gear and moved her Tahoe to block Thad Griffin's view of his driveway. She then returned to Ann Griffin's body and motioned for Amy to help her turn the victim over.

"Her head's mush and she's got several broken bones," Susan warned. "She'll probably flop around a little."

Amy nodded, but Susan noticed that the muscles in her jaw were tight and she was staring down at the ground with an intensity that hadn't been there earlier.

"You okay?" she asked.

Amy took a breath, nodded, and mumbled, "Morning—er, afternoon—sickness. Things that never bothered me before are kicking my ass now."

"I can get someone else to help," Susan said quickly. "You don't need to do this—"

"Nonsense." Amy waved her off, but still didn't look up. "I'm fine. I get to eat the same Chinese food I ate for lunch, but I only have to pay one price. What could be better than that?"

The comment was so unexpected that Susan lurched forward and snorted, trying hard not to laugh out loud. She quickly checked to make sure her Tahoe was blocking Thad's view of the scene. It was, and she was thankful for that small miracle. As had all of her officers, she had long ago become acclimated to death and destruction, and it was easy to find humor even in the worst of situations.

While many people outside of law enforcement would never understand it, a healthy sense of humor was an absolute necessity in their line of work. Those who didn't possess one usually left the job early, and they often needed mental health treatment in order to cope with what they had witnessed during their time on the job. It didn't make them weak, but just human.

The officers who did possess a healthy sense of humor seemed impervious to even the most horrific of scenes. Sure, there were situations that brought a tear to the eye or a lump to the throat from time to time, but the officers who were able to slog through the blood, guts, and near-death experiences of the job without being fazed were cut from a different cloth.

Although she was trying really hard to keep her food down at the moment, Amy was one such officer, and Susan could tell it pained her to show even the slightest hint of weakness at a crime scene.

CHAPTER 11

Once Amy had worked past the wave of nausea that had overtaken her, Susan cradled Ann Griffin's head in her gloved hands and carefully rotated it while Amy flipped her torso over.

Ann's body settled limply onto what was mostly her back. She was too damaged for them to be certain. Susan changed gloves and began searching the pockets of Ann's shorts until she located a cell phone. Amy had recovered fully and walked over to look over her shoulder.

"We're in luck," Susan muttered. "There's no passcode."

Amy grunted. "She must be a good girl."

Susan raised an eyebrow in Amy's direction.

"Oh, if her phone's not locked, then she's definitely not sending boob shots to her husband," Amy explained. "You don't want that kind of thing escaping into the cloud, you know."

"Amy!" Susan gasped. "You do *not*!"

Amy glanced down at her engorged breasts and shrugged. "Why not? I don't know what'll happen to these after I have our baby, and I want Baylor to remember his ladies how they were."

Shaking her head from side to side while trying not to laugh, Susan navigated to Ann Griffin's recent text messages. The last one had come a little after two o'clock in the afternoon from someone named *Bestie*, and it read: *Hey, hooker, Whatcha doing?*

Ann had apparently seen the message, but she hadn't responded.

"That's rude," Amy said. "If that's her bestie, why'd she leave her on read? Unless she was killed right after opening it."

Susan didn't answer. Instead, she navigated to the call log, and it was there that she located a call to Bestie at around the same time the text message had come in. She held it so Amy could see.

"She called her instead."

Amy whistled. "I guess they are best friends after all."

"Yeah, and they talked for almost an hour." Susan studied the phone number. The area code was 710. She showed it to Amy and asked if she recognized it.

Amy shook her head and dug out her own cell phone. After a few seconds, she said, "It's in northern Georgia. Covers a pretty large area."

"What about the prefix?" Susan asked.

"On it." A few more seconds later, Amy announced that it narrowed the area to a few smaller towns, which included Plain Ridge, where the Lexus was registered. "I typed in the whole number, but it doesn't come back to any businesses or people."

Susan raised her head and looked into Amy's eyes. "It's quite possible this was the last person to ever speak to our victim."

"Unless the husband killed her," Amy said. "Then he would be the last one."

"Think I should call it or wait?"

"I'd call it," Amy said. "She might be able to tell us something we can use right now."

Susan nodded, but before she could pull out her cell phone, the transport van from the coroner's office arrived.

"I'll handle the body if you want to call that woman and find out what she knows," Amy offered.

Susan wanted desperately to know if the friend would offer anything useful, so she nodded and walked toward the edge of the concrete driveway to make the call. The phone rang several times and then went to voicemail.

"Hey, this is Susan Wilson," she said, disappointed that no one had answered. "I'm the police chief in Mechant Loup, Louisiana. I need to speak to you about Ann Griffin. It's urgent. Please call me back at this number…"

She then provided her number and ended the call. She looked up to see Amy helping the coroner's investigator slide Ann's body on top of an open body bag. She wanted to tell Amy to be careful, but she knew it would be useless. Amy was careful anyway, but she would do what she wanted to do.

Just then, her cell phone rang. She glanced down at the screen and saw the same out-of-state number she'd just called displayed across it.

"Hello, this is Susan," she said, quickly answering it. "Are you friends with Ann Griffin? And are you in Plain Ridge, Georgia?"

"Yes, ma'am," came a hesitant voice. "Why? What's going on? Did you say you were the police chief?"

"Yes, ma'am, I am." Susan took a breath. "Now that you know who I am, do you mind telling me who you are?"

"Don't you already know?" the woman asked. "You called my number. Hey, how'd you get it anyway?"

Susan had no clue what Ann meant to this woman, and she didn't want to make a death notification over the phone, but she knew it might be inevitable.

"Well, Ann has your number," she said simply. "So, can I ask you about the last time you and Ann spoke?"

"Um, sure, I guess." The woman sounded confused. "I talked to her earlier today. About three hours ago."

"And what's your name?"

"Carrie Young."

"Nice to meet you, Carrie." Susan paused for a split second, hoping she could get her questions answered before having to spill the beans about Ann. "And how are you related to Ann?"

"We're not related," said Carrie. "We're friends. We've been best friends since grade school."

"Oh, nice. Did anything unusual happen during your conversation with Ann today?" Susan asked.

"Like what?"

"Like, did you hear any voices in the background? Did she say anything out of the ordinary? Did she talk about any problems she might've been having?"

"Ma'am, you're starting to scare me!" Carrie's voice was beginning to take on a hint of panic.

"I don't mean to," Susan said. "I'm working a case and it would be extremely helpful if you could tell me everything you remember about that phone call."

"But why?"

Susan hesitated. She didn't want to reveal too much, but she also didn't want to downplay the severity of the situation. It was a fine line she would have to walk if she was to get information from her victim's friend.

"All I can say right now," she began slowly, "is that there's been a terrible accident out at the house. If you could—"

"Oh no!" Carrie cried. "What kind of accident?"

Before Susan could answer, there was a loud noise that sounded like the phone had dropped.

"Carrie?" Susan called. "Carrie, are you still there?"

There was no response.

"Shit!" Susan pursed her lips, guilt flooding over her. It would've been better to have an officer from Carrie's hometown show up and make the notification, but that could've taken a long time…and time was not a luxury they enjoyed at the moment.

"Carrie, are you okay?" Susan raised her voice hoping Carrie would be able to hear her even though the phone was away from her ear. It didn't seem to work. She checked her phone to make sure the connection was still live. It was, but she couldn't hear Carrie in the background.

She was thinking she would have to call Clint and let him know what was happening. He might have an idea of how to best proceed. The last thing she needed was for Carrie to fall apart, but there would be no helping that now.

That was when Ann's phone began to ring. She picked it up from where it was resting on her crime scene box and checked the number that was calling. Curiously, it was from the same area code and prefix as Carrie Young's number.

Susan groaned, hoping Carrie hadn't contacted Ann's loved ones. She hadn't stopped to consider Carrie's proximity to Ann's family. In Southeast Louisiana, many families lived on the same lane as each other and their childhood friends. She was certain it was the same in other small towns across the country, and she knew it would be devastating if Carrie had run next door and told Ann's family that there had been a terrible accident out at her house.

She was still trying to decide if she should end Carrie's call or not when the woman came back on the line.

"It's Ann, isn't it?" she asked, sounding more desperate than earlier. "It has to be Ann, because I just tried calling her from my house phone and she doesn't answer. She always answers my call. It has to be her."

Susan hesitated for a brief moment, and then said, "Look, it's very important that I find out what y'all talked about. I'd rather have this conversation in person, but you're in Georgia and I'm in Louisiana, so it's not possible."

"I want to know what's going on!"

"Look, if you answer my questions," Susan bargained, "I'll tell you everything I can about what's going on."

"No!" Carrie said stubbornly. "I'm not saying anything until you tell me what's going on. She's my best friend. I deserve to know what's happening with her."

"Okay, I'll tell you, but you have to sit down," Susan finally said. "And you have to promise you'll hold it together."

There was some rustling sounds in the background, and then Carrie mumbled that she was sitting.

"And you can't tell anyone what I'm about to tell you," Susan said. "I can't have this getting out before we can locate her family."

"I promise."

"Okay." Susan paused for a brief moment, and then spilled it. "We received a call from Thad Griffin earlier saying that he found his wife lying in the driveway. She was unresponsive."

Carrie let out a bloodcurdling scream that pierced Susan's eardrums and sent a chill reverberating up and down her spine.

CHAPTER 12

It took Susan every bit of five minutes to get Carrie Young calmed down enough to start answering her questions again. After getting her to reaffirm her promise not to contact Ann Griffin's family, she began by asking what she and Ann had talked about earlier in the day.

"We...we just talked about what was going on in our lives," Carrie said, her voice low and shaky. "I was telling her how much I missed her, and wanting to know how life was in the swamps."

"Did she sound happy?"

"Yeah, she did," Carrie said. "She always does."

Susan caught movement in her peripheral vision. She looked up to see Amy walking toward her from their vehicles, a camera dangling from her neck and a notepad tucked under her left arm. When Amy reached her, Susan turned the cell phone to speaker so Amy could hear the conversation, and both women headed for the front door of the house.

"Did she say if she had any plans today?" Susan asked once they were inside. She remained near the doorway while Amy began documenting the condition of the interior of the home with photographs, notes, and diagrams.

"Not really," Carrie said. "I don't remember her saying specifically that she had any plans, but I know she always picks Wess up from the bus stop around three o'clock."

"Were y'all on the phone at three?"

"We hung up just before then, if I remember right."

"Did you hear any voices in the background while y'all were

talking?"

"No, ma'am," Carrie said. "It sounded like she was alone, and she didn't say anyone was with her."

"Did she say what she's been up to lately?"

"Not really. She talked a lot about Thad. She even defended him when I said he was selfish for dragging her to the swamps just to write his books."

Susan cocked her head. "Was there a disagreement about moving down here?"

"Not between the two of them," Carrie acknowledged. "I guess I was the one being a little selfish. I didn't like that Thad moved my best friend so far away. Jim and me don't get to take a vacation every year, so I'll never get to see her anymore, unless they come back home to visit. I did take that hard, and I guess I did blame Thad for losing my best friend."

It sounded to Susan like there was some bitterness in Carrie's voice, and if Thad had been the one murdered, Susan would definitely have wanted to ascertain Carrie's whereabouts.

"How did Ann react to you questioning Thad's intentions?" Susan asked.

"Oh, like she always does…good naturedly. She said it was best for Thad to live where his characters lived. She said he needed to be close to the swamps to write with *authenticity*." Carrie emphasized the last word and grunted. "She never used big words like that before Thad got famous. I even joked with her about it."

"Did she laugh?" Susan asked. "Did she sound happy?"

"Oh, yeah, definitely," Carrie said. "She was her same old happy self. That's why I don't understand what's going on. What did you mean when you said she was unresponsive?"

Susan ignored Carrie's last question, and asked, "Did she and Thad ever fight?"

"Do you mean did they argue?" Carrie asked. "Or do you mean did they fistfight?"

"Both."

"They had arguments from time to time, but nothing serious." Carrie grunted. "Carrie would never let a man hit her. If Thad would've ever hit her, she would've cut his pecker off—and I would've helped her. Just like that song by the Dixie Chicks about Earl getting his ass killed."

Susan chuckled, and then asked if Ann had talked about having trouble with anyone in town.

"No, ma'am," Carrie said. "Ann said she liked the place. She always told me she wished I could move down there with her. She said we would rule that town."

"She sounds like a lot of fun," Susan said with a smile, careful not to speak of Ann in the past tense.

"She is!" Carrie's voice grew excited. "She's the best friend any girl could ever have. She has your back no matter what. She always has, ever since we were kids. She even fought a boy for me in school when we were five. The boy pulled my hair, and she ran up and punched him right in the nose. She drew blood, so she got in trouble. We found out later that the snot nosed boy actually liked me, and that was why he pulled my hair." Carrie paused and grunted. "Can you believe I ended up marrying that son of a bitch when we grew up?"

There was more bitterness in Carrie's voice, but it didn't seem to have anything to do with the present case as far as Susan could tell, so she ignored it.

"Did Ann have any enemies in Georgia?" Susan asked. "Someone who might've wished her ill?"

"Wait a minute…did someone hurt her?" There was real panic in Carrie's voice at that point. "Is that what this is about?"

"We're looking at every possibility," Susan said, trying to keep the conversation going before Carrie could read too much into her questions. "Did she have any enemies?"

"Oh, no, everyone loved Ann."

"What about Thad?" Susan continued quickly. "Did he have any enemies there?"

"Thad didn't grow up around here, so he wasn't well known in town until after his alligator books took off," Carrie said. "As far as I know, he didn't have any problems with anyone. Like, I know he never got in any fights with anybody. He wasn't that type of person."

"Where's he from?"

"A place called Copper Head, Tennessee, which is about an hour north of here."

"How long has he lived in Plain Ridge?" Susan asked, making a note to tell Clint to look into Thad's background in Copper Head.

"He moved here when he and Ann first got married." Carrie paused for a second, seemingly thinking about it. "Let's see, Wess is eight now, so that would've been nine years ago. His mom followed him after his dad died, and I actually saw her in the grocery store the other day. She told me she misses him and she's worried that he's working too hard."

"Do you have her name and number?"

"I don't know her number, but her name is Esther."

Susan jotted the information in her notes, and asked, "Does Thad have any friends in Plain Ridge?"

"Oh, yeah, he's got some friends here," Carrie said. "At first, he only knew my husband and a few of Ann's and my friends, but after he sold that first alligator book, more people started noticing him. Now, though, after those books really took off, everybody in town wants to be his friend. And even though he's not originally from here, they all claim him as a local, since he's married to one of our own and he wrote the first three books in town."

"And no enemies that you know about?"

"No, ma'am."

Susan asked more questions that dealt with Thad and Ann's experiences in Plain Ridge, and then she turned her attention back to Carrie's conversation with Ann.

"That's about all that was said," Ann explained. "She told me that Thad was leaving and she had to go, and that was it."

Susan's pen froze over her notepad. "What'd you say?"

"Um, that's all that was said between us?" The statement sounded more like a question.

"After that," Susan pressed. "You said something about Thad leaving."

"Oh, yeah," Carrie said. "Ann told me that she thought Thad had finished his work for the day, and she said she wanted to spend some time with him before he left."

"She said Thad was leaving to go somewhere?"

"Yeah, and she said she wanted to go see if he needed anything." Carrie paused briefly. "Ann was always thoughtful like that. Oh, and she also told me to call her tomorrow. Will...will I be able to do that?"

Susan didn't hear the last question, because she had walked to the front door and was staring out the window toward the porch of the neighbor's house. The sun had slid deep into the western horizon, and shadows were starting to form, making it hard to see the expression on Thad's face from that distance.

"You've got some explaining to do, mister," she said quietly, before mumbling a "thanks" to Ann and ending the call.

CHAPTER 13

Mechant Loup Police Department

I looked over Lindsey's shoulder as she pointed out some things in one of Thad Griffin's books that might be pertinent.

"In this chapter," she said, "a couple get into a fight over the son wanting to quit playing football. The husband insists that he should play, but the wife is worried that the boy will get hurt. Things get physical, and the next thing you know, the husband is dead."

"Did you read to the end yet?" I asked. "Do you know who killed him?"

"Oh, yeah, I finished it about ten minutes ago," she said. "The son killed him."

"Why?"

"He didn't want to be forced to play football."

"Good enough reason, I guess." I suddenly wondered if the character was eight years old. It was a rare event, but there had been cases of young kids committing murder. While it was usually of their own doing—albeit a byproduct of their environment—kids had sometimes killed at the behest of an adult, and I had to wonder if Thad had put his son up to murdering his mom. "The boy in the book—how old was he?"

"Seventeen."

I grunted, but had another thought. "Did he run over the dad with a black Lexus?"

"I wish!" Lindsey sighed. "No, he hit him on the head with an axe. He then wrapped the body in an old rug and buried him in a shallow grave behind the barn, but we don't find out about that until the end. The book starts when an alligator digs up the body and drags it into the water, where it's found by a fisherman two days later."

I straightened and scrunched up my face. "Would an alligator really do that?"

"It's fiction," she said with a shrug. "Sometimes you have to suspend disbelief for a story to work."

"Well, I like my fiction a little more realistic." I thanked her and headed for the door, calling over my shoulder, "Please let me know if you hear anything on that Lexus."

Once I reached my Tahoe, I began driving the streets of Mechant Loup again. I had already made a few rounds through each neighborhood after leaving the scene earlier, but vehicles weren't static, and what wasn't there one minute might very well be there the next.

A dozen sheriff's patrol deputies had joined me in searching the town, but we hadn't come up with anything. We had pulled them from town earlier and sent them north, asking them to search all of the neighborhoods heading into Central Chateau. Other deputies had headed to the interstates leading out of the parish, while neighboring parishes had also flooded their streets searching for the Lexus and the missing boy.

Baylor and Homer had headed south along Old Blackbird Highway to look for the car, but last I heard, they hadn't seen any sign of it. We knew nothing about our suspect, and it was starting to worry me. I was heading toward the east side of town when I received a call from my wife.

"What's up, Sue?" I asked, slowing my Tahoe in anticipation of having to head back to the scene.

"I think we might have something," she said quickly. "A girl named Carrie Young was on the phone with Ann Griffin moments before she died. Carrie said Ann mentioned that Thad was finished with his work for the day and was leaving to go somewhere. She said Ann wanted to spend some time with him before he left."

"What time was the phone call?"

"A little after two o'clock."

I stomped the brakes and whipped my SUV around on Washington Avenue. "He lied to me!"

"He did?"

"Yeah, he said he went in his office around five in the morning and didn't leave until after five in the afternoon," I explained, speeding up Washington and heading north on Main. "If she says he was leaving the house at two, then he lied his ass off."

"Then there's a good chance he ran her over and then headed for the bus stop to get Wess."

Although she couldn't see me, I nodded my head. "Is he still at the neighbor's house?"

"Yep, I'm looking at him now."

"I'll be there in a minute." I dropped my cell phone to the console and slowed as I rounded the curve on my approach to Tiger Plantation Boulevard. My mind was racing as I headed toward the back of the street. I needed to be careful how I approached Thad.

I couldn't let him know about the phone call. He had to think I was only trying to gather information to help find his son, otherwise he might become defensive and clam up. Worst yet, he might lawyer up if he thought we suspected him. If that happened and he was responsible for his wife's murder and his son's disappearance, we might never locate Wess.

Thad was pacing in front of the neighbor's house when I parked on the street. He was talking on his cell phone, but he quickly ended the call when I exited my vehicle. I saw a sheriff's deputy with a police social services patch and the name *Bradley Naquin* embroidered over his shirt pocket. I gave him a nod before approaching the—real or fabricated—grieving father.

"Did you find Wess?" Thad asked, his eyes wide with anticipation. "Is he okay?"

I shook my head. It was possible he might be lying about his involvement in his wife's murder and his son's disappearance, but I needed to remain cordial in case we were wrong.

"No, sir, but we've got officers searching everywhere." I took a breath. "Can you come with me to the police department, so I can pick your brain some more about what happened out here today?"

"I already told you what I know."

"I've got a few questions," I explained. "They're important ones, and they could help us find your son."

He took a frustrated breath, but gave a short nod.

I asked the PSS deputy to follow us to the police department, so he could be available to keep an eye on Thad in the event that I had to leave for something. He agreed and headed for his marked car.

"Do I have to ride with you?" Thad asked hesitantly.

"It would be better," I said.

He gave a nod and slipped into the passenger's side seat. He didn't say a word as I drove us to the office and led him to the interview room. Once he was seated across from me, I asked him to recount everything that had happened at his house, beginning with when he woke up in the morning and entered his office.

"Like I told you earlier," he explained, "I went in my office at five this morning. I went right to work on a difficult scene in my current book."

"What time did you wake up this morning?"

"It must've been four-thirty." He thought about it, and then nodded. "Yeah, it was four-thirty. Ann fixed me a cup of coffee and I took it to my office with me."

"Did you see Wess this morning?"

Thad shook his head. "I never usually see him in the morning. He doesn't wake up until six, and I'm usually already in my office by then."

I couldn't imagine not seeing my kids at the start of my day, and my expression must've shown my thoughts, because Thad quickly said, "I get to spend a lot of time with him in the afternoon when he gets home from school. I help him with his homework, and I read to him, and we play games. We have a good time every night. He really looks forward to our evenings together."

I nodded. "Did you leave your office at all during the day?"

Thad shook his head.

"Did you see Ann again after getting the coffee from her?"

Again, he shook his head.

"Can you tell me in great detail what happened when you wrapped up your work for the day?" I asked. "Start from the moment you left your office, up until the time you found Ann on the driveway. Don't leave anything out."

Thad took a deep breath. He held it for a second, exhaled slowly. He finally nodded, and said, "Okay, I'm ready."

CHAPTER 14

Earlier...

Upstairs at the Griffin Home

Thad Griffin checked the counter at the bottom left-hand corner of the Word document. He removed his headphones and sighed. He had finally reached his goal of 2,000 words per day. He usually reached that mark before noon, but that day's session had been a particularly rough one. He had been having a hard time trying to describe a fight scene between his main character and a large alligator, so it had taken him much longer to reach his word count. While he didn't know exactly what time it was, he knew it had to be at least a few hours past noon, because that had been when he'd stopped for lunch.

Since he'd never fought an alligator himself, he had been forced to do extensive research in order to find out what it felt like to go toe-to-toe with the prehistoric lizards, and he still wasn't sure he'd nailed it. He had interviewed a few men and one woman who had survived alligator attacks a few weeks earlier, but there were certain questions he'd forgotten to ask, and he'd found himself scrambling for information earlier in the morning. He hadn't even known he needed to ask those questions until he was neck deep into the scene.

After hours of watching YouTube videos of alligator and crocodile attacks—most of them completely and utterly useless—he had finally found one where a man had been attacked underwater while wearing a GoPro, and it had provided enough elements of realism to help him finally push through to the other side of the action scene. Shortly afterward, he had reached his goal for the day.

He sighed as he saved his work in three different places—his computer's hard drive, an external hard drive, and a flash drive—and then drank the last of his Diet Coke. Mondays were always the hardest writing days for him. After spending two free days of doing anything he wanted, it always felt like a punishment to lock himself in his office and remain there until he had reached the desired output. He had often thought of scaling back to 1,000 words per day, but then it would take too long for him to finish a book, and his readers were waiting on him for the next Gator Haven installment.

Although the morning had been rough, things had gotten easier as the day dragged on and he had started getting into the scene. Now, he couldn't wait for the next day to come around, so he could jump back into the story. Just like his future readers, he was excited to see what would happen next. He knew from past experiences that the motivation would carry him through most of the week, and then Friday would roll around and he'd start getting excited about his two days off again. It was a vicious cycle, but it wasn't nearly as vicious as "working for the man."

Thad glanced around at the mess in his office and grunted his disgust. He hated that he always became so absorbed in his work that he let his office get so out of hand. It wasn't that it was cluttered that bothered him, but the fact that Ann would always sneak inside and clean up his trash. He didn't like that she worked so hard picking up after him.

"It's the least I can do," she once said. "Thanks to your talent and dogged determination, I don't have to work a grueling nine-to-five job anymore for bosses who don't appreciate me. Hell, if you'd let me, I'd spoon-feed every meal for you and wipe your ass."

He had been taking a sip of his Diet Coke when she'd made the comment, and he had laughed so hard that the soda had shot up his nostrils and singed his nose hairs.

Making a mental note to clean up his own mess this time, he headed downstairs to thank Ann for the hot breakfast biscuit and sweet note she had left for him that morning.

"Hey, Honey, where are you?" he asked when he reached the landing to the stairs and looked around for her. "I loved the breakfast biscuit!"

Although he was the sole breadwinner, he felt bad about her waiting on him hand and foot, and he wished he would be more mindful of cleaning up after himself.

"Ann?" Thad called, stopping briefly in the kitchen to look for his wife. She wasn't there. It was dark inside the kitchen, and that confused him. He wasn't sure what time it was, but it had to be getting into the afternoon. While many of his fellow authors wrote for a certain number of hours per day, that kind of schedule didn't work for him. When he entered his office, he wasn't allowed to leave until he had written the prescribed number of words for that day. It didn't matter if it took three hours or fifteen.

In fact, he didn't allow clocks in his office, and he had put a piece of masking tape over the time stamp on the bottom right-hand corner of his computer. He didn't even want to know what time it was. He ate in his kitchenette when he was hungry, so there was no need to know when it was noon. If he got thirsty, he grabbed a drink from his office refrigerator. He called the process "doing time," and he had to get his work done before being released on good behavior.

"Ann, where are you?" he asked, stopping to listen. "What time is it?"

Nothing. No answer, and not a sound.

Confused, he headed for the back door to see if she had gone for a swim. It was May in southeast Louisiana, and just about every day of the month was hot enough for a swim. However, Ann wasn't in the pool.

He pulled out his cell phone and pressed the side buttons to turn it on. He was never sure which one activated the phone, so he just pressed all of them at the same time. While waiting for it to fire up, he called out Ann's name a few more times while he walked around checking the spare bedroom upstairs, Ann's craft room, and Wess' bedroom, but she wasn't there.

Puzzled, and more than a little concerned, he headed to the garage to see if Ann's car was there. He couldn't help but remember when she had called 9-1-1 when she had been worried about him, and he promised himself he wouldn't make the same mistake. Warm air gushed in when he opened the side door, and he frowned when he saw that her car was gone.

"Huh, where is she?" he muttered to himself. "Did something happen?"

Thad slid his finger across the screen to wake up his phone. It had finally come to life, so he navigated to his contacts and pushed the icon for Ann's cell number. He was starting to worry as he pulled it to his ear. Not since they'd first gotten together had she just disappeared like that, and back then it had been because she'd received a call from her sister saying that her mom was in the hospital. He hoped nothing like that had happened. It would be like her to not want to disturb his work, but she also hated to leave without saying goodbye.

Her phone had been ringing in his ear—it was going on the third one—when he realized he was hearing something else. The sound was coming from outside the phone's speaker. He glanced toward the noise, which appeared to be emitting from beyond the closed garage door. Not only did it match the rhythm of the ringing in his ear, but it also matched Ann's ringtone.

"Ann?" he called again, reaching blindly for the button to the automatic garage door. "Ann, are you out there?"

When the phone went to voicemail in his ear, the ringing on the outside stopped. He watched curiously as the door slowly retracted. More and more of the concrete driveway came into view as he waited. He wondered why Ann wasn't answering him. Surely, if he could hear her cell phone, then she could hear him hollering her name. It wasn't like her not to respond.

The sunlight spilled in and brightened up the interior as the door completed its cycle. Thad had to lower his head and shield his eyes against the unexpected light, and it was then that he noticed a pair of burnout marks on the concrete. They began where Ann's rear tires would've been parked near the opening, and proceeded out into the driveway.

"What in the hell?" he asked out loud.

Those marks hadn't been there the last time he had entered the garage. He couldn't remember exactly when that had been, but it must've been during the weekend. That would mean they were made that day, but that didn't make sense. Why would Ann have left in such a hurry that she would've left burnout marks on the concrete?

Keeping his hand in front of his face to block out the sun, Thad lifted his head to follow the burnout marks with his eyes. He sucked in his breath when he saw a bundle of some sort lying in the middle of the driveway. It didn't make sense at first. The bundle was wrapped in tattered clothes that closely resembled what Ann had put on that morning, but that was impossible. What would her clothes be doing in the driveway?

"Dear God!" he said suddenly, realization hitting him so hard that his knees got weak. "No!"

Thad rushed forward and dropped to the ground in front of his wife. He retched violently. When he was done, he began screaming hysterically for someone—anyone—to come and help him.

CHAPTER 15

South of Mechant Loup

Homer Verdin's head was on a swivel. He and Baylor Rice had driven all the way to the end of Old Blackbird Highway—turning down every street and cruising through every neighborhood along the way—in search of the stolen vehicle and the missing boy. While they had seen several Lexus vehicles, none of them had been black with dark tinted windows.

"Do you think the dad had something to do with it?" Homer asked as they made their approach to the southern end of town. He didn't take his eyes off of his surroundings when he asked the question.

"I actually hope so," Baylor said, slowing as a black sedan approached them from the north. It wasn't a Lexus, so he picked up speed again. "If the dad killed the mom, there's a good chance we'll find the boy alive. If some deranged individual did it, God help the kid."

Homer gritted his teeth, thinking about his younger siblings. If anyone ever hurt one of them, he didn't know what he would do to them. *Well, I do have an idea what I'd do,* he thought wryly, remembering what he'd done to the former terrorist who had called himself Spider.

"Let's check out the east side again," Baylor said when they entered town. He veered slightly right onto Back Street and headed for Market Street Bridge, which crossed Bayou Tail and connected the two sides of town.

Baylor had explained to Homer earlier that the east side was their high crime area, and he said it was there that he would expect to find a stolen vehicle.

"If a stranger stole the car and kidnapped the kid," Baylor had explained, "my money is on him ditching the car and transferring the kid to a getaway vehicle." After a moment of silent reflection, Baylor had continued. "I hope I'm wrong, because that would be the scariest scenario."

"Couldn't the dad have ditched it, too?" Homer had asked. "Just to make it look like a stranger killed his wife and kidnapped his kid?"

Baylor had grinned and turned to look at Homer. "You haven't been a cop for a full day, and you're already starting to think like one."

It had made Homer feel good to receive such a compliment from an officer that he was quickly growing to respect, but he hadn't had much time to dwell on it. He had been too busy trying to scan the interior of every car that drove by, just in case the kidnapper had really switched rides. He was thankful for the photo that Clint Wolf had sent them, and when he wasn't looking at an approaching car, he was staring at it in hopes of burning a permanent image in his mind.

"What's going on over here?" Baylor asked as they approached the bridge.

Homer turned to see what he was talking about, and he saw two women and three young boys standing on the shoulder of the road just past the bridge. The women had their backs to them, but he could see the faces of the boys, and they looked excited. One of them held a fishing pole in his right hand and a tackle box in the left one, and he was waving both items around as he spoke in an animated fashion.

"Let's check it out," said Baylor, passing up the bridge and pulling the cruiser to the shoulder of the road.

Homer had unsnapped his seatbelt the very second Baylor had mentioned the incident, and he was out of the car in a flash. When he spun to face the group of people, he stopped dead in his tracks, but only for a split second.

"What is it?" Baylor asked, noticing the sudden—albeit brief— change in his partner's posture.

"Oh, it's nothing," Homer said quickly, and moved toward the group with Baylor.

"Hey, what's up, Ali?" Baylor asked when they reached the two women and the young boys. "Is something wrong?"

Homer was familiar with Ali Bridges. She was a beautiful woman with long brown hair and brown eyes—much like many women in his tribe—and she was a reporter for the Mechant Voice. She had interviewed him after he'd gotten the award, and he remembered being extremely nervous to talk to her. Not because she was beautiful, but because he had never been interviewed for a story before, and he just knew he had messed up most of his answers.

His mom had somehow gotten her hands on a copy of the story, and she said the article had made him sound smart and official. He told her it wasn't him who had been smart or official. He informed his mom that it had been Ali Bridges who had made him sound that way, because she had fixed all of his mistakes.

And while he recognized Ali from before, he had never seen the younger woman who stood beside her in the jeans and black form-fitting shirt. The top of the shirt was what he'd heard one of his former girlfriends refer to as a "scoop neck," and there were several fashionable rips across the upper thighs of the jeans. The girl's athletic legs filled out the fabric perfectly. The parts of her firm legs that were visible through the rips appeared as smooth and tanned as her upper chest, neck, and face, and her long blonde hair was accentuated by her complexion.

Ali Bridges was Homer's senior by a few years, but this girl had to be his age. He dropped his eyes for a brief moment, searching her left hand for a ring. There was none. He did notice that her arms and hands were also bronze colored and perfectly sculptured, and her nails were painted a glossy red.

She was tall—only about three inches shorter than his own five-ten frame—and she reminded Homer of a female volleyball player. In his short life, he couldn't remember ever seeing a girl who looked so appealing. As he stood there wondering who she was, she turned to look at him. Her green eyes sparkled, and they seemed to bore deep into his soul when their gazes locked. His pulse quickened. He fought the urge to lick his dry lips. However, he couldn't help but swallow hard when her mouth curled slightly at the corners, forming a subtle smile. Her lower lip jutted out just a little. It was full and her lipstick glistened in the waning light.

Despite himself, Homer wondered what it might feel like to kiss those luscious—

Homer was suddenly snapped from his trance by the sound of Ali's voice mentioning a black Lexus. It was only then that he remembered he was a cop and he was working an important assignment. He quickly looked away from the girl and turned his full attention on his training officer. His face was flushed with embarrassment for having lost his concentration, and he hoped no one noticed.

CHAPTER 16

"We had just heard about a black Lexus being involved in a hit and run on Tiger Plantation Boulevard," Ali explained to Baylor and Homer. "We were heading out there when these boys waved us down to ask us to call somebody about a black car that almost ran them over. They said it was a Lexus."

"Are you sure?" Baylor asked, turning to the young boys. "Do y'all even know what a Lexus looks like?"

"Yes, sir!" A sandy-haired kid with orange freckles nodded his head up and down for emphasis. "My aunt's got one, but hers is older. This one was shiny new."

"And where'd you see it?" Baylor asked.

"We was waiting to cross Cypress Highway over there," the boy said, lifting the fishing pole and pointing it toward the east, "and the car came speeding by, heading up the bayou. It almost ran us over."

Homer had grown up in the swamps of Chateau Parish, and he knew "up the bayou" meant that the car was heading north. He also knew that Cypress Highway ended in that direction, so the car couldn't have gone far.

"Did you see who was driving?" Baylor asked.

The boy shook his head. "No, sir. It was going too fast and the windows were really dark. It looked like my uncle's truck. He's got illegal tint."

Homer noticed that Baylor stifled a chuckle before turning to the other two boys to ask if they had noticed the presence of any passengers, but they shook their heads in unison.

"Are you boys sure?" Baylor pressed.

"Yes, sir," the sandy-haired boy said. "We couldn't see anything inside."

"Yeah," piped up one of the others. "It could've even been empty. My brother told me they got cars that drive themselves now, and they wreck all the time. That one looked like it was going way too fast, so I bet it was one of them kind of cars and I bet it wrecked when it got to the end of the road."

"He's right," rejoined the sandy-haired boy, pointing toward the north. "The road ends way up there, and I bet that car didn't have time to stop before it ran into the bayou."

Baylor nodded and asked a few more questions. Homer paid close attention to every word that was spoken. He wanted to retain the information for later, and he wanted to learn how to question potential witnesses.

Finally, Baylor got the names, addresses, and phone numbers for the boys and their parents. He thanked them and let them go. After they had scurried off, he turned to Homer.

"I'll give Clint a call and see what he wants to do." Baylor looked directly into Homer's eyes and shifted his head slightly.

Homer felt his face redden. He nodded and turned to the new girl. He stuck out his hand. "I'm Homer Verdin."

"Remi Walton," said the girl, sticking out her own hand. It was cold and soft, but she had a nice grip. "Well, my name's Remington, but everyone calls me Remi."

"Nice to meet you, Remi."

"Okay, break it up you two," Ali said, stepping closer to Homer. "What's going on with this black Lexus?"

Homer shrugged. "You know I'm new here, so it's not my place to say anything."

"And here I was thinking we were friends." Ali folded her arms across her breasts and shook her head in a feigned expression of sadness. "You seemed like such a nice guy the first time we talked. I guess I was wrong about you."

"A friend wouldn't try to get me fired on my first day," Homer shot back playfully, to which Remi burst out laughing. He smiled inwardly at her reaction. His dad used to always say, *If you can make a girl laugh, you're halfway to her heart.* He was sure there were exceptions to that rule, but he hoped it applied in the present case.

"Touché," Ali said with a nod. She turned to look at Baylor, who stood in the doorway to the Charger talking on his cell phone. "Maybe I should've let Remi ask the question."

"I would've given the same answer," Homer blurted without

thinking. After he said it, he quickly glanced at Remi, whose green eyes appeared glassier than earlier, thanks to the glow from a nearby streetlamp that had come on. "I mean no offense."

Remi smiled. "None taken."

Homer nodded, not sure what else to say. He also didn't know what to do with his hands, so he shoved them in his pockets. Thankfully, Baylor reappeared and bailed him out.

"Okay, let's go," Baylor said. "We've got a dozen deputies scattered around, and Clint wants us to go across the bayou right away."

"Hold up, Baylor," Ali said. "What's going on with the black Lexus?"

"Pretty much exactly what you heard."

Ali's eyes narrowed. "Then why am I sensing there's a whole lot more to it than that?"

"You can call Clint and see if he'll give you more," Baylor said. "It's his case, so he decides what gets released. I just do what I'm told. I do appreciate your help, though."

Ali nodded her resignation and waved for Remi to follow her. Homer noticed that Remi glanced at him before following Ali, and that made his pulse quicken a little.

"I think she likes you," Baylor said when they were in his Charger and heading for the Market Street Bridge. "Did you get her name and number?"

"I got her name, but I didn't ask for her number." Homer scowled. "Should I have?"

"Definitely." Baylor slowed to turn onto the bridge and shrugged. "You'll get another chance. They're heading to Tiger Plantation now to cover the story. Knowing Ali, she'll stay on this thing until the very end, so we'll cross paths with them again."

Homer was quiet for a long moment. Baylor drove across the bridge, navigated his cruiser through the east side of town, and then headed north on Cypress Highway. Homer kept his eyes peeled the entire time, ever searching for the black Lexus. His mind kept wanting to wander to Remi Walton, but he fought to remain focused on the search.

"Hey, Baylor," he finally began, guilt tugging at his chest, "is it wrong to think about a girl while I'm on the clock? I mean, we're out here trying to find a missing kid, and all I can think about is Remi. I'm trying not to, but I can't help it."

Baylor let out a hearty laugh that rang through the cruiser for several long seconds. When he finally stopped laughing, he said,

"Homer, you're not RoboCop. You're allowed to have feelings and emotions."

"Who's RoboCop?"

Baylor took his eyes off the road for a brief moment to stare at Homer. "You've never heard of the 1987 movie RoboCop?"

"Nah, that was way before my time."

"It was before my time, too, but I've seen the movie at least a dozen times growing up." Baylor was thoughtful. "Do y'all have televisions out in the swamps?"

"We do, but I don't watch it much," Homer admitted. "I'm more interested in what's going on outside. I don't like being cooped up in the house."

"I don't blame you there." Baylor slowed as they approached the Bayou View Apartments. "I can't stand watching TV when it's light outside. Amy and I will watch movies in the evenings sometimes, but we never have the television on during the day unless it's to catch the news."

"I hear you." Homer was thoughtful, and then frowned. "Hey, what was your point about this RoboCop movie?"

"RoboCop could mimic human emotions, but he didn't have any," Baylor explained. "You and me, we might work in law enforcement, but we're humans first. While we're expected to keep our feelings and emotions in check, we're still allowed to have them."

"We can have them, but not act on them?"

"Right. It's perfectly normal for you to get angry when you have to arrest a child predator. You might wish him dead, or want to kill him yourself—like any normal man or woman might wish or want to do." Baylor paused to shake his head. "But the difference between you and any other man or woman is that you're a cop, and you have a code to follow. You don't have the luxury of acting on your feelings and emotions. You have to rise above them and remain disciplined at all times."

Homer was confused. "Are we allowed to act on our feelings sometimes, or do we have to be like RoboCop all of the time?"

"Well, falling in love is one of the greatest human emotions there is," Baylor began. "If you're single, then you're free to—"

"I'm not falling in love!" Homer blurted. He suddenly realized he'd sounded a little too defensive, so he quickly cleared his throat and tried again, but with less emphasis. "I'm not falling in love. I was just asking about other stuff."

"If you say so, Romeo," Baylor said with a laugh, turning onto

Bayou View Lane. "Just know that I fell in love with Amy while we were working together, and I still got my job done. When it's go time, you forget everything and—"

"There!" Homer said, subtly pointing out the passenger window toward the north, where a vehicle had just rounded a bend in Cypress Highway and passed under a streetlight. "A black Lexus!"

CHAPTER 17

Mechant Loup Police Department

I had listened carefully to Thad Griffin's statement, not interrupting him once. Unlike most of my witnesses, he had needed no prompting from me. The man was definitely a good storyteller, and this made my job harder. On the one hand, I found myself believing everything he'd had to say. On the other, I found myself wondering if being a writer of lies had made him a good liar.

"Mr. Griffin, what would you say if I told you we had evidence suggesting you left your office much earlier than you're saying?" I asked after he had finished his story. I glanced at my notes. "It would've been around three o'clock, actually."

Thad scowled. "I would say that's impossible. As soon as I left my office, I searched the house just like I said, and I know that didn't take but a few minutes. When…when I found Ann, I started screaming for help. I was in shock, I admit it, but I know it wasn't more than a few minutes before my neighbors came running to help. I'm pretty sure they called 9-1-1, because you guys arrived shortly thereafter."

"What if this information came directly from your wife?" I asked, studying his expression carefully. "Would you call her a liar?"

"What do you mean?" His face was twisted in horror. "What are you saying?"

There was no strategic reason not to withhold the details of the phone call between his wife and her best friend, so I went ahead and described it to him. As I talked, he became more and more vexed. By the time I was finished, his mouth hung open.

"Are you saying she thought I was leaving the house?" he asked in a weak voice. "She thought I was leaving, so she went to tell me bye, and then she died? Are you saying that she died thinking I did this to her?"

"That's impossible for anyone to know," I quickly explained. "We can't exactly recreate her final moments, but it does appear that she thought you were finished with your work for the day, and that you were leaving in one of the vehicles."

He buried his face in his hands. "Dear God," he murmured, "how can this be happening?"

I sat quietly for a few minutes, allowing him to process what he'd just heard. When I thought he'd had enough time, I asked if he was denying leaving the house at three o'clock, or thereabouts.

"I'm absolutely denying it," he said, not lifting his head from his hands. "I didn't leave my office until around five—like I've already told you multiple times." He groaned in desperation. "How is this happening?"

"Mr. Griffin, did you run over your wife—either by accident or intentionally?" I suddenly asked, without warning.

He lifted his head and stared directly into my eyes. "No! I would never hurt my wife. I loved her. She was the mother of my son. We were building a life together. Everything was finally going right for us. Why would I destroy everything by killing her?"

I didn't answer him, and I gave no indication as to whether or not I believed him. I simply asked the next question, and the next. He answered each of them without hesitation, as I subtly tried to pick apart his story, attacking each aspect from different angles. However, all of his answers were consistent with his story. No matter how many times I asked the same questions in different ways, he never wavered, and he never grew defensive.

While I knew he could be good at deception, given his occupation, I found myself believing him. His grief for his deceased wife seemed deep and genuine, as did his concern for his son. Had he stashed Wess away somewhere and knew that the boy was safe, I doubted he would be able to put on such a performance—and I doubted he would've continued to interrupt me to ask if we'd found his son, as he had been doing throughout the entire interview.

"Mr. Griffin, you said earlier that no one wanted your wife dead, and that if they wanted anybody dead, it would've been you," I began after a time, deciding to change gears. "But then you said no one wanted y'all dead, that y'all were good people. Do you recall that?"

Thad nodded.

"Good people are attacked all the time and for different reasons." I leaned forward, resting my elbows on the table. "Your house was in pristine shape. Nothing seemed out of place, so we can probably rule out a burglary. The Lexus was taken, though, which would usually spell robbery, but there's the issue with your son being taken. That throws a big wrench into all of our best theories."

I paused and waited for a response from Thad. There was none. He simply stared back at me, his face a twisted mask of horror, despair, and confusion.

"Being famous comes with its own risks and challenges," I continued. "Have you received any threatening mail, emails, or messages from anyone?"

Thad shook his head quickly. "None at all."

"Have you had any complaints?" I pressed. "Maybe you killed off a favorite character? Or wrote about a controversial topic?"

Again, he shook his head instantly. "The feedback I get is 100% positive. Now, I'll get some low ratings and negative reviews on Amazon or Goodreads from time-to-time, but nothing out of the ordinary."

"What do they complain about in the negative reviews?"

"It's mostly over the killing of alligators," he said with a shrug. "The bad guys in my stories are usually alligators, and the good guys track them down and kill them. Some people don't like hunting of any kind, and they're quick to condemn an author who writes about it. It comes with the territory. I'm not bothered by it at all. It's better than having them say the storyline was unrealistic or the main character was unlikeable or that it's a copycat of some other author's work, like they did with my first detective series."

I would never rule out any person or motive without cause, but I doubted someone would murder his wife and kidnap his son merely because he wrote about hunting alligators. I also wouldn't take his word for anything. As I was interviewing him, Susan and Amy were carefully going through his house, office, computers, and other electronic devices in search of a motive. They would also be searching through all of his wife's things, looking for any hint of a reason why evil had paid a visit to this family.

"What did you do before you became a writer?" I asked, listening with interest as he detailed his entire employment background. He began with his first job working as a farm hand in East Tennessee at the age of fifteen, and took me all the way to his latest book. There seemed to be nothing untoward in his work history, so I asked about his love life, and if there were any disgruntled girlfriends or wives in his past.

"Aren't they all?" he asked with a chuckle. When I didn't respond in kind, the smile left his face and he shook his head. "No, nothing like that. Ann was my first serious girlfriend. All of my other relationships only lasted a short time. The longest was about six months. Most of them probably don't even remember my name."

"Did you hurt any of them?" I asked. "Or cheat on them with Ann? You know what they say about a woman scorned."

He shook his head. "I had been single for about two years when I met Ann. Besides, the girls I dated usually broke up with me to go out with someone with more money or who drove a big truck. One girl left me because I wore Lee jeans. She said I dressed like a bum, and that she was embarrassed to be seen with me."

"How'd that make you feel?"

"I didn't care," he said. "My dad wore Lee jeans all his life, and he married my mom, so I'd say he did just fine. And I ended up with Ann, so every breakup was a good thing. If any of those relationships would've worked out, I might never have found her. She's the best thing that happened to me."

It sounded like he was about to break down again, so I asked about his family, and whether or not there was any animosity between any of his relatives and his wife. It was the wrong move if I wanted to keep him talking, because at the mention of his family, he dropped his head and broke down crying harder than earlier.

"They don't even know what's going on yet," he said in a choking voice. "I haven't had the courage to call them. I...I don't even know how to begin to tell Ann's mom and dad."

I frowned. "If you want, I could have some officers from your county notify your family and Ann's family."

Thad raised his sorrowful face. "You would do that for me?"

"For sure."

"But...but I thought you suspected me of killing my wife," he said. "Why would you help me?"

"I don't necessarily suspect you," I explained. "I just haven't ruled you out yet. And even if you were our prime suspect, I'd still send someone to contact Ann's family. They did nothing wrong."

He nodded his acknowledgement and provided me with addresses for members of both families, as well as the names of the sheriff's offices for both jurisdictions. That saved me some research, and it only took me a few minutes to make arrangements for them to be notified. I was still standing outside the interview room when Lindsey stuck her head out of the opening to the dispatcher's station, her eyes wide.

"Clint, it's Baylor and Homer!" she hollered. "They've spotted the Lexus!"

Before I could respond, the door to the interview room jerked open and Thad rushed out.

"They found Wess?" he asked, his voice shrill with emotion. "Is my boy okay?"

Lindsey hesitated, looking at me before offering an explanation. Based on her expression, I didn't think the news was very good.

I gave a nod, thinking that Thad deserved to know what was going on. Based on my interview with him and his most recent reaction, I was leaning more and more toward eliminating him as a suspect. Unless he was an excellent actor, he hadn't been responsible for the murder of his wife and the kidnapping of his son.

"What's going on?" I asked Lindsey.

"As soon as they spotted the Lexus, it began running," she said. "They were heading south on Cypress Highway, but they just crossed onto Old Blackbird, still heading south. The vehicle's driving erratically and with the headlights off, so they're backing off a little, hoping it'll slow down. We don't have any units south of them, so they'll probably lose it—"

"No!" Thad screamed, lunging toward Lindsey. "Tell them to keep going! They need to stop that car at all costs! They can't let it get away!"

I stepped forward quickly and wrapped an arm around Thad before he could reach Lindsey. I pushed him against the wall and told him to calm down.

"They need to stop the car!" he repeated, his voice filled with despair. "If they don't, the chances of getting Wess back alive are nil! You know—"

Right at that moment, Thad's sentence was cut off by the sound of Homer Verdin's voice calling authoritatively over the radio.

I didn't recognize it as Homer at first, because I had never heard him use that tone before. He sounded much older and more mature than his years, and I found myself feeling like a proud father at that moment.

His demeanor was calm, as though he were reporting that a bridge was out or that he and Baylor were stepping out of the car for lunch. However, when his transmission echoed through the building and the message sank in, my heart dropped to my boots. Lindsey gasped and rushed to the radio, while Thad began screaming like a man possessed. It was all I could do to keep him from smashing his head through the nearest window.

CHAPTER 18

Mechant Loup East

Although the sun had set and he figured the driver of the black Lexus couldn't see inside their patrol cruiser, Homer still refrained from turning his head to follow the suspect vehicle's path, while Baylor continued to cruise nonchalantly down Bayou View Lane.

"Easy does it," Baylor said softly. "As soon as he gets out of sight, we'll whip it around and go check it out."

Homer could see his training officer tracking the vehicle in the rearview mirror. "Do you think it's the one?" he asked, stealing a glance behind Baylor's head. He could see the taillights disappear around a curve in the road. In that same moment, Baylor whipped the marked cruiser around on the lane and sped toward Cypress Highway. He barely slowed when he reached the intersection, and the tires squealed when he made the turn.

The engine roared and wind whistled against the light bar as the car rapidly picked up speed. For the second time in one day, Homer felt a rush of adrenalin surge through him. Only this time, it was much more intense.

Homer expected to see the black Lexus when they rounded the corner, but scowled when he saw that the highway in front of them was empty. He looked over at Baylor. From the glow of the dash lights, he saw a hard expression spread across Baylor's face.

"He's running!" Baylor said, stomping the accelerator and activating the lights and siren. "Let dispatch know we've spotted the Lexus and we're in pursuit! Give our location, direction of travel, and speed."

Homer snatched the mic from the clip on the dash as the Charger shot forward. He'd never traveled that fast before—not in a car or boat or any other vehicle—and he was pumped.

"Headquarters, we're in pursuit of a black Lexus," he said, surprising himself with how calm his voice sounded. "We're heading southbound on Cypress Highway at"—he leaned over to see the speedometer—"eighty miles per hour and climbing. We're approaching the intersection of East Main and Cypress."

"Ten-four," Lindsey called back.

It wasn't until they reached a speed of ninety and had passed East Main that Baylor announced he could see the vehicle up ahead. Homer leaned forward and squinted. He didn't see any taillights like he'd expected, and that confused him a little. He did notice a dark blur in the distance and several sets of headlights approaching, but having never been involved in a high-speed chase, he wasn't sure what he was looking at.

"He's running without lights and there's traffic coming the opposite direction," Baylor said. "This is getting dangerous. Let Lindsey know what's going on and tell her we're backing off a little. We've got no officer to the south, so we can't set up a roadblock, and we can't spike the tires at those speeds with a kid inside. Our only option is to slow down and turn off our lights and siren. If he thinks we're giving up, he might slow down."

Homer did as he was told. They had reached a long stretch of highway, and he could see for about a mile. Far in the distance, he caught intermittent glimpses of the dark blur zigzagging in and out of the left lane, causing several approaching vehicles to swerve out of its path.

"What in the hell's he doing?" Baylor asked. They had slowed to about seventy, and the blur in the distance was getting harder to see. "We're not even close to him. This asshole must have a death wish."

Homer winced as a set of headlights swerved severely to its right, cut back to the left, and then fishtailed from lane to lane before coming to a complete stop sideways in the middle of the highway. Baylor slowed, eased to the rough shoulder, and zipped past the stopped vehicle. Homer could see that a woman was driving, and the expression on her face was one of sheer terror. He couldn't imagine how she must've felt to be driving along the highway, minding her own business, and then suddenly having a blacked-out vehicle appear in her headlights. Given the circumstances, he thought she had done well for herself, and he wasn't sure if he could've come out of the situation without crashing.

"What're we supposed to do?" he asked Baylor after they had traveled another mile, or so, and the vehicle continued to outdistance them.

"At this point, all we can do is observe and report," Baylor explained. His jaw was set, and it was obvious he didn't like the position in which they found themselves. "If we press too hard and he crashes, it's on us. And forget liability. While that's an issue, I just don't want some innocent child's death on my conscience."

Homer nodded and continued leaning forward, squinting to see. Although it didn't improve his visibility, it made him feel better. Several more cars drove by the Lexus without incident. Some of them had probably not even noticed that there was a vehicle traveling in the opposite direction at a high rate of speed with the headlights off.

When they had driven another couple of miles, brake lights suddenly lit up the roadway in front of them.

"He's slowing down," Baylor said. "We're approaching the bridge, so I think he's crossing."

The brake lights went dark for a second, and Homer could see the dark shadow of the car shoot across the bridge, crossing to the opposite side of the bayou. When the Lexus reached the end of the bridge, the brake lights came on again and the car veered left, heading south on Old Blackbird Highway.

Since the car was out of sight, Baylor sped up and quickly crossed the bridge, making up a little distance. He flipped the headlights off when he reached the opposite end, and headed south after the suspect vehicle.

Homer took a breath and leaned back in his seat, not wanting to be so close to the windshield while they were speeding down the highway in total darkness.

"Can you see?" he asked Baylor, trying to keep the nervousness from his voice.

"Good enough," came Baylor's response. "We're gaining on him, and he doesn't suspect a thing."

"How can you tell?"

"Because he's slowing down."

That made Homer feel a little better, but he was still apprehensive about driving in the dark.

"Don't ever do this," Baylor warned after a minute of driving in silence. "It's too damned dangerous."

"One of those *do as I say and not as I do* moments?" Homer

asked.

"Exactly," Baylor said with a chuckle. "In all my years of police work, I've never had to do this, but I've never faced a more reckless suspect. This asshole wants to get away at any cost, and that makes him extremely dangerous."

"Do you think he's armed?"

"In this business, everyone's armed until you prove otherwise."

Homer filed that nugget of wisdom away, sure that he would need it someday, while keeping his eyes straight ahead. The brake lights came on again briefly before the car disappeared around a bend in the road, and Homer felt Baylor speed up some more.

When they rounded the same curve, Homer was not prepared for what happened next. Up ahead of them, a vehicle with bright headlights was approaching the Lexus from the south. It appeared to be a small sedan, and just as the two vehicles passed each other, the suspect sideswiped the unsuspecting vehicle. Orange sparks shot into the air as metal scraped violently against metal, and the sedan swerved off the road to the right, over-corrected to the left, and ran directly into a small tree that grew along the shoulder of the road.

"Shit!" Baylor called, immediately turning on his headlights and fighting the steering wheel to keep the Charger from colliding with the sedan, which spun out of control after clipping the tree.

With nothing else to do, Homer held on for dear life as he was jerked from right to left with the swerving of the police car. When Baylor finally brought it to a halt, Homer jerked his head around, searching for the sedan. He finally spotted it several dozen yards behind them.

It had come to a stop with the rear tires resting in a ditch and the front tires on the fog line of the northbound lane. Smoke was spewing from under the hood. There was a large hole in the passenger side of the windshield, and he let out a rare curse when he saw what looked like a young woman sprawled in the roadway. Before he or Baylor could utter a word, the car burst into flames.

As Baylor jumped from the driver's seat and rushed to render aid to the injured woman, Homer keyed up the mic on the police radio. Speaking in an oddly calm voice—one that he didn't recognize as his own—he let Lindsey know about the crash, the injured woman, the burning car, and the fact that the Lexus was getting away.

Homer could hear sirens far away in the distance, and he knew that help was on the way. He had exited the patrol cruiser and was approaching Baylor at a quick run. Baylor had quickly checked the woman for signs of life and then begun chest compressions.

Homer had almost reached Baylor and the woman when he suddenly wondered if he should turn back around, jump in the patrol car, and continue the chase. Since Baylor was tending to the victim, he didn't think it would be proper to interrupt his training officer with such a question. He also didn't know if that was the kind of decision he should make on his own, given it was his first day on the job.

He was still heading toward Baylor when he heard a shrill scream that chilled him to the bones. He skidded to a stop. He turned toward the sound. He couldn't be positive, but it sounded like the scream had come from the sedan. He hoped that wasn't right, because flames were rising up from the engine area, and growing ever larger with each passing second.

That's when he heard another scream coming from somewhere inside the burning car. It was definitely from a woman, and it sounded more desperate and terrified than the first. He quickly keyed up the mic attached to his lapel and said, "Headquarters, be advised someone's trapped in the burning vehicle. We need fire rescue ASAP!"

CHAPTER 19

After sending the radio transmission, Homer's first reaction was to head straight for the burning car, but Baylor barked out some information that sent him in another direction.

"In the trunk!" Baylor hollered, not stopping what he was doing. "I've got a fire extinguisher!"

Homer gave a quick nod and dashed toward the patrol cruiser. He had never trained for such a situation, but he somehow managed to find the trunk release button and activate it without trouble. He removed the fire extinguisher from where it was strapped to the inside of the trunk, and returned to the burning sedan in what seemed like record time.

When the sedan had crashed into the small tree earlier, not only had the female passenger squirted through the windshield, but the hood had been severely damaged and had snapped open. Aiming the nozzle of the fire extinguisher at the large flames that licked up from behind the engine, Homer gave the release lever a squeeze.

As Homer worked, he caught a fleeting glance of the driver and saw that she was a young woman. In that brief moment, he saw that she had blonde hair, blue eyes that sparkled in the orange glow from the fire, and deep red lipstick. He didn't know it then, but he would never forget the look of terror on her face as she struggled with the interior door handle, choking on the smoke and yelling for help.

Homer almost cried out in triumph as the white powder shot from the nozzle and smothered the flames. Soon, the orange glow gave way to a thick white cloud and even more smoke, and he found himself coughing along with the trapped woman. He didn't let go of the lever until the fire extinguisher had given one last, dry gasp. He dropped the empty cylinder and headed for the driver's door.

"Hang on," Homer called out as he reached for the door handle. "I'll get you out!"

He fumbled with the handle for a split second before realizing that the door had been so damaged when the Lexus had sideswiped it that it couldn't be opened. Muttering to himself, he rushed around to the other side of the sedan. He breathed easier when he pulled on that door handle and it opened. While he had initially felt a sense of relief that he was able to gain access to the cab of the car, that brief moment of triumph was wiped away when he noticed that the fire had come back, and it seemed to be spreading faster than earlier.

Sucking in a deep breath of fresh air, Homer squeezed into the tight quarters of the smoke-filled cab, and reached for the button to the driver's safety belt.

"I'm stuck!" the girl said in a choking voice, her minty-fresh breath breaking through the putrid smell of melting plastic and burning fuel. "It's my legs. I can't move them."

Homer gave a nod. He jerked the seatbelt free and pulled it over her left shoulder. The steering wheel was pressed snuggly against her breasts, and he had to use some force to remove the belt.

He didn't want to hurt the girl by yanking on her arm to free her, so he wrapped his left arm around her back and clasped his hands together under her armpit. Bracing his left knee against the seat and his right boot against the floorboard, he gave a giant tug, intent on pulling her free in one quick motion.

He knew the move might injure her, but he figured it would be better than a series of repetitive jerks. To his dismay, the girl let loose with a blood-curdling scream that pierced him to the eardrums, and her body remained trapped.

"I'm sorry!" Sweat broke out on Homer's forehead, and it wasn't just from the heat that was rolling into the cab. "I have to get you out of here. The fire's coming back."

In the orange glow from the rising flames, Homer noted a strawberry-looking abrasion on the girl's forehead. He figured it was from the deflated airbags that draped across the girl's legs. He pushed them out of the way to get a look at her legs. They were twisted and bloody, and a bone could be seen protruding through the skin that surrounded her right shin. He quickly looked away.

"What's your name?" he asked, readying himself for another strong tug.

"Lisa Grant," the girl said between fits of coughing. Tears of pain streaked down her cheeks, but on her face was a look of determination.

Homer took short breaths, trying to keep the smoke from his lungs, and said, "Hang on, Lisa. This'll hurt a bit."

Lisa bit down hard on her lower lip and nodded to let Homer know she was ready. Blood appeared almost instantly on the flesh beneath her bright teeth, and Homer knew she was suffering greatly, but bravely.

Bracing himself again, he gave an even harder jerk. There was an audible popping sound from somewhere beneath the draping airbags, and Lisa let out a muffled moan. Homer knew he had broken a bone, and it made him sick.

"I'm so sorry," he said, pausing briefly to survey the mangled dash. He wondered fleetingly if a pry bar might help, but he didn't have one, so he dismissed the idea. The jerking he'd done had pulled Lisa sideways in the seat, so the steering wheel was no longer a hindrance. It seemed that the only thing keeping him from dragging her free was the underside of the dashboard pressing against her legs.

He shot a quick glance toward the highway. He could see that Baylor was still performing CPR on the other girl, and he knew his training officer couldn't stop what he was doing. To do so would mean his victim would surely die. The sirens seemed to be growing closer, but they were still far off, and they would never arrive before the flames overtook the cab of the sedan. So, it meant Homer was on his own, and he would have to do whatever he could to get Lisa out of that car—even if it hurt her.

Smoke was billowing into the cab and it was getting hard to breathe. Homer opened his mouth to apologize for what he was about to do, but he sucked in a mouthful of smoke and began coughing. Ignoring his own discomfort, he gave another jerk...and another...and another.

Each time he tugged on Lisa, she let out a guttural gasp, and each utterance was immediately followed by a violent fit of coughing. Homer apologized profusely between his own coughing fits, but kept jerking as hard as he could. He used every ounce of strength that the good Lord had given him, but he couldn't seem to pull the young girl free. He knew he was causing damage with each tug he gave, but he couldn't free her legs from the clutches of the twisted metal.

I should've ripped her legs off by now, he thought, as he readied himself for another attempt. Just as he braced himself, flames reached through the break in the windshield and licked at the fabric attached to the roof. At that same moment, he heard tires screeching and he caught sight of a sheriff's patrol cruiser coming to a stop a dozen yards away. The deputy jumped from the driver's seat and headed for the trunk, where Homer knew he was going for a fire extinguisher.

Ignoring the melting fabric that dripped across his bare forearms, Homer continued jerking on Lisa, his energy levels rising and his hope renewed. Backup had arrived! Soon, the fire would be out, and the deputy would be able to help him rescue Lisa from a certain and horrifying death.

CHAPTER 20

The white powder shot from the spout of the fire extinguisher and into the cab of the sedan. Although it choked him almost as bad as the smoke, Homer didn't care.

"I'm here to help you," he hollered to Lisa. "You're gonna be okay!"

Although he was certain the deputy would soon enter the wreckage to help him free Lisa, he didn't slack off. He remembered how quickly the fire had reignited earlier, and he was afraid the same thing would happen as soon as the deputy's fire extinguisher emptied. There had to be a fuel leak somewhere under the engine. Unless it could be plugged up, there would be no stopping the fire from returning time and again.

As he struggled to free Lisa, Homer kept wondering why the car hadn't exploded yet. When he'd first entered it, he'd been positive that it would blow up with him inside, and that he and Lisa would both be immediately incinerated. With each new second that passed and saw them still alive, he felt grateful.

Homer took a break from jerking and squeezed his body closer to Lisa's. He ran his left hand down her left leg until he felt where the metal met her flesh. He was searching for a break in the bone—for a place to make a clean cut if it became necessary. He knew he would probably get in real trouble for cutting her leg off, but he didn't want the poor girl to burn to death. He knew if he were in a similar situation, he would gladly give up his legs so he could live, and he figured she would feel the same way.

Homer was having a hard time finding an obvious break in the leg bones, so he decided to try pulling her free again. Just as he backed out from under the cramped space beneath the dash—and to his shock—he spotted an orange glow through several holes near the brake pedal. The fire was spreading again!

"Deputy, give me a hand!" Homer hollered when he had regained his spot on the seat beside Lisa. "I need some help getting her out of here!"

Wondering why the deputy hadn't come to his aid, Homer wrapped his arms around Lisa and began jerking on her again. She screamed out with each of his attempts, and every outcry brought with it a violent fit of coughs.

Homer found himself coughing more frequently, thanks to the noxious smoke that poured into the cab through the opening in the windshield. The heat was growing more intense, as well, and Homer was getting desperate. He called out for help again as he continued to pull on the girl for all he was worth. Despite his efforts, it didn't seem like he was making progress.

During one of his heavy jerks, Homer's hands slipped free and he fell backward, almost out of the car. He was trying to right himself when a gust of wind blew in from the bayou. It helped to blow the smoke clear of the interior of the sedan, but it also fanned the flames that were rising up from the engine compartment. Without warning, the fabric along the roof ignited, and began spreading rapidly.

Ignoring the melting plastic that dripped down on his bare arms and the back of his neck, Homer reacquired his grip on the young girl and started jerking like a man possessed. He knew his muscles should've been fatigued by that point, but he felt a surge of energy as he worked. He prayed out loud, begging God to help him save Lisa. Heat and flames were all around him. He felt the molten plastic dig deep into his flesh, but he ignored the pain. His only thought was saving the young girl beneath him, and if God willed it, he would die in that car with her.

Homer was so focused on his work that he hadn't heard the multitude of cars arrive, and he hadn't seen the four burly deputies approach the passenger side of the sedan. His first awareness of their presence came when both of his legs were trapped in vice-like grips and he was jerked so hard that he nearly lost his hold on Lisa.

Confused as to what was happening, he turned and glanced toward the doorway. Through the flames and rolling smoke, he saw several figures getting set to regrip his legs.

"Let go of me!" he hollered, pulling and kicking with his legs in an attempt to break free from their grasps. "Get in here and help me save her!"

As more of the plastic rained down, Lisa let out a bloodcurdling scream that chilled Homer to the core. He turned quickly toward her again and saw that her hair was ablaze. He reached out to beat back the flames with one of his hands, but the deputies gave another jerk and broke his hold on Lisa. With a third jerk, they snatched him completely out of the car.

Homer hit the ground with a thud, landing directly on his stomach and chin. At first, he thought the deputies had pulled him free so they could go in and rescue Lisa, but when none of them moved toward the car, he suddenly realized they weren't there to help him, but rather, to save him.

Never taking his eyes off of Lisa, he immediately began throwing elbows and swinging his fists to beat the deputies off of him. He was covered in sweat from having been exposed to the intense heat of the car fire, and he was able to pull his slippery arms away from the deputies. He broke free for just a second and had barely scrambled to his feet when he was tackled roughly to the ground again.

Homer tried to fight free again, but there were too many of them and they were too strong and heavy. Two of the deputies had landed squarely on his legs and wrapped them up. A third had twisted Homer's right arm behind his back. He had landed a left elbow to the fourth deputy's face, and he could see that man rolling on the ground in his peripheral vision, but it hadn't helped him escape.

With nothing else to do, he stared straight ahead, watching Lisa's shadowy figure writhe about amidst the billowing smoke and growing flames. She seemed to be struggling with the handle on the driver's side door, as though trying to get it open. She repeatedly cried out for help, and it spurred Homer on.

"Let me go!" he hollered, fighting for all he was worth with one arm while pulling and kicking with his legs, trying desperately to free himself from the three deputies who held him down. "Get the hell off of me!"

"Settle down!" one of the deputies yelled back. "There's nothing you can do to save her! She's trapped!"

Refusing to give up, Homer continued to fight. He even tried to bite one of the lawmen, but the fourth deputy had recovered from the elbow strike Homer had thrown earlier, and he secured Homer's head in the crook of his own beefy elbow. Homer strained against their holds, but it was no use. They had apparently worked in unison on many occasions to take down unruly suspects, and they had him thoroughly wrapped up. All he could do was stare in shock at the flames that were enveloping Lisa's body.

Lisa's screams were more than he could take. She swayed from right to left, seeming to move in harmony with the flames, and her arms flailed about. In the glow from the fire, he could see her pale flesh slowly transforming to a blistering mess, and her screams turned guttural. He felt utterly helpless. Had his right hand been free, he figured he would've considered pulling his gun and shooting her in the head to spare her the agony that she was enduring.

Even as the thought crossed his mind, he dismissed it as ludicrous. He was pretty sure mercy killings on humans were frowned upon—probably even illegal—and he would've felt horrible if a fire truck would've arrived in time to save her.

As Homer continued to watch, Lisa's thrashing movements slowed considerably, and he knew she was fading quickly.

"We have to help her!" he pleaded in desperation to the deputies who had him pinned to the ground. "If y'all won't do it, then get the hell off of me and let—"

Before he could finish his sentence, a loud *pop* sounded from the car, and the four deputies all jerked in their skins. Homer had seen what caused the noise—one of the tires had blown out—so he hadn't started. As for the deputies, they must've thought the car was about to explode, because they peeled themselves off of him and hurried away, hollering for him to follow suit.

Ignoring them, Homer instead scrambled to his feet and rushed forward, intent on saving Lisa. However, he stopped dead in his tracks when he caught sight of the girl again. Her hair had been completely burned away. Her body had been reduced to a charred and lifeless figure, resembling that of a dark mannequin. She made no more sounds as the flames continued their relentless and brutal assault on her flesh.

As he stared in horror at what remained of the young girl he had failed to save, he sank slowly to his knees, and then to his haunches. His mind was numb. The bright orange glow of the flames turned to a blurry mess as a flood of tears formed in his eyes and spilled down his face. He ignored the intense burning sensation he felt along his neck, back, arms, and legs. The minor injuries he had sustained were nothing compared to what Lisa had endured during her last minutes on earth.

Homer also ignored the cries of the deputies to get away from the car before it could explode. At that moment, he didn't care about the car exploding or of dying himself. Even when he was actively inside the car trying to free Lisa, he hadn't thought about his own safety.

All he cared about then and now was the senseless and tragic death—no, *murder*—of an innocent girl who was simply going about her life, minding her own business, when an asshole in a stolen car decided to sideswipe her.

With a torrent of tears streaming down his face and his heart breaking like it never had before, Homer swore to God and to Lisa that he would avenge her death. He would find the man responsible and make him suffer the way Lisa had suffered.

No, he thought, *I'll make you suffer much worse, you miserable piece of shit!*

CHAPTER 21

Mechant Loup Police Department

It had been all Deputy Bradley Naquin and I could do to keep Thad Griffin under control when Homer had mentioned a fiery crash, and the man nearly went berserk when Homer came back on to say that someone was trapped inside the vehicle.

"It's not your boy!" I hollered in Thad's face after we'd been forced to take him to the ground. "It's another car that's on fire. The Lexus got away. It hit another car, and it's that car that's on fire!"

It had taken Thad a long moment to comprehend what I'd said, and when it had hit him, he'd let out a long choking sigh and sank to the ground, crying like a newborn who was seeing the light for the first time.

Once he'd calmed down, I had been able to convince him to wait in the interview room with Deputy Naquin while I headed for the scene to find out what was happening. Everyone except for Lindsey had vacated the police department at the first mention of a fiery crash, and I had been a little apprehensive about leaving Thad alone with Deputy Naquin. I was worried that he might not be able to handle the man if he lost his composure again, and if he broke free from the deputy, he might enter the dispatcher's station and give Lindsey trouble. When I voiced my concern to Lindsey, she assured me she would keep the radio room door locked.

"If he tries to break in," she'd said as I had been on my way out the door, "I'll shoot him...a lot."

All of our dispatchers were P.O.S.T. certified, which meant they had received the same law enforcement training as the rest of us, and Lindsey was the best shot of all of the dispatchers. Susan had offered her a patrol assignment on many occasions, but she had declined each offer, saying that her position was too important to give up. She was right. Our dispatchers were the heartbeat and lifeline of our department, and without them, law and order would cease to exist.

When I reached the scene of the crash, members of the fire department were already there, and the blaze had been put out. I had heard bits and pieces of radio traffic while trying to get Thad under control, and I knew that there was one fatality, and one victim had been resuscitated. I had passed an ambulance on the road, and I also knew that the young woman who had been resuscitated was en route to the hospital in critical condition.

There were also about a dozen marked and unmarked cruisers on the scene, and I had to park about fifty yards from where the crash had taken place. While walking to the site, I saw a familiar face sitting in the back of an ambulance—it was Homer Verdin.

I quickly veered in that direction and stopped outside the door. A medic was applying some kind of solution to the back of Homer's uniform shirt, and I noticed that it had melted to his skin in several large spots. I also noticed a number of black blotches on the back of his neck and up and down his arms where molten plastic and fabric had melded to his flesh. That told me all I needed to know—he had spent way too much time inside the car trying to save the young girl who had perished.

I sighed inwardly when I saw a number of crooked, vertical streaks in the black soot on his face. He wasn't crying at that moment, but I knew he had shed some tears for the girl who had died. Having been there myself, I knew his heart was heavy and I knew he blamed himself for not saving her.

"Hey, Homer," I greeted in a low voice. "How're you holding up?"

He turned toward me and forced a smile. "I'll be fine. Nothing but a few scratches. As soon as they peel these off of me, I want to get back to work."

"We're not peeling anything off of you," the medic said. "You're heading to the hospital. This stuff is burned into your flesh."

"No, I don't have time to go to the hospital." Homer shook his head in defiance. "I have to get back on the road. We have to find that Lexus."

"Burns are highly susceptible to infection," the medic explained. "If we don't care for these properly, you'll be spending more than a couple of hours in the ER—you'll be admitted and hooked up to IVs for God knows how long."

"It's okay, Homer," I said. "As soon as they release you, we'll let you back in the saddle."

"I wouldn't recommend it." The medic shook his head. "They'll put him on narcotic pain medication. He won't be able to drive, much less carry a gun."

"Something tells me he won't be taking any pain meds," I said. "This kid's as tough as they come, and he can come back to work whenever he says he's ready."

Other than a solemn nod, there was no reaction from Homer. I knew he was too distraught and angry over losing the young girl to care about anything else, and I also knew he was dead set on catching the one responsible for her horrific demise. Having seen what he'd done to the man who had killed his friends two months earlier, I knew of what he was capable. I didn't think he would do that sort of thing again, especially under the color of law, but I definitely wanted someone close to him in case he happened to encounter our suspect.

It wasn't that I didn't trust him to do what was right. This was his first shift and it had been a rough one for him. I simply wanted a veteran officer around to help him navigate the various emotions and feelings he would be experiencing throughout the night and into the coming days.

Before I could comment further, Baylor walked up. The front of his uniform was covered in crimson and his hair was wet with sweat. Blood was even smeared around his mouth, and I knew it was from performing CPR on the injured victim. From what I'd heard, the fact that he'd brought her back was a miracle on its own, and it was a testament to his dogged determination. However, it would take another miracle for the young lady to survive the night.

"How're you holding up, Partner?" Baylor asked Homer.

"I'm okay." Homer forced another smile. "I heard you brought your girl back from the dead. Thank God at least one of us was able to do some good."

Baylor pulled at his chin. "Look, you did a great job back there, and no one will ever say different. Even the deputy you dropped said you're the bravest and craziest kid he's ever met."

I raised an eyebrow, turned from Baylor to Homer, and then back to Baylor. "He dropped a deputy?" I asked incredulously.

"When the S.O. arrived, they saw Homer inside the burning car trying to get Lisa out," Baylor said with a nod. "They thought the car would explode with him inside, so they grabbed him and pulled him to safety. Even though the car was fully engulfed, Homer was still trying to get inside to save the girl. They said he fought like a cornered mountain lion, and although there were four of them holding onto him, he was able to drop one of them with an elbow that swelled his eye shut. That dude said it's the hardest he's ever been hit. He said he saw his grandpa, and that man's been dead for thirty years."

Homer didn't even crack a smile at Baylor's joke. He only lowered his head and mumbled, "I didn't fight hard enough, apparently. I couldn't get her out."

"Homer, no one could've done more than you did," Baylor said in a soothing voice. "Her legs are so tangled up in the twisted metal that they'll have to use the Jaws of Life to free her. Trust me when I tell you that no one could've gotten her out—not you, not those four deputies, and not even ten strong mules."

"I don't know." Homer took a breath. "I just keep thinking if only I would've been stronger or something."

"You did more than most people would've done," Baylor continued. "Years ago, my best friend died in a helicopter crash during a military training exercise in California. He survived the crash, but he was trapped in the harness and he was burned alive."

"Oh, no!" A wave of genuine sorrow seemed to sweep over Homer. "I'm so sorry to hear that!"

"The pilot escaped without a scratch," Baylor continued. "Instead of running into the fire to try and save my friend—like Marines are taught to do—he ran away from the helicopter. He later said he was afraid it would explode." Baylor paused, shook his head. "If that coward would've had half the brass balls that you've got, my best friend would definitely still be alive today. Don't doubt yourself over this. You did more than most brave men would've done."

"Even Melvin lost someone to a car fire once," I interjected. "It's normal to second-guess yourself. It means you give a shit, and that's a good thing. You just need to understand that we can only do so much. We'll win some, and we'll lose some, and that's okay. The important thing is that we did our best, and today, you did much more than that."

"Yeah," Baylor agreed with some relief. "I'm glad those deputies showed up when they did. I was so intent on trying to save my victim that I didn't realize what was happening with you. They said they pulled you out just in time, and that it looked like you were willing to die with the girl if you couldn't get her out."

I saw the muscles in Homer's jaw bulge as he bit down hard, no doubt trying to fight back the tears. He was a tough kid and he was able to keep his eyes dry, but the pain he had endured was written all over his face. I'd seen it way too many times on the faces of other officers throughout my career, and I had even seen it in my own reflection on more than one occasion.

Although we wore badges and uniforms, and some folks viewed us as larger than life, we were all human. We hurt like anyone else would, especially when we failed in our job. We felt anger and grew sad. There were times when we were afraid. We sometimes experienced doubt about our abilities and our decisions. But the difference was that we had to put on a brave and strong face, remain professional, and continue doing our jobs—no matter what.

From what Baylor had said, Homer had done much more than was expected of him, and then some, but he still felt like it hadn't been enough. That spoke volumes about him. Going forward, our job was to convince him that he had done all he could to save Lisa's life, and that was all that could be asked of him. While we wanted to save everyone in every situation, there would be times when we would fail. Once he could come to terms with that, he would be fine. If he couldn't, it would be a long and painful road ahead, and he might not last in law enforcement.

As for my betting money, it was on him turning out okay. He was smart, he was resilient, and he had come from good stock. Susan had outdone herself when she'd hired him, and we were lucky to have him. Of this, I was positive.

CHAPTER 22

Three hours later...

Chateau General Hospital

Baylor had ridden in the ambulance with Homer when it had left the scene much earlier, and I had given Amy a ride to the crash site to retrieve Baylor's marked cruiser.

"I've been reduced to a valet," she had grumbled when I'd dropped her off. "I'm not allowed to bust down doors, I can't make arrests, and I can't respond to active scenes, but I can do the most dangerous job a police officer does every day—drive a damned car. Please make it make sense."

I had laughed and driven away, heading for the southern part of the parish, where the sheriff's deputies and the rest of our available officers had flooded the area in search of the stolen Lexus. I had spent a couple of hours searching myself, and then headed for the hospital to check on Homer.

Since he worked directly for Susan, she had followed the ambulance to the emergency room. After making sure Homer was okay, she had asked the sheriff to send his helicopter to pick her up and bring her to the Dark Swamps, so she could notify Homer's family of his injuries. She had returned to the hospital about an hour before I arrived, and when I walked into Homer's hospital room, the first person I saw was his dad, Romain Verdin.

"Hey, Mr. Romain," I said, holding out my hand and smiling. "It's good to see you again. I'm sorry it's under these circumstances."

"Yeah," Susan called from the opposite side of Homer's hospital bed. "I'm worried his parents won't let him come back to work, considering this happened during his very first day on the job."

"He's a grown man now. He makes his own decisions." Mr. Verdin took my hand and gave it a squeeze. He turned to Susan and gave her a nod of approval. "At his age, my pépère was killing Nazis, so our family understands the risks. I raised him like my pépère raised my dad, and how my dad raised me. He'll be fine."

Every time I talked to the man, I liked him more and more. After greeting Homer's mom and siblings, I moved to his bedside, where only the lower portion of his tanned body and one leg were covered with a white sheet. He didn't appear to be in any pain, which was remarkable. I asked him how he was feeling.

"I'm ready to get back to work," he said. "They got my clothes and the melted plastic off of me, so I don't know why they're waiting to release me."

While he talked, I looked over the many bandages on his arms and the sides of his neck that were visible in his supine position. There were also bandages on his left leg and the right side of his torso, and I figured there were many more on his back. The white dressings stood out against his olive complexion, and I could see a number of smaller bright pink burns up and down his arms.

In addition to his fresh injuries, I noticed a number of dark scars on his bare torso, and they included the gunshot wound in his shoulder that he had sustained two months prior when his friends had been murdered. I had my own share of scars, and each of them told a story. I couldn't help but wonder about the many stories that the new officer in front of me already had at such a young age.

"The doctors are concerned about his risk of infection," Homer's mom cut in. She didn't seem impressed with her son's toughness. "I think he needs to listen to their advice and stay in the hospital until they say it's safe to leave. And"—she turned to look directly at Homer—"you need to take the pain medicine they're offering you. You've got nothing to prove, Boy."

Homer frowned. I had fully expected him to offer some kind of objection, but he didn't. And he didn't seem even a little embarrassed that his mom was scolding him in front of his boss and fellow officers. He took it all in stride, and I knew that meant he had great respect for her.

"Come, now, Mother," said Mr. Verdin, "he's a man now, and we need to let him make his own decisions. You promised you would respect his wishes."

Mrs. Verdin huffed, but didn't argue the point. Instead, she leaned forward, kissed Homer on the forehead, and begged him to be safe.

I was about to excuse myself when I heard movement and voices at the doorway. I turned to see a nurse standing there with a man and woman, both of whose eyes were red and swollen. The woman clung tightly to the man's arm, and she stared straight ahead, as though in a daze. I couldn't be positive, but I guessed she was on something.

The nurse spoke quietly to them, and they stepped hesitantly into the room. The woman was clearly too distraught and spaced out to say anything, so it was the man who spoke up.

"Officer Verdin?" he asked, his eyes focusing on Homer. "Are you the police officer who was out at the scene of the crash?"

Homer instinctively pulled the white sheet over his chest and sat upright in the bed. His easy manner was gone, and his expression quickly turned somber.

"Um, yes, sir." Homer shifted uneasily, but met the man's gaze directly. "I…I was there."

"We heard you almost died trying to save our daughter, Lisa," the man continued, his voice cracking as he spoke. "We also heard you got burned pretty badly."

"No, sir, I'm fine," Homer quickly said. "I'm okay, really."

"Well, we just wanted to say thank you, and we wanted to let you know that the firemen said there was nothing you could've done to get her out. We wanted to let you know that, on behalf of our family, we appreciate you risking your own life to do what you did." He paused and glanced around at the others in the room. Everyone was crying, and the tears were falling freely down his own face. "Can…can we say a prayer for you?"

"Yes, sir," Homer said, his voice trembling. "I would like that very much."

CHAPTER 23

After Lisa Grant's parents had finished praying with Homer and had left, Dr. Bruce Evans entered the room and smiled down at Homer.

"You've been such an outstanding patient that I'm here to break you out early on good behavior," Dr. Evans said, holding a stack of papers. "These are your discharge and care instructions. They're the same ones the nurse went over with you earlier, including that you can't go swimming until the wounds are completely healed. She said you moaned a bit when she went over that one."

Homer smiled sheepishly. "I love the water."

"Well, you'd hate getting a bacterial infection more." Dr. Evans' expression turned somber. "If you think spending a few hours in the ER is inconvenient, try having an infection turn septic and then being forced to spend days or months in here fighting for your life. Trust me; you don't want to play with this one."

Homer gulped and nodded.

"Good, I'm glad we understand each other." Dr. Evans handed Homer the paperwork. "Now, are you sure you don't want some pain meds? I understand not wanting any scheduled drugs, but I can get you some prescription strength Tylenol, if you want."

"No, sir." Homer shook his head. "I don't need anything."

"If you *sir* me again," Dr. Evans said with a chuckle, "I'll put Takecia on you. I hear she's tight with the chief of police."

Homer muttered an apology, and shot a worried glance at my wife. Not only was Takecia an officer with the Mechant Loup Police Department, but she was also one of Susan's closest friends. She had been dating the ER doctor for a while now and he had met Homer a couple of times, so they weren't strangers. And it had been the fifth or sixth time since landing in the ER that Dr. Evans had warned Homer not to call him that. Still, Homer was a polite kid, and those kinds of good manners seemed to die hard.

While they continued joking about it, Susan and I stepped out of the room and headed for the elevator. Once we were inside, she asked what I thought about letting Homer go back on patrol. He still had about six hours left of his shift, and we both knew he wanted to finish it.

"How many times have you refused to stay away from work when you were hurt?" I asked.

"It's different when you're in charge, and you know it," she said. "I feel responsible for each and every one of them. Hell, I feel responsible that he got hurt. If he would've been killed out there…"

She allowed her voice to trail off, and I frowned.

"You heard his dad," I offered. "He's a man now, and he knows the risks. No one forced him to jump in that car. He did it because he's a brave man, and he'll make a great cop."

"I'm just afraid he doesn't know when to back off. You heard what the deputies said. If they hadn't pulled him out, he would've burned to death right alongside that girl."

Susan was right, and I acknowledged it.

"He'll be okay," I said as the elevator stopped on the first floor and opened. "It's his first shift. He doesn't know what's expected of him, and what's not. He'll grow up fast. He's got some good teachers."

"You're right."

When we stepped out of the elevator, she glanced up and down the connecting halls to make sure we were alone, and then she leaned close and kissed me on the mouth. Her lips were soft and her tongue moist. She pushed her breasts firmly against my chest as we kissed, and I felt a stirring deep inside of me. When she pulled back, breathless and her eyes shut, I whispered, "When this case is over…"

"Promises, promises," she murmured, and then opened her eyes and took a breath to calm her racing heart.

"It ain't no promise," I retorted, in my thickest Cajun voice. "It's a threat."

She laughed and slugged me playfully on the chest, and then grew serious. "What time are you going in?"

It was almost midnight, and I hadn't heard any traffic come across my portable radio in some time, so I figured the search for the

Lexus wasn't going well.

"I want to talk with Thad Griffin a little more," I said. "He's got to have an idea who might want to murder his wife and kidnap his son. This is highly personal, so it has to be someone from his past—or someone he recently pissed off."

She nodded her agreement. "I'll head home and get some sleep, so at least one of us will be well rested in the morning. There's no telling where this case might lead us."

We walked to the parking lot together and kissed briefly before climbing into our separate vehicles and heading south. On the entire trip back to the police department, I kept wondering if Thad was keeping something from me. I was fairly certain he hadn't murdered his own wife, but I figured he had to know someone who wanted her dead, or who wanted to make him pay for some wrongdoing—perceived or real—he had perpetrated at some point in his life.

CHAPTER 24

I spent the rest of the night sitting across from Thad Griffin. I dredged up every aspect of his life, but I came nowhere closer to figuring out who might've had the intent to murder his wife and kidnap his son. It left me wondering if I had missed something, and if he might've been behind the crimes. It was possible he was a great actor. After all, he was a writer, and that meant he told lies for a living.

I figured the measure of a good writer would be based upon his sales numbers. After all, if a book sucked, the word would get around, and no one would buy it. Based on what I could see, Thad had sold a lot of books. Thus, I'd have to rate him as a good writer. If being a good writer was synonymous with being a good liar, then I had my work cut out for me. Still, I hadn't picked up on any verbal or nonverbal cues that would indicate anything was amiss with the man.

Finally, at six in the morning, I ended the interview and drove the exhausted man home. When he stepped out, he hesitated, and turned wearily to me.

"I…I don't know if I can ever sleep in my house again," he said. "I don't…um…it doesn't feel safe anymore."

Was he acting? It didn't look like it to me, but I needed to keep my guard up with him.

"I can put you up in a hotel," I offered. "There's one in town."

He glanced inquisitively toward his neighbor's house. I followed his gaze and saw that the lights were on inside the kitchen. Through the thin curtains, I could see someone bustling around. The sun was just coming up, and early risers were already beginning their day.

"I can stay at my neighbors," he said. "At least until I figure something out."

I nodded and watched him walk across the street and knock on the door. After a brief exchange between him and the husband, both men disappeared inside. I waited for a long moment before turning my Tahoe around and heading up the street.

I had asked him about every friend, enemy, lover, employer, and acquaintance of his since his earliest memory, but we hadn't come up with a single viable lead. My next best guess had been that it was somehow related to something he had written, but he'd given me full access to his website email account, and I couldn't find a single angry message from a reader, or anyone else, for that matter.

With nowhere else to turn, I headed back toward the police department to speak with Lindsey. Throughout the previous day and night, she had plowed through the three books in his alligator series, and she had started reading an older series he'd written that had been set in Atlanta. I was hoping she had something for me, but as it turned out, I would have to wait much longer to find out, because the radio suddenly erupted in chaos.

"Headquarters, I've got the Lexus!" called an unfamiliar voice over the police radio. "We're heading south on Old Blackbird, about ten miles south of town, traveling in excess of ninety miles per hour!"

I cursed out loud and sped up. Buses would be rolling soon, and the last thing we needed was for that Lexus to slam into one of them. We'd already lost one innocent life. We couldn't afford to lose another.

Homer called over the radio to say that he and Baylor were heading in that direction from the east side of town, and several other deputies radioed that they were also en route. Melvin was about twenty miles south of the pursuit, and he radioed that he would set up a roadblock.

"I'll set up to deploy some spike strips," he called. "We need to disable this vehicle at any cost."

I wanted to drive much faster than I was, but it would've been reckless to speed through town, so I cruised at about fifty until I reached the southern end of Main Street. When I finally rounded the last curve in town, I let my horses run.

The blaring of my sirens, the flashing of my lights against the passing trees and buildings, and the excited chatter over the radio caused my heart to pound. I wanted desperately for the chase to end without more officers or innocent civilians getting hurt. The closeness with which we'd almost lost Homer did not escape me, and the horrific murder of the innocent young girl weighed heavy on my heart. Part of me wanted the suspect to meet with the same ending, but another part of me wanted him to survive.

I had a ton of questions for the asshole, and if he were killed, I'd probably never get them answered.

I had gone about another three miles south of town when the deputy who had initially given chase called out to say that the vehicle had turned down an old cane field road beside a cemetery.

"He's driving reckless and at a high rate of speed on the shell road," he called. "There's no way he can maintain control." There was a pause, a scratch, and then he said, "Be advised, Headquarters, the suspect just threw something out the driver's window. It appears to be a clear baggie, about a gallon size. It'll be in a shallow ditch near a large tombstone with a cross on top— Oh, shit! Headquarters, the suspect has lost control of his vehicle. Be advised, the vehicle has crashed into the ditch about a half mile down the road."

The radio went silent for a moment, and I let out a triumphant shout, punching the roof of my Tahoe at the same time. I continued speeding to the scene, eager to hear an announcement that the suspect was in custody and Wess was located safely. But when the deputy came back on, that was not what had happened.

"Headquarters, be advised I'm involved in a foot pursuit!" The deputy's voice was shaky, and it was obvious he was running as he talked. "We're heading south through the cemetery. Correction, we're now heading east. The suspect is a black male, six foot, about a hundred and eighty. He's wearing blue jeans and a white shirt."

I drove even faster. I knew exactly what cemetery the deputy was talking about, and I realized I was still about ten miles away. There were other officers closer—including Homer and Baylor—and I soon heard another sheriff's deputy go out at the location.

For the next thirty seconds or so, we only heard several grunts and an unintelligible utterance from the first deputy, while the second deputy repeatedly called out for the first one to give out his location again.

And then there was a long moment of radio silence. It was eerie, and I began to worry. I even leaned closer to my speaker, wondering if there was something wrong with my unit. I wanted desperately to hear that the suspect was in custody, and that the chase was finally over. Not only did I want the suspect caught, but I also wanted Wess to be found safely.

With every hour that had passed since we'd first realized the boy was missing, I'd grown more and more worried about him. Was he in the wrecked Lexus? If so, had he been hurt in the crash? What about the crash from the previous day? That had been one hell of a collision, and the Lexus would've received extensive damage. If Wess had been inside and he hadn't been strapped down, he could've been seriously hurt.

What if he's...?

I shook my head to clear it. I didn't want to think about the worst case scenario. I did wonder what I'd do if Wess wasn't in the car. If not, then where could he be? That question brought on a new set of concerns. While the suspect deserved all the horrible things he had coming to him for what he had done to Lisa Grant and Ann Griffin, I didn't want him to die until we had Wess safely in our hands.

Finally, after what seemed like eternity, the second deputy came back on the radio. There was a hint of desperation in his tone that immediately told me something wasn't right.

"Headquarters, be advised the suspect's swimming the bayou. He's halfway across. We need a chopper in the air ASAP." There was another long pause. "117 to 112, what's your twenty?"

He was asking for 112's location, but there was no response from the other deputy.

"117 to 112," he called again, this time with more urgency, "come in!"

The radio traffic wasn't jumpy, so it meant the second deputy was no longer running. The dispatcher asked him if he had a visual on 112, but he responded and said he did not. He was quiet for another long moment, and I figured he was walking around searching for the first deputy. Baylor came over the radio to say he and Homer had arrived at the scene. Far ahead in the roadway, I could see flashing strobe lights, and I wondered if it was from their unit.

"Headquarters," the second deputy finally called over the radio, "I can't find Deputy Richmond. Be advised, I believe he jumped in the bayou after the suspect. He...he hasn't resurfaced. I repeat...he hasn't resurfaced! Be advised, Deputy Stan Richmond is lost!"

CHAPTER 25

When I turned down the cane field road, I only had to drive for half a mile before I came to the area of the crash. Two sheriff's patrol cruisers were parked on the grassy shoulder to the right of the shells, and Baylor's cruiser was parked on the left side. Straight ahead, a tube gate was blocking the way, and there was a long line of skid marks leading from the center of the shell road to a large ditch on the right. Based on the evidence in front of me, the driver of the Lexus had apparently tried to stop suddenly in the road in order to avoid driving through the gate, and he had lost control of the vehicle.

The Lexus had spun out of control, entered the deep ditch backwards, and come to rest with the headlights pointing toward the sky. I stopped directly in front of the crash scene and jumped from my Tahoe with my flashlight in hand. Saying a silent prayer, I slid down the steep embankment and tromped through the soft mud toward the vehicle. I called out to Wess as I approached, hoping against hope to hear a young voice call back to me.

I had no such luck.

The sun was rising fast, but the rows of sugarcane along the ditch cast deep shadows over the Lexus, so I flipped the switch on my flashlight as I neared the driver's side of the vehicle. The front window was down, and I nearly dove through it in anticipation of finding our missing boy. My flashlight was bright and it lit up the interior, so I was immediately able to see that it was empty. I turned my attention to the back seat, but it was also empty.

"Shit!"

I hesitated for a brief moment, but then I had an idea. I propped my boot on the rear tire to get some lift, and I pulled myself through the window so I could look between the front seats. I wanted to make sure Wess hadn't been slammed to the floorboard during the crash. I looked left and right, but blew out my breath when I realized he wasn't there. I quickly slid from the tire and was about to climb out of the ditch when I considered the trunk.

Of course, I thought. *He's in the trunk!*

The engine was still running, so I leaned back into the window and jabbed the trunk release button with my index finger. I heard an audible *click*, and pulled free of the window.

"Wess, are you in here?" I asked, dropping to my hands and knees in the mud and jerking on the trunk lid. The back of the Lexus had buried itself into the mud a little, and the lid snagged.

"Wess!" I hollered, trying desperately to force the trunk open. "Are you in there?"

I received no response from inside, so the boy was either not there or he was nonresponsive—and neither case was good.

As I worked feverishly to get the trunk open, my portable radio droned on in the background. At one point, I heard an unfamiliar deputy say that the suspect had almost reached the opposite side of the bayou, and that he was escaping.

We couldn't let that happen, and I knew I had to do something in a hurry. I dug my boots into the mud and propped them against the rear bumper for support, and then strained with all of my might to pull the trunk open. It budged just a little, and I dropped to my knees and shoved my light into the crack that I'd created. Scattered about was a jack, an action figure, a box of books that had flipped over, and a thick sweater—but there was no kid.

Not wasting another second, I scrambled out of the ditch and sprinted for my Tahoe. As I ran, I radioed Lindsey to let her know that Wess Griffin was not in the crashed vehicle, and that he was still missing and in danger.

I gritted my teeth as I slammed the door on my Tahoe. I wanted to get to the bayou at the back of the sugarcane road as fast as I could to help catch the suspect, and the quickest way was either directly through or around the tube gate in front of me. There was some room on the right side of the post that held the gate, but it would be a tight squeeze, and I might end up sliding into the ditch. The tombstones were too close to the post on the left side, so I did the only thing I could do—I revved up the engine and sped straight forward, aiming the front of my Tahoe at the weakest point of the gate.

I knew I would be personally responsible for the damage I was about to cause, but I didn't care. At that moment, I was singularly focused. My only goal was capturing the suspect and finding out what he had done with Wess Griffin.

The gate offered little resistance as I plowed through it and sped forward on the shell road. I soon drove past the last set of graves and came to an open field. It stretched from the cemetery westward to the bayou that cut from north to south along the back side of the property. The rays from the rapidly rising sun sparkled off of the water in the distance, and I was almost positive I saw a dark figure emerge from the depths and disappear into the trees that skirted the western edge of the bayou. There were at least four uniformed sheriff's deputies standing on the eastern bank of the bayou, but they seemed more intent on searching the water directly in front of them, rather than tracking the escaping suspect.

I tried to keep my eyes focused on the spot where the suspect had disappeared, but in my periphery, I saw something that shocked me. In addition to the deputies standing on the eastern edge of the bayou, there were several more uniformed officers running for all they were worth in their direction. I recognized Baylor at the forefront of that group, but a hundred yards ahead of them, there was a streak of a uniform closing in on the side of the bayou.

I blinked in disbelief. I had never seen a human being run so fast. The uniform was ours, so I knew it had to be Homer Verdin. I also knew he was running way too fast to stop. And he didn't. Hell, he didn't even slow down. When he was still about five feet from the edge of the bayou, he jumped high into the air and dove headlong into the murky water.

"No!" I hollered out loud as he disappeared from sight. "Don't do it!"

Forget that it was dangerous to dive into any canal or bayou in southeast Louisiana due to the risks of striking underwater debris or getting stuck in the soft mud. Homer was under strict orders not to get his wounds wet because of the dangers of contracting a bacterial infection, and the brackish water into which he had just jumped was anything but sanitary.

CHAPTER 26

Earlier...

When the elevator door opened on the first floor of the hospital, Homer stepped out without looking up. He was too busy trying to straighten out the uniform shirt that Baylor had loaned him. It was a little big, but he didn't mind one bit. He was just thrilled that Chief Wilson had allowed him to finish out his shift, and he was eager to get back into the patrol car with Baylor.

Homer's mind had been working overtime during his time in the hospital. Sure, he had been interacting with his visitors and caregivers, but he had come up with a dozen questions for his training officer—questions he had never considered until the fiery crash had happened. There were so many things he had yet to learn as a police officer, and he felt like he needed to learn as many of them as possible, and as quickly as he could, before he found himself in similar situations. He also wanted to know how Baylor had managed to save the victim who had been thrown from the—

"Hey, Homer, how're you feeling?"

Homer lurched to a stop at the suddenness and unexpectedness of the sweet voice that called out to him from inches away. He looked up to see Remi Walton standing there. Her cheeks were puffy and her green eyes glassy. She had changed since he'd last seen her, and currently wore a pair of sweatpants and an oversized T-shirt. Her hair was up in a ponytail and she didn't have a shred of makeup on.

"I...I'm good," he said, his face scrunched up in confusion. "What are you doing? Why are you here?"

"Lisa's mom told me you were upstairs," she explained. "I was going up to find you."

That confused Homer even more. "You know Lisa's mom?"

"I…I was good friends with Lisa." Tears formed in Remi's eyes and her bottom lip jutted out even more than it naturally did. "We grew up on the same street. She…she was like a sister to me. I still can't believe she's gone."

Remi put a hand to her mouth and wept softly. Homer hesitated, but only briefly. He stepped closer and opened his arms. There was no hesitation in the young woman.

"I'm so sorry, Remi!" Homer wrapped his strong arms around her and pulled her close. "I…I had no idea y'all knew each other."

Remi hugged him back and rested the right side of her head against his left shoulder. He could feel her warm tears spill onto his neck and slide down his chest.

"I've never lost anyone close to me," Remi said in a low voice. "I…I don't know what to do, or…how to act."

Homer rubbed her shoulders and nodded. "I don't either."

After a long minute or two, Remi pulled back and scrubbed the tears from her face. "I'm sorry for that."

"Don't be."

Remi stood there nodding and looking down at the front of Homer's uniform. She then turned her attention to one of the bandages on his right arm. As she ran her fingers lightly across it, she asked if it hurt.

He shrugged. "It still burns from time to time, but it's not as bad as it was earlier."

He wanted to tell her it was nothing compared to the hell that Lisa had endured, but he dared not. No one needed to know how bad the young woman had suffered during her last moments on earth.

"I felt so bad when they told me it was you who had tried to save her," Remi continued. "I mean, on one hand, I was glad it was you, because I knew if anyone could save her, it would've been you. On the other hand, I didn't want you to have to carry around that burden."

Homer shifted his feet. "What made you think that?"

"Think what?"

"That I could save her."

Remi looked up and studied him for a long moment. A tear or two still leaked down her face, but she seemed to be in control of her emotions again.

"I'm not sure," she said thoughtfully. "Something in your eyes.

You have this intense look about you. Like, if you set your mind to doing something, you won't let anything get in your way, and you won't let anyone stop you from accomplishing your goal."

Homer couldn't meet her gaze. The guilt was too strong. "That didn't work out last night."

Remi reached up and took a hold of his chin. She turned his face until their eyes locked and he was looking down at her.

"You did everything you could to save Lisa," she said softly. "One of the deputies at the scene told Ali that they had to pull you out of the burning car. He said you would've died right there beside her if they hadn't dragged you from it and that you kept fighting to get back in the car to save her. He said you wouldn't quit, no matter what. I mean, look at all of your injuries. You...you did all you could."

Homer shifted his feet. He didn't know what to say, so he said nothing.

"Thank you for trying so hard to save my friend," Remi said after a long moment. "It means a lot to me, and I know it means a lot to her family."

"I...I just wish it would've turned out differently," he said. "Maybe if I had more experience or if I was better trained, I might've been able to save her."

She shook her head. "Ali and I were there when they freed her from the car. We were standing behind the police line, but we could see and hear everything that was going on. The firemen had to cut her free with the Jaws of Life, and they even had a hard time getting her out. I...I overheard them say there was nothing anyone could've done."

"Really?" While he felt relief at learning the news, Homer tried not to show it. "Did they really have trouble getting her out with the Jaws of Life?"

"Yeah." She bit down hard, but continued. "They said the metal was so twisted around her legs that it was almost impossible to get her out. They said even if you would've had the Jaws of Life with you, you wouldn't have been able to get her out in time to save her from the fire."

He nodded slowly, and then asked about the other girl. "Do you know her, too?"

"I know her name is Judith Landry, but that's about it," she said. "Lisa's mom said they expect her to make it."

"That's good."

They stood there looking at each other for a long moment, and then the elevator *dinged*.

Homer blinked and Remi took a breath.

"Well, I guess I have to get back to the lobby," she said. "I promised Lisa's mom I'd check on her before I left."

"I can walk you out, if you like," Homer offered, hoping he didn't sound too eager. Remi didn't seem to mind, and she fell in beside him as they walked toward the lobby.

They had almost reached the end of the long corridor when Remi suddenly stopped and reached for Homer's arm.

"Homer," she said breathlessly, "I've been thinking."

He stopped, too, and turned toward her. There was something in her tone that got his full attention. "Yeah? What is it?"

"Um, if you're willing to risk your life for a perfect stranger, then I know you're willing to risk it for someone you love," she said. "Do...do you think that's true?"

"I guess so." He thought about it for a moment, still not sure what she was driving at. "I never really thought about risking my life for a stranger. I mean, yeah, I'd die for someone I love, but I never gave the other thing any thought."

"You just risked your life for Lisa," she pointed out, "and she was a perfect stranger. What made you do it?"

"I...I don't know." He shifted his feet again. The conversation was making him feel uncomfortable. He had failed miserably and someone had died. Those were the cold, hard facts. As for *why* he had done what he'd done, he had no clue. He had simply reacted. After what seemed like too long, he finally said, "I was just doing my job, I guess. I just did what I thought any other officer would do."

"It was more than your job, and not many officers would've done what you did." Remi pursed her lips and studied his face. "It says a lot about you as a man. It lets a girl know that you would lay down your life to protect her."

Homer cocked his head to the side. The conversation had taken an unexpected turn, and he didn't know what to make of it.

"What do you mean?" he asked.

"My mom has always told me that a girl just wants to feel safe," she explained. "I've never felt that way in a relationship. Your girlfriend is lucky."

"But I don't have a girlfriend," Homer blurted out loud before he could stop himself.

For the first time since he'd run into her outside the elevator, he saw Remi's face light up a little. And for the first time since he'd failed to save Lisa Grant's life, he felt a hint of happiness.

CHAPTER 27

From the moment he'd left the hospital with Baylor Rice, Homer Verdin never took his eyes off the road. He was in constant search of the black Lexus, hoping against hope that they would spot it before the end of his first shift. Not only did he want the killer off the streets, but he wanted to be present when the arrest was made. And the sooner, the better. The last thing anyone wanted was for the suspect to injure or kill another innocent civilian.

While they drove around, Homer posed more than a dozen different scenarios to Baylor, trying to learn as much as he could from his training officer about how to deal with a number of law enforcement situations. The crash from the previous evening had made him think of things he'd never thought about before. He also had lots of questions about the techniques Baylor had employed to save Judith Landry. He didn't think he could save someone under similar circumstances, and that scared him. Although he understood that there was nothing more he could've done to save Lisa, he still felt like he had already failed once, and he didn't want that to ever happen again.

Baylor wasn't much for conversation, and neither was Homer, so things got quiet in the squad car after Baylor had answered most of Homer's questions. There was intermittent radio traffic throughout the night, with several phantom sightings of the black Lexus, but things remained relatively quiet. As for them, they hadn't spotted a single black Lexus, despite having driven down every street from Mechant Loup to the coast, and they were starting to think it might be resting at the bottom of Bayou Tail.

"People like to ditch stolen vehicles in the bayous around here," Baylor said after they'd turned around in the Spearmonger Dive Shop parking lot and headed back north. "As soon as the sun comes up, we'll start searching the bayou for oil slicks. I haven't seen any tire tracks leading off the roadway yet, but that doesn't mean they didn't ditch it. We'll have to go over the shoulders with a fine-tooth comb."

Homer nodded and glanced toward the east, where the dark horizon had subtly grown a shade lighter over the past few minutes. He shook his head. It felt odd to be sitting inside a police car wearing a uniform while watching the night slowly begin to give way to the day. On any normal Tuesday at that time, he would be heading to his boat for the long ride to school.

Never again, he thought. *This is your life now.* He sighed and turned his attention to the shoulder of the road, searching for any indication that a vehicle had left the roadway.

It was approaching the end of his first shift. He thought back to all that had happened during the course of the evening and into the night, and he couldn't believe how much he had experienced in twelve short hours. He also couldn't believe how close he had come to dying or getting seriously injured on his first day. Had the deputies not pulled him out when they did, he would've become fully engulfed like Lisa had. He shuddered to think how his family would've reacted to receiving that sort of news, but quickly dismissed the notion. People died every day in all kinds of ways and doing all kinds of jobs.

As Baylor had pointed out earlier, the important thing was that he had survived the night.

"Now, your number one job is to survive the rest of this shift," Baylor had continued. "And tomorrow, when you get back on duty, your number one job will be to survive your second shift. And so on."

Both officers rode in silence for the next twenty or thirty minutes, and they soon found themselves on the eastern side of the bayou heading north.

"Where're we going?" Homer asked curiously, hoping Baylor wasn't heading for the police department to end their shift.

"I want to check out the Waxtuygi Nature Park again," he said. "The Lexus was coming from that direction when you first spotted it. Maybe they came from the park."

Homer had been there many times as a kid, but he had never accessed the park from the highway. He had always gone the back way by boat. He'd heard about a murder that had happened back there when he was in middle school, and he asked Baylor about it.

Just as Baylor began to tell him the story, the radio scratched to life and a deputy's voice spat from the speaker.

"Headquarters, I've got the Lexus!" he said. "We're heading south on Old Blackbird, about ten miles south of town, traveling in excess of ninety miles per hour!"

Homer snatched up the radio mic and let dispatch know that he and Baylor were heading in that direction. "We're leaving the east side of town," he said, holding on to the roof as Baylor slowed rapidly and made a violent U-turn to head in the opposite direction.

The radio exploded with traffic, but Homer tried to drown out every voice except for that of the original deputy. He listened intently to his every word. He wanted nothing more than to be in the car with the deputy, and to be present when the suspect was captured. He didn't know what he would do—or what he was even allowed to—but he wanted to do something to avenge Lisa's murder.

Melvin came over the radio to say he was setting up spike strips to the south, and Homer began to worry that the suspect would reach Melvin long before he and Baylor got in on the chase. But that was when the original deputy radioed that the suspect had turned down a sugarcane road near a cemetery.

Homer glanced at Baylor. "You know the place?"

"Yep. We're not far."

Baylor had crossed the bayou and they were racing south on Old Blackbird Highway when the deputy called that the Lexus had lost control on the shell road and crashed into a ditch. A little later, the deputy came on to say he was involved in a foot chase.

Homer cursed under his breath. He could feel the heel of his boot bouncing on the floorboard. He wanted to urge Baylor to drive faster, but he refrained. After all, he was the trainee, and what did he know about high speed pursuits? What he did know was that there were other deputies closer to the crash site, and they would arrive before he and Baylor did. There was no way he would be involved in the chase or the arrest.

Homer sank back into his seat. He accepted the fact that he would not get to confront the suspect, and he tried to will himself to be grateful that the suspect would soon be in custody. As long as he was held responsible for his crimes, what did it matter who captured him?

The radio traffic became chaotic. It was all confusing to Homer, who was not accustomed to deciphering all the codes and signals in real time and at high speed. However, there was one bit of traffic that came in loud and clear, and in plain English for all to understand: *"Be advised, Deputy Richmond is lost!"*

CHAPTER 28

"Does that mean he's dead?" Homer asked Baylor as they turned onto the sugarcane road. "Is Deputy Richmond gone?"

"It sounds like he jumped in the bayou and disappeared," Baylor said, working the steering wheel to maintain control of his cruiser on the loose shells. "He probably got stuck in the mud. If they don't find him fast, he'll drown."

Homer unsnapped his seatbelt and waited for Baylor to stop. They didn't have to go far. About a half mile down the road, they came to the spot where the Lexus had crashed into the ditch on the right. Two sheriff's patrol cruisers were parked on the grassy shoulder on that side of the road. Homer's hand was already on the door handle when Baylor stopped his cruiser on the left side of the road. Before Baylor could put it in gear, he was out the door and running straight for the tombs.

Homer had understood enough to know that the bayou was due west of the graveyard, so he ran straight in that direction. The sun was coming up behind him, and it brought color and details to what would've been dark shadows had they arrived at nighttime. He was glad for the daylight. It would make it harder for the suspect to hide, and therefore make it easier for them to take him into custody.

As Homer raced toward the back of the property as fast as his legs could carry him, he quickly overtook and passed a couple of deputies who were also heading for the bayou. Off in the distance, he could see a line of trees stretching from north to south, and he figured they marked the opposite bank of the bayou. If he were to guess, he would say it was half a mile away.

He cursed under his breath for the umpteenth time during his first shift. If the deputy had been lost in the bayou, that meant the suspect had also jumped in the water. It had been about a minute since Homer had first heard that the deputy was lost. If the suspect were a decent swimmer, he would've had ample time to reach the opposite side of the bayou and disappear into the thick trees beyond. Homer couldn't let that happen. If he had to, he would shoot the suspect to stop him. After all, the man was a murderer.

As Homer neared the bayou, he saw several deputies huddled together near the edge of the bank. One of them was talking excitedly and pointing while two others were stripping down to their boxers. They were entering the water to search for their friend, and that made Homer feel better about continuing the chase.

As he closed in on the bayou at warp speed, his arms pumping like pistons on steroids, Homer scanned the trees along the opposite bank. In the next second or two, he caught movement along the surface of the water. It was a little to his right. As he watched, a dark figure emerged stealthily from the shallows and slipped into the trees that skirted the opposite edge of the bayou.

The suspect!

Upon seeing the man that was responsible for Lisa's murder, a surge of electricity shot through Homer's veins. His legs and arms seemed to pump even faster. Every part of him felt numb. It was as though he were in a dream, and none of it was real. Just like when he had been in the car fighting for Lisa's life. He hadn't had time to think. He had simply reacted, and that was exactly what he was doing at that moment.

When he was still about five feet from the edge of the water, he leapt high into the air and twisted his body sideways. He wanted the left side of his ribs to make contact with the water at the same time his outstretched hands did. That way, he would skirt across the water like a skipping rock, rather than plunging into its depths, and his hands and arms would protect his head and neck from any debris that might be lingering beneath the surface.

As luck would have it, there was no underwater debris, and his giant leap had helped him clear the shallow area. Water instantly saturated his uniform and filled his boots, but he was a strong swimmer. Kicking his feet rapidly and taking long strokes with his arms, he sliced through the water like the old reliable dugout that his grandfather had made for him when he was a kid. He figured it would only take him thirty or forty seconds to reach the opposite bank. Without the boots and gun belt weighing him down, he could've done it much faster. Still, he was confident he could make it to the other side a lot faster than the suspect had. Once he reached dry land, he would be able to quickly overtake the suspect. He was sure of it.

Even if the suspect disappeared from sight, Homer would be able to track him with ease. The criminal was desperate to escape, so he wouldn't be taking any time to cover his tracks. And if he did try to conceal his passing, his efforts would leave a trail almost as easy to follow as his—

Suddenly, there was a violent splash in the water right beside Homer, and then an explosion sounded in the distance. It was followed by another, and another. He knew without looking what was happening.

That asshole! Homer thought. *He's shooting at me!*

Just as he registered the attack in his mind, he heard returning gunfire from somewhere behind him. He didn't know who was shooting at the suspect, but someone had his back, and he was extremely grateful. It would've been difficult for him to draw his pistol and return accurate fire while treading water.

Homer took a quick breath and descended deeper into the water, but he didn't change course. He was going to make it to the other side and he was going to capture Lisa's killer—or he would die trying. He had learned a lot from Baylor in the hours they'd been searching for the black Lexus, and he figured he'd learned enough to give himself a fighting chance against the gunman.

One of the lessons had included the importance of utilizing cover and concealment in making an approach to an armed suspect, and that information had prompted his immediate descent toward the bottom of the bayou. He'd learned as a young boy that water could stop bullets, so he decided to use the water as his cover. He had gotten a quick look at the opposite bank as he'd launched himself into the air, and he had seen a large weeping willow leaning precariously over the water. It had been a little to the north of where he'd gone in, and it would offer excellent protection from the suspect's bullets, so he angled himself in that direction.

Before long, Homer could see the water above him brighten, and his hands brushed the soft mud of the bottom. With a quick twist of his back, he lifted his head from the water to check on his progress. He smiled inwardly and dipped back under the water. His senses hadn't failed him. He was about twenty feet from the large willow, and the suspect was nowhere in sight.

After swimming as close as he could, he pulled himself to his feet and slogged through the shallow waters as fast as he could travel. He was making noise now, so he had to move as rapidly as he could. According to what Baylor had taught him, it was imperative that he didn't remain in the open for long.

Although his legs were pumping like pistons, it felt like he was moving in slow motion in the soft mud. It didn't help that his uniform was clinging to his flesh and his boots felt like sandbags. He had almost reached the nearest branch when three more gunshots sounded from the trees in front of him.

"Shit!" Homer dove to his left and landed face first in the soft mud. He cursed as he began sniper crawling through the slop. There was nothing gracious about his movement. His legs and elbows sank deeper with each push, and it seemed to take minutes for him to reach the trunk of the willow tree.

Once there, he pulled himself to drier land and jerked out his own pistol. Resting his left hand against the tree, he waited and listened, not daring to peek out from behind cover just yet. He needed to make sure the suspect wasn't waiting for him to do just that, but he didn't know how long he should wait. While he knelt there, the suspect could be getting away.

Since the sun was to Homer's back and shining directly into the suspect's eyes, the suspect should be at a disadvantage and shouldn't be able to get a good bead on Homer. However, his first few shots had been way too close for comfort, and Homer wasn't about to take any chances. He wanted the man to pay for what he had done to Lisa. If he killed Homer before that could happen, he might disappear forever.

Thinking quickly, Homer grabbed a nearby twig and pushed it out from behind the tree. Nothing happened. He then dropped the twig and leaned his head out from behind cover, moving a centimeter at a time…and that's when he saw the suspect.

CHAPTER 29

The suspect was on the run, zigging and zagging between trees, making a hasty getaway. He was a little over a hundred yards away, and he was moving faster than Homer had initially thought he would.

Figuring it was fear that spurred the suspect on, Homer wasted no more time. He leapt from behind the Willow and began racing after the fleeing felon. He thought about shooting the man in the back, but he wasn't sure he could hit him from that distance with a pistol, and especially while they were both on a dead run.

As he sprinted forward, Homer heard shouts coming from the opposite side of the bayou. He also heard a car door slam and somebody yell for an ambulance, but he didn't stop to look back. At that moment, his only concern was catching the man who was responsible for Lisa's horrific murder.

Sure, it's probably not a murder in the technical sense of the word, he thought as he ran, *but that's what it is, and you still deserve to die for what you did!*

Having lived in the swamps his entire life, Homer whisked through the trees with all the grace of a large buck, and he had soon closed to within thirty or forty yards of the suspect. It seemed the suspect could feel Homer breathing down his neck, because he turned to look over his left shoulder and his dark eyes widened. Letting out a screech, he whipped around and—running backwards—began firing his pistol as fast as he could pull the trigger.

Homer was running too fast to stop. He veered slightly to the left to put a young pine tree briefly between himself and the suspect, and he began firing his own pistol. The noise was deafening, but neither of them noticed. The suspect seemed to be pulling the trigger with reckless abandonment, stumbling backwards as he did so, trying desperately to kill the young lawman coming for him.

Meanwhile, Homer was trying to see his front sight as he pulled the trigger, but it bounced roughly up and down with each pounding step he took. He wasn't surprised that his pistol fired after having been submerged underwater for about a minute or two, because a large alligator had once flipped his pirogue over, but he had still been able to bring his rifle to bear and fire a killing shot before the gator had gotten a hold of him. However, he was surprised that the suspect was still standing when the slide locked back on his empty pistol.

Homer had come to within ten feet of the suspect by the time he had shot his pistol dry. The suspect's handgun was also empty, and he immediately raised his arm to throw the firearm at Homer. He was too late. Without slowing down, Homer jumped into the air and executed a flying side kick that landed with a thud to the suspect's chest. The suspect went down hard, and Homer landed lightly on his feet.

Homer's heart was racing a bit. Not from the run, but from the adrenalin that coursed through him. He couldn't believe he hadn't been hit by any of the suspect's bullets, and he couldn't believe none of his bullets had found their mark. As he reached for the magazine release button with his right thumb and pulled a fresh magazine from his pouch with his left hand, he strolled calmly toward the suspect.

"Please," said the suspect between gasps. "I…I didn't mean to shoot at you. I…I was scared."

Homer didn't say a word as he shoved the fresh magazine into his pistol and released the slide. He kept walking until he was standing directly over the young man.

"I…I'm sorry," the suspect continued. "I didn't know that…that you was the law. I thought you was trying to rob me. I swear!"

Homer calmly aimed the pistol at the suspect's face. Finally, he asked, "What's your name?"

"Jerome."

"Jerome what?"

The man swallowed hard. He had been rubbing his chest rigorously with both hands, but he stopped and raised them high in the air. "I'm Jerome Folse. I…I'm not resisting arrest. I'm not armed. I give up."

When Homer continued staring down at him without saying a word, Jerome pressed the insides of both wrists together.

"I give up," he repeated. "Go ahead and take me in."

"You killed her," Homer said in a low voice. "She burned to death because of you."

Jerome licked his lips, his eyes darting wildly about. "I…I don't know what you mean. Who burned?"

"Lisa Grant." Homer placed his finger on the trigger and took up the slack. "You sideswiped her car last night with that black Lexus you were driving. She crashed into a tree and her car burst into flames. She…she burned to death inside."

Homer was talking through gritted teeth, and he was doing his best to keep the dam in his chest from bursting. He wanted so bad to shoot Jerome Folse in the face…to make him pay for what he had done, but he was having a hard time pulling the trigger. He kept hearing a voice in the back of his mind. He was trying desperately to ignore it.

Tears began to flow down Jerome's face. He shook his head from side to side. "Sir…Officer, you have to believe me! I…I didn't mean for that to happen. I just wanted to make that car zigzag in the road a little. You know, to throw y'all off the trail. I…I didn't mean for nobody to die, and I definitely didn't mean for no girl to burn up in the car."

"I don't give a shit if you meant it or not," Homer said. "You murdered her."

"No, sir, I didn't—"

"You ever read the Bible?"

The question was so unexpected that Jerome stopped crying for a split second. "What?"

"Have you ever read the Bible?" Homer repeated. "Specifically, the Old Testament?"

Jerome nodded his head vigorously up and down. "Oh, yeah, I used to read it all the time with my Mom when I was little. Every line. In fact, I was getting ready to start going back to church with her this weekend."

"Then you know what it says about paying life for life." Homer leaned closer and pressed the muzzle against Jerome's head. The front sight shook violently over the enormity of what was about to happen, and how it would impact his life. "I just wish I had time to set you on fire before everyone else gets here."

"But…but you a cop!" Tears were once again flowing freely down Jerome's face, and his dark complexion had turned a shade lighter. "You…you can't just murder me, man! You the law!"

Homer took a breath and closed his eyes. When he did, he saw the sweet face of Lisa Grant looking up at him while fire raged all around them. The image caused the many burns about his body to sting. *Or was it the exposure to the water?*

Homer shook his head and opened his eyes. He was about to pull the trigger when the voice at the back of his mind moved to the forefront.

"It's perfectly normal for you to get angry when you have to arrest a child predator. You might wish him dead, or want to kill him yourself—like any normal man or woman might wish or want to do, but the difference between you and any other man or woman is that you're a cop, and you have a code to follow. You don't have the luxury of acting on your feelings and emotions. You have to rise above them and remain disciplined at all times."

Homer sighed and eased up on the trigger, as Baylor's words from the previous day played over and over in his mind.

"Get on your face," he said sternly to Jerome, "and put your hands behind your back. If you give me half a chance—"

"I won't give you even a little bit of a chance!" Jerome quickly flipped to his belly and placed his arms behind his back. "Take me to jail...please!"

CHAPTER 30

The end of Cemetery Road

Before I could bring my Tahoe to a stop at the end of Cemetery Road, I saw the water around Homer explode in action. There were several small sections of what looked like geysers shooting into the air, and they were within inches of his body. Since there were no geysers in Southeast Louisiana, I knew instantly that the suspect was shooting at him. My blood instantly began to boil.

I slammed the brakes. My Tahoe skidded several feet in the loose shells before coming to a halt sideways in the road. I snatched up my AR-10 and threw open my door. I heard several pistol rounds going off from the area where the deputies were searching for their missing comrade, but I knew the distance was too great and there were too many trees for them to be effective.

I rested the handguard of my rifle in the crook of the driver's door, but before I could bring it to bear, I saw the suspect fleeing through the trees, heading west in a zig-zagging motion. I turned my attention toward where I'd last seen Homer, and my heart fell. Other than the rippling of water, there was no sign of him.

"Damn it!" I threw my rifle in my Tahoe and slammed the door shut. Breaking out in a run, I turned my head to see how far Baylor had gotten. While I was only twenty yards, or so, from the edge of the water, he was still about fifty yards away, but he was closing fast. His intentions were written all over his face. He was swimming the bayou, just like I was, and it was a race to see who would hit the water first.

I was about two jumps from the bank when I saw a head break the surface on the opposite side of the bayou. I let out an audible sigh of relief when I recognized Homer's tanned face rising from the murkiness. The saturated uniform clung to his sinewy frame as he made his way through the shallows. He was heading toward a large Willow, and I was glad he was utilizing the cover that was available, rather than rushing blindly into the trees after the armed suspect.

A quick glance over my shoulder showed that Baylor had gained some ground on me, but I reached the bayou first. I leapt high into the air and twisted sideways, turning my ribs toward the approaching water. I wasn't interested in breaking my neck on any debris that might be just under the surface.

Right as I hit the water, I heard three rapid gunshots from across the bayou. I didn't have time to react, and soon found myself submerged. I began kicking for all I was worth, trying to get back to the surface as quickly as I could. Once there, I began swimming for the opposite side, while trying to catch another glimpse of Homer.

After about a dozen strokes, I finally saw him through waterfilled slits in my eyes. It was a fleeting glance, but he looked to be moving with purpose, running from one tree to the other. I was relieved that he hadn't been hit, but I had hoped he would wait for backup before pursuing the suspect. Of course, there was also the chance he had no idea that backup was on the way. None of the other deputies had hit the water in pursuit, so he might've thought it was solely up to him to bring in the killer.

At a year and two months shy of forty, I still considered myself a young man, but it hadn't seemed as difficult the last time I'd swum a bayou. When I reached the opposite bank, I found myself winded and spent, but I forced myself to go on without a break. For all I knew, Homer could be in trouble and might need my help. He had been there to save London, Melvin, and me, and by God, I was going to die before giving up on him.

Heaving to get wind in my lungs, I rushed through the trees, heading for the last place I'd seen the suspect. I thought I'd heard a fierce gun battle while I had been swimming the bayou, but everything was quiet at that point. I didn't like it one bit. My own gun was in my palm, but I was starting to wish I'd lugged my AR-10 along. It would've been more difficult to swim the bayou with the rifle in tow, and I wouldn't have gotten there as quickly as I did, but it would've been a better choice.

I was still running as hard as I could when I heard something crashing through the brush behind me. I glanced over my shoulder to see Baylor catching up. I cursed my aging legs, while also pushing them to move faster and longer. One of my recent favorite country songs was Toby Keith's *Don't Let The Old Man In*, and I was determined to obey the lyrics.

Baylor and I were rushing forward, almost neck and neck, when we both drew up at the same time. A dozen yards ahead, in a small clearing, Homer was helping the black male suspect to his feet. The suspect was in handcuffs, and neither of them appeared hurt.

"I heard a bunch of gunshots," Baylor said, barely out of breath. "It sounded like a warzone."

I nodded, breathing in slowly through my nose to calm my racing heart. After an exhale and another deep breath, I answered him. "I heard some shots, too, but they both look okay."

It was then that Homer lifted his gaze and saw us. His face broke into that boyish grin of his, and he waved us forward.

"I got him," he said. "His name's Jerome Folse. He admitted to sideswiping Lisa Grant's car to throw us off his trail."

"I didn't mean to kill nobody." Water dripped down Jerome's face, and I could tell the drops were mixed with tears. "I was just trying to get away. I wasn't trying to hurt nobody. I swear it."

By the time Homer reached us with the suspect, I had calmed my racing heart enough to talk without sounding like I'd just swum the bayou and sprinted a few hundred yards. I began by reading Jerome his Miranda rights, and then I asked about the gunshots he'd fired at Homer.

"Are you going to swear you weren't trying to hurt our officer, too?" My voice was a little more heated than I'd intended, and he lowered his head.

"No, sir," Jerome said. "I won't lie to you like that."

I was surprised by his answer. "So, you're saying you were trying to kill our officer?"

"I mean, I don't think I was trying to kill him." He sounded sincere. "I was just shooting at him so he wouldn't catch me. I was scared, don't you see?"

"Scared of what?" I wanted to know, as I took the suspect by one of his arms and helped Homer escort him back toward the bayou.

"Scared that he would shoot me."

"You're lucky he didn't," I said, bristling. "You would've certainly deserved it."

"I sure tried, but I missed every time," Homer said sheepishly. "I was running while I was shooting, and Baylor said I shouldn't do that. He said I should run between cover, and shoot from behind it.

He said shooting on the run is a waste of ammo. I guess I was so caught up in the moment that I forgot to listen."

"We've all been there," Baylor said. "How else would we know what *not* to do?"

That seemed to make Homer feel better, and he walked for a ways without talking. I wanted to begin asking the suspect questions as soon as possible, but I needed to record every word he said, and I wasn't sure if my cell phone had survived the earlier plunge. The protective case was allegedly waterproof, but I wasn't sure to what depth.

Although the sun was coming up, no one had alerted the mosquitoes, and they were swarming all over us. They always seemed worse when people were wet. They apparently didn't want to disappoint us on that morning, because they attacked with a vengeance as we tromped through the trees. Jerome complained almost nonstop about being helpless to defend himself because his hands were cuffed behind his back, and he threatened to sue us if he contracted West Nile. None of us responded to him.

I didn't know what was on Homer or Baylor's mind, but my thoughts were on the deputy who was missing, and also on young Wess Griffin. It was imperative that I get Jerome to confess to kidnapping the kid, and I needed him to tell me where to find him. If he refused to talk, we might never know what happened to the boy.

As we pushed through the trees and neared the water's edge, I realized that Jerome had stopped complaining. I glanced in his direction and saw that he was staring off in the distance, his eyes wide. I didn't need to look to know that he was watching the recovery efforts taking place on the opposite side of the bayou. He looked concerned, and he was right to feel that way. If the deputy died, he would be responsible.

"What...um...where'd that deputy go?" he asked when we stopped on the bank. "The one that was chasing me."

"He's missing," I said. "He likely drowned."

Jerome's shoulders slumped, but he didn't say another word.

"Chief...I mean, um, Clint," Homer began, "do you mind if I help them find Deputy Richmond?"

"Sure," I said. "They've got a boat and some divers coming—"

Before I could finish my sentence, Homer had kicked off his boots and was removing his gun belt. He handed it to Baylor and asked if he would keep an eye on it.

"You're not going back in the water, are you?" Baylor asked. "Your wounds could get infected, remember?"

"I already got them wet once," Homer said with a shrug. "I can't do much more damage. Besides, the tide's moving out. If we wait for the divers to get here, Deputy Richmond's body could get pushed into the lake, and we might never find him."

"Do you think you can locate him?" I asked Homer.

"Yes, sir." He quickly corrected himself. "I mean, yeah, I can find him."

I gave a nod and told Jerome to sit on the ground. While keeping one eye on the suspect, I watched Homer slip in the water and disappear from sight. A long time passed before he finally reappeared in the middle of the bayou.

"How long was he under?" Baylor asked. "That seemed like a long time."

"Shit, it had to be longer than three minutes," I said. "It was probably close to four."

Homer took a few breaths, and then descended into the murky water again. I glanced at my watch. He remained underwater for just over three minutes, and then reemerged closer to where the deputies were still searching the shallow area on the opposite side of the bayou. He repeated his underwater search several times, and each time he surfaced, he was at a different location. He seemed to be covering a lot of ground.

"He moves like an alligator in the water," Baylor commented at one point. "And he runs like a cheetah."

Jerome, who had been silently watching the search, let out a curse. "I've run from a lot of cops," he complained, "but I ain't never seen one of y'all run that fast. I knew my ass was in trouble. That's why I shot—"

Jerome clamped his mouth shut and mumbled something I couldn't hear. I wasn't positive, but I thought he was starting to get cold feet about talking.

I was about to strike up a conversation with him to make him feel at ease, when Homer came up for the dozenth time. Only, this time was different. In the crook of his left arm, we could see the top of someone's head. That's when all hell broke loose from the deputies on the opposite bank. A couple of them jumped in the water and swam to help Homer land Deputy Richmond's body.

"He dead?" Jerome asked, his lower lip quivering. "That…that deputy…he dead?"

"It sure looks like it." I shook my head at the sight of the deputy's lifeless body being dragged across the water. His pistol was still in his holster, but he had lost a shoe and his uniform shirt was torn.

"Did he make contact with you?"

"Oh, no, sir!" Jerome shook his head from left to right. "I got out of that car and ran like my life depended on it. Nobody got close enough to touch me. Well, except for that Indian-looking dude, there at the end. He's one fast mother—"

"That would be Officer Verdin to you," I said, trying to keep the hate from my voice. Although I was angry with him, I needed to remain professional and cordial to get him talking. It would be no easy task. He was already responsible for the severe injuring of one innocent person, the killing of another, Homer's injuries, and now the killing of a deputy.

I shook my head. On the one hand, I secretly wished one of Homer's bullets would've found their mark. On the other, I was glad Jerome was alive and alert, so I could get him to talk himself into the death penalty—and hopefully tell me where to find Wess Griffin. At that point, I was certain we would be looking for a body.

"Say, Mr. Policeman," Jerome began in a slow voice. "Am I getting charged for killing that cop?"

"Oh, yeah," I said simply. Anything more would've revealed how I really felt.

"Will I get the death penalty?"

I let his question hang on the air. He could think what he wanted, and I didn't mind if he feared the worst. It might actually work to my advantage.

CHAPTER 31

About twenty minutes after Homer had located the body of Deputy Richmond, the divers with the sheriff's office had arrived with a boat, and they had ferried Jerome, Baylor, and me to the eastern bank of the bayou, where all of the action had been taking place.

One of the divers hadn't looked happy about Homer recovering the body of his comrade. While he hadn't dared say anything directly to Homer, I did overhear him ask his captain why they'd been called out if some cowboy was going to jump in the bayou and do their job for them.

"Shut your mouth," the captain had said. "It doesn't matter who found Stan's body. The important thing is that he was recovered before he started decomposing or the marine life got to him. This way, his family will get to hug him one last time."

The original diver had clamped his mouth shut and nodded his apology. He had gulped a few minutes later when he'd seen Homer sitting in the back of the ambulance getting his burn wounds cleaned and rebandaged.

"Is that the same guy who also tried to save that girl from the burning car?" he had asked the captain of the dive team.

"He's had an eventful first shift," the captain had said with a nod.

"Wait, this is his first shift?" the diver had asked, seemingly not believing what he'd heard. "Like, first shift ever?"

"Yep." The captain had stared wistfully at Homer. "If only I had two like him…"

I had chuckled to myself and turned to stuff Jerome into the back of Takecia's patrol cruiser. She had arrived a few minutes earlier, right behind Melvin, and they were talking with Homer while he was being worked on.

Susan and Amy had also arrived a few minutes earlier. They had started processing the vehicle and the scene of the crash, while two of Sheriff Turner's detectives had taken a boat across the bayou to begin processing the scene of the shootout between Homer and Jerome.

Keeping one eye on Jerome in the back of the patrol cruiser, I sidled up to the rear of the ambulance and leaned against a door. Homer looked up and his face fell.

"I'm really sorry about wasting ammo," he said. "I guess the chief will have to take sixteen hours off my check."

I scrunched up my face. "Huh?"

Melvin and Takecia burst out laughing.

"I told him we get docked one hour for every shot we miss in the line of duty," Melvin said. "I told him it's done to encourage firearms proficiency. You know, to keep innocent bystanders safe."

I chuckled, but Homer seemed concerned. Not only did he say he was embarrassed for missing every shot he'd fired, but he expressed concern that he might've injured an innocent party.

"First off, you would've handled it differently if you were in the middle of downtown," I said with confidence. "Secondly, Jerome Folse is worth more to us alive than dead. Had you killed him, we might never know what happened to Wess Griffin. I just thank God that he didn't kill or injure you."

That seemed to satisfy Homer a little, but he still seemed to be beating himself up on the inside.

"Would you like to sit in on the interview?" I offered. "Since you're the one who captured him, it's only fair."

His eyes lit up at that, and I told Homer to meet me at the front of the street when the medics were done treating his wounds.

"I'm going to put in a call to Bruce," Takecia said to Homer in her thick Jamaican accent, as I walked away. "I'll tell on you for getting your burns wet. He won't be happy."

I didn't hear his response. My mind had already returned to the case at hand, and I was several yards away from the ambulance. Once I made it to my Tahoe, I got in and drove toward the front of Cemetery Road. I stopped at the gate and dismounted. I surveyed the damage briefly. I figured it would cost me a few hundred dollars to get it repaired, but it would be worth it.

I looked toward the crashed Lexus and saw Susan squatting near the back of the vehicle, trying not to slip in the soft mud. She had a DNA collection kit in her hands. As I strode toward the southern edge of the ditch, she plucked something from the underside of the bumper. Once I was close enough to make out what was happening, I saw that she had removed a clump of hair from the vehicle. Even from that distance, I could see that the flesh was still attached to the strands. It matched Ann Griffin's hair color.

"This is definitely the car that killed Ann Griffin," she said once she had straightened and backed away from the vehicle. "There're more chunks of flesh and some fabric stuck to the frame. I'll get it towed to the sheriff's motor pool and have their crime scene unit process more of it there. Meanwhile, I'll have Amy send this sample to the crime lab along with the DNA samples she'll get from the autopsy."

"Is it scheduled?" I asked about the autopsy, turning to look in Amy's direction. She had put an evidence flag on the road near where the suspect had discarded a bag of marijuana, and she was walking back toward us, searching both sides of the shell road for more evidence.

"Yeah." Susan made some notes on the DNA recovery kit and secured it in her crime scene box. "Dr. Wong set it for ten this morning."

Dr. Louise Wong was our coroner and a forensic pathologist, and she performed almost all of our autopsies. While forensic examinations were important pieces of the investigative puzzle, I wasn't expecting any surprises with Ann's autopsy. The most important evidence would be a known DNA sample from our victim, as that would link the crime scene to the Lexus, and, in essence, also to Jerome Folse. Although we had an overwhelming amount of evidence to place Jerome inside the Lexus, Susan and Amy would also swab the car's interior for his DNA. In my world, there was no such thing as too much evidence, and I wanted to recover everything we possibly could to make our case airtight.

I expected that they'd also find Wess Griffin's DNA in the car, but that wouldn't tell us much about his kidnapping. He had been in the car countless times, so the presence of his DNA was to be expected. I was just hoping they wouldn't find any blood. Since I had the thought, I asked Susan if she had noticed any in the car.

"Nothing on the inside," she said. "Thank God for that."

Although there was an absence of blood, we still couldn't say definitively that no harm had come to Wess, but at least it was a small piece of good news.

When Amy drew up beside us, she gave me an angry look. "You know this is bullshit, right?"

I nodded, knowing what was coming.

"You get to run around with my husband and his new best friend and chase bad guys, while I'm stuck babysitting a crime scene." She blew a tuft of blonde hair away from her eyes. "I mean, y'all are swimming bayous and getting in gunfights, and what am I doing? Marking a bag of marijuana in the grass!"

I didn't tell you to get pregnant, I thought, but didn't dare to say. Instead, I nodded sympathetically. "As soon as you have that baby, you can be the lead on every major case we get for the rest of the year."

"Promise." She said it as a command, not a question.

"I promise."

"Okay, I guess I forgive you."

"*Forgive* me?" I shook my head in astonishment. "What did I do?"

"I already said it, and I'm not repeating myself." She glanced at Susan. "Any sign that the boy was in the car?"

"Not a one." Susan shook her head. "But his mom's all over the undercarriage."

CHAPTER 32

Two hours later, Homer and I were seated across from Jerome Folse in one of the interview rooms at the police department. He had refused to speak when we'd first walked him into the room and I'd asked if he remembered me reading him his Miranda rights in the swamps.

"I ain't saying nothing," he had said, "unless I can get some clean clothes and some food."

"Is that it?" I'd asked.

"No." He had hesitated for a long moment before continuing. "And I want you to promise me that I won't get the death penalty for killing that cop, because I didn't do it and I didn't mean for him to die."

I had started to tell him to shove it, but that would've been reckless. I needed him to tell Homer and me where to find the missing boy.

"I can't make any promises," I had explained, "but if I can get the district attorney's office to state that they won't seek the death penalty against you for the killing of Deputy Stan Richmond, will that work?"

"Yeah."

"And if I do that, will you answer all of my questions?"

He had nodded his head. It had seemed a little noncommittal, but I'd accepted it and placed the call to the district attorney's office anyway.

Now that we were back in the interview room and Jerome was wearing warm clothes and munching on a hamburger, I slid a printed copy of an email from the district attorney's office toward him.

"You got your warm clothes and your burger," I said. "Now, here's a note from the district attorney's office stating they won't seek the death penalty against you for the death of Deputy Richmond."

Since the circumstances surrounding Deputy Richmond's drowning death didn't meet the elements of a first degree murder charge, Jerome couldn't be sentenced to death anyway, but he didn't know that. Had he asked for an attorney, he would've found out that the most he could've been charged with was manslaughter, and that might've prompted him to keep his mouth shut.

However, luck had swung our way for the first time since the inception of the case, and I had wanted to take advantage of it as much as possible. If I could just get him talking, I should be able to convince him to admit to murdering Ann while in the process of robbing her of the Lexus, and all for the purpose of kidnapping Wess. As long as the facts of the case matched the elements of first degree murder, the district attorney's office would have the option to seek the death penalty for what had happened to Ann, and I was hoping for the maximum. It didn't seem appropriate for Jerome to spend the rest of his life with three "hots and a cot" after having left behind so much suffering.

Jerome looked over the note from the DA's office, nodded, and took another bite of his burger.

"Okay, I'll tell you whatever you want to know," he said after swallowing his food. "But I want to reserve my right to shut up whenever I want to."

"Agreed." I watched him wolf down the last of his food, and then I asked him how he came to be in possession of the Lexus. "Start from when you first arrived at the house."

"What house?" he asked, wiping his mouth on the sleeve of the shirt I had given him to wear.

"The house where you acquired the Lexus." I was careful not to use the word *stole*. I wanted to put him at ease, and get him comfortable with talking to me. If I started throwing around labels like *stole*, *kidnapped*, or *murdered*, he might get defensive and shut down. I needed him to acknowledge taking possession of the vehicle, backing out of the garage, and picking up Wess from the bus stop, and I would frame it as casually as possible at first. Once he opened up, I would talk about the woman who had been behind the car when he backed out of the garage. But I needed to get him slowly to that point.

"I didn't get the car at no house," he said. "I found it on the road."

"What do you mean you found it on the road?" I tried to keep the annoyance out of my voice, and I was careful not to make any leading statements. I needed him to say he got it from a garage without me offering that detail.

"I mean it was parked on the road."

"Jerome, you said you would tell me the truth if I got the DA's office to take the death penalty off the table for killing Deputy Richmond," I said slowly. "I held up my end of the bargain. Now, I need you to do the same."

"I am."

To make sure he wasn't playing word games with me, I asked, "Where'd you get the black Lexus that you crashed in the ditch next to the cemetery?"

"On the road to the park."

I decided to play along and see where he went. "What park?"

"Um, the Indian park over on the east side."

"The Waxtuygi Nature Park?" I asked.

"Yeah, that's the one."

"When you say it was on the road," I began, "what do you mean?"

"I mean it was on the road leading to the park," he said. "It was not far down neither. You could see it from the highway. I was just riding my bike down the road, and I looked over and saw it parked there."

While I remained stone faced, a seed of panic was planted deep inside my chest. "Are you saying the black Lexus was parked there with the keys inside, and you just so happened to ride by on your bike?"

He cocked his head to the side, as though thinking about it carefully, and then straightened and nodded. "Yeah, that's what happened."

"What time did you see the car there?"

"Oh, it was later in the day." He was thoughtful again. "What time do the kids get off of school?"

"About quarter to three."

"Then it was around that time, because I left the trailer when my sister's kids got home from school." Jerome shifted in his seat. "I'm staying with her until I can get another job, but I don't like it. Her kids are noisy. I can't hear myself think half the time. So, I usually ride my bike around town when they get out of school. Yesterday, I went to the park, and that's when I saw the car."

"Where's your bike?" I asked, still not sure if I believed him.

"I stashed it in the trees next to where I found the car," he said. "It's next to where this big oak tree is growing on the left side of the road. I covered it with a broken branch I found so nobody steals it. It's not even my bike, really. It's for my nephew. My sister would probably kick me out if I got it stolen."

I was thoroughly confused, but I didn't let it show. "Describe how you approached the car."

"Oh, I just turned around and went down the road," he explained. "I rode right up to it and tried to look in the window. I could hear that it was still running, so I thought somebody was inside. The windows are dark. I couldn't see anything, so I knocked on the glass. When nobody stepped out, I opened the door. It was empty."

Jerome took a breath and then continued.

"I called out to see if somebody was around, but nobody answered." He shrugged. "So, I decided to take it for a ride."

I leaned forward. "Jerome, this is very important; was anybody in the car?"

He shook his head. "Nope."

"Are you sure?"

"Positive."

"Did you check the back seat?" I pressed.

"I didn't need to," he said. "There was nobody back there."

I leaned back in my chair and stared across the desk at him. If what he was saying was true, Wess Griffin hadn't been in the car when he found it. And if that was true, we were in real trouble.

"Jerome, if I call one of our officers right now and ask them to go search that road," I began, "will they find your nephew's bike hidden in the trees?"

"Yeah," he said hesitantly. "I mean, unless somebody stole it."

I nodded slowly. Finally, I pulled out my cell phone and called Takecia. When she answered, I asked if she could ride to the Waxtuygi Nature Park and locate Jerome's nephew's bike. I described where he had stashed it, and then I made small talk with Jerome while she set out to carry out my request.

As I waited, I prayed she would call back and say she couldn't find the bike. I needed Jerome to be lying.

Finally, after about ten minutes of idle talk, my cell phone rang. I glanced down and saw that it was Takecia.

"Hey, did you find it?" I asked quickly, barely able to handle the suspense. "Was it there?"

"Yep. It was right where you said it would be."
Shit! I thought. *He might be telling the truth!*

CHAPTER 33

I stepped out of the interview room and asked Takecia to secure the area until Susan and Amy could get out there, and then I called Susan to let her know what was going on.

"No way!" After a long pause, she continued. "So, this isn't over yet, is it?"

"Not by a long shot." I paced back and forth in front of the interview room door, my mind racing. "This ain't good."

"Okay, we're almost finished here," she said. "We'll head to the park in a few minutes."

I thanked her and ended the call. I took a deep breath and let it out slowly. I relaxed the muscles on my face and tried to put on a pleasant air.

"Good news," I said to Jerome when I stepped back into the interview room. "Your nephew's bike wasn't stolen. Our officer found it and is securing it as we speak."

"Oh, that's awesome," he said. "My sister would be pissed if it got stolen."

"What happened after you took the car?" I asked, feeling completely deflated.

I had always expected that once we found the Lexus, we would either find Wess or discover what had happened to him. Now, I had no clue what to think. If Jerome was telling the truth, someone had murdered Ann, kidnapped Wess, and then abandoned the car on a desolate road. What happened next would be anybody's guess, but the suspect had either stashed a getaway car at that location or had arranged for an accomplice to pick him up. Either way, the suspect and Wess were likely hundreds of miles away—and they had probably left the area long before we had even begun our search.

"Well, I drove the car around a little bit," Jerome said. "I stopped at one of my buddy's houses and showed it to him. He asked me if it was hot. I told him that I found it. He got all nervous and told me to get the hell out of there with it. He said he didn't want no stolen car in his driveway. I told him it wasn't stolen, but he didn't care. He threatened to call the law if I didn't leave, so I left."

"Where does your buddy live?" I asked.

"On the east side."

"Where on the east side?" I pressed.

"You not gonna talk to him, are you?" he asked, almost pleadingly. I don't need him thinking I'm a rat.

"I'm talking to everybody," I said. "This is a pretty important car, and I'm going to have to retrace every single step you took to make sure you're telling the truth. Trust me when I tell you that you don't want to lie about this."

Jerome must've sensed something in my tone, because he let out an audible gulp. "Um, he lives at the end of Camp Street."

"What did you do next?"

"Um, I just drove around a bit," he said. "I crossed over and headed down the bayou. I wanted to show another one of my buddies the car, but he wasn't home, so I turned around and headed back up the bayou."

"What road were you on?" I asked.

"Cypress Highway."

"Do you remember seeing three boys at some point?"

He scrunched up his dark face. "Were they white?"

"Yeah, and they were…" I turned to Homer. "How old?"

"About eleven or twelve," Homer said, and he went on to describe what each boy looked like.

Jerome nodded. "Oh, yeah, I saw them boys. They was trying to cross the road. They acted like I was gonna run them over or something."

"What makes you think that?" I asked.

"Because they was waving these sticks in the air and yelling at me like they was mad or scared," he said. "Come to think of it, those sticks might've been fishing poles, because I think one of them had a tackle box."

"Were you driving fast?" I asked.

"It's a Lexus." Jerome smirked. "Of course I was driving fast!"

"What happened after you saw the boys?" I asked.

"Not much." He lowered his head to think about it. "I drove around for a bit longer. I got bored after a while and decided it was time to go back to my sister's house."

He stopped talking, as though he were done with his story, and I had to prompt him to continue.

"Well, I thought I should bring the car back to where I found it," he explained, "so I headed back in that direction. When I started to turn down the road to the park, I saw some people jogging—I think it was a man and a woman—so I kept going. I didn't want nobody seeing me in the Lexus, so I turned around and headed back toward my sister's house. That...um...that's when I saw the cop car by the apartments."

"What'd you do at that point?"

"I played it cool for a minute until I passed them, and then I hauled ass." Jerome shifted in his seat. "They...um...they caught up to me a ways down the road, and started chasing me. We crossed over to this side and kept going down the bayou. After a while, they dropped back, but I know the game. I know they was calling some cops up ahead to spike strip me. I needed to cross the bayou and head back in the opposite direction, but I couldn't do that with them on my tail, so I...I...well, I kind of accidentally rubbed a car that was coming my way—"

"When you say you accidentally rubbed a car," I interjected, "don't you mean you sideswiped it?"

"Uh-huh," he said. "That's what I meant to say. I kind of swerved into it and it went out of control. I didn't mean for it to catch fire or nothing, and I wasn't trying to hurt nobody. I was just trying to use that car to run the cop car off the road, you see?"

"Oh, yeah, I see." I reached into my folder and pulled out the extensive criminal record on Jerome Folse that I'd received from Lindsey. "And why were you running from the officers?"

"I mean, I didn't steal that car, but I figured it was stolen," he said. "And I can't be caught in no stolen car."

"Why is that?"

Jerome indicated the criminal record with a nod of his head. "You got my sheet, so you know why."

I nodded. Jerome was out on parole for drug possession and a vehicular homicide from out of New Orleans after only having served six months of an eight-year sentence. He had five additional felony convictions on his record, all of them out of Orleans Parish, and three of them were crimes of violence. The fact that he was running around was a testament to the failures in our judicial system.

However, I knew one thing for certain: his reign of terror was over. No jury from Chateau Parish would let him see the light of day again.

"Where'd you go after you sideswiped that car?" I asked, curious as to where he had gone and what he had done throughout the night.

"I just laid low," he said, not lifting his head to look at me.

"Where?"

"Do I have to say?"

"It's your call, but honesty is best in this situation," I explained. "If you lie about where you were, I've got to think you're lying about accidentally killing Deputy Richmond."

"That *was* an accident!" He finally lifted his head and looked me in the eye. "I didn't want that deputy to die."

I almost asked if he had wanted Homer to die, but I refrained. "Where'd you go?" I asked instead.

"Please, I don't want to involve nobody else."

I had a hunch, and I played it. "Look, I can go arrest your sister right now, or you can just tell me the truth."

He threw up his hands. "Okay, okay, I'll tell you. Just please leave her out of it."

I studied on it for a second, and then said, "I might take her statement, but I won't arrest her if all she did was let you hide the car."

"That's all she did, I swear," he said in desperation. "I had crossed the bayou and drove back to her house. I…I woke her up and told her I was in trouble, and she let me hide the car in her father-in-law's garage. I swear to God, she didn't know what all I had done until the next morning when she heard about the girl in the fire. That…um…that's when she told me to get that car out of there and to get rid of it. Not long after I left her house, that's when that cop that drowned saw me and started chasing me."

Jerome paused and shook his head. "This place was crawling with cops. There was nowhere I could go to dump the car. I thought about just stopping and telling the cop the truth—that I found the car—but I had ten ounces of weed on me, so I knew I was screwed either way."

I questioned him about the car chase, the crash, and then the foot pursuit through the cemetery and swamps. He recounted everything accurately and in surprising detail, except when it came to shooting at Homer. He claimed he intentionally missed, and that he only shot to scare Homer and make Homer stop chasing him.

"But he wouldn't quit, and he wasn't scared one bit. Back in the day, I swam some drainage canals in Orleans and Jefferson, but the cops never swam after me." Jerome paused to look at Homer and shake his head. "You're one crazy son of a bitch. I thought for sure you would kill me."

Homer wasn't one bit moved by Jerome's show of admiration. He didn't even acknowledge that the criminal had addressed him. I hadn't known Homer long, but I could already read a few of his expressions. The one currently displayed on his face told me that he'd just as soon rip Jerome's throat out than say hello to him. However, I noticed that he also appeared more restrained than the wild kid I'd first met in the swamps two months earlier, and I knew he would make a fine officer.

I continued with the interview, gathering more details about Jerome's hours-long crime spree in our town. Once I'd satisfied all of the elements to all of the crimes he'd committed, I pressed him for more information on the Lexus, and whether or not he remembered seeing anyone in the vicinity. He was able to provide a pretty descriptive drawing of the area where he'd found the abandoned car, and I sent a picture of it to Susan. I continued to press him, but try as I might, none of my probing questions stimulated his senses. Alas, I had to acknowledge he had nothing more to offer, and I ended the interview.

Since he hadn't been responsible for robbing Ann Griffin of the Lexus, murdering her, and then kidnapping Wess, I couldn't charge him with a capital offense. However, I did announce that he was under arrest for attempted first degree murder, two counts of manslaughter, resisting arrest violently, and theft of a motor vehicle.

"But I didn't steal the car," he said after stammering a bit. "And I...I didn't commit no manslaughters. And two of them? Who was I supposed to do manslaughters on?"

"When you resist arrest and an officer dies, that's manslaughter," I explained. "Even if you didn't mean for the officer to die."

His jaw slacked opened. "But you said I couldn't get in trouble for that!"

"Nah, we just told you it wouldn't be a first degree murder charge, and that the DA's office wouldn't seek the death penalty."

"Wait a minute..." His brow furrowed. "It was a manslaughter all along?"

I nodded.

"You...you tricked me!"

"Yep."

"You can't do that!"

"Unfortunately for you," I said, "we can."

He stammered for a while, and then asked about the second manslaughter charge.

"That's for Lisa Grant," I said. "You intentionally sideswiped her vehicle and caused her death, and that's as clear cut a manslaughter as it gets."

Jerome sank back into his chair. It was his turn to feel deflated. "But…but I don't understand what's happening," he finally said. "Why are you doing this to me? This is a set up!"

"Stop playing games." I had all the information I needed from him, so there was no need to be overly nice. I wasn't going to be hostile to him, but I didn't need honey to catch bees anymore. "You've been in the system long enough to know what you did, and you understand what's happening."

"But I'm on parole!" he said with a wail. "I'm a fourth or fifth time loser!"

"That's true." I nodded. "We can't put you to death for all the crimes you committed in our town, but I can pretty much guarantee that you'll spend the rest of your life in prison."

"Life?" His eyes widened for a second, but then a grin slowly played across his face. "Man, I ain't getting no life. I might do three, four years, but I ain't getting no life."

"You're in for a rude awakening," I said, leaning forward in my chair. "You're in the country now, and we don't play."

CHAPTER 34

After writing up the arrest report and locking Jerome Folse in a holding cell, I called the lieutenant on duty at the Lafourche Parish Detention Center and explained that Sheriff Buck Turner had made arrangements to have Jerome housed at their facility, given he had been responsible for the death of one of his officers.

"I've been made aware," said the lieutenant. "I've got a van en route back from court. I'll send them your way as soon as they get back here."

After thanking him, Homer and I headed to the Waxtuygi Nature Park to meet up with Susan and Amy.

Susan pointed at Homer when he exited my Tahoe, and said, "You need to get some sleep for the night shift."

"Oh," he said, glancing at me. "Should I leave now?"

"No, you can wait until we're done here," she said, "and then you can sleep in one of the interview rooms. We've got cots in the back. They're rough, but you're young and shouldn't notice it."

Homer smiled. "I've slept on rocks before, and it didn't bother me too much."

"While y'all are talking about rocks," Amy jumped in, "my baby's throwing kicks like Bruce Lee on speed to let me know he's hungry. We need to search this area so I can—"

"Hold up," Susan blurted. "You're having a boy?"

"Oh, shit!" Amy clamped a hand over her mouth. "I wasn't supposed to say anything! Baylor doesn't know."

"Cat's out of the bag now," I said. "The only way three people can keep a secret is if two of them are dead. There are five of us here, and we're all very much alive."

"And I'm telling Baylor as soon as I see him tonight," Homer sang out in a teasing manner. He then held his hand out, palm up. "But…I do accept bribes."

"You little devil!" Amy nodded her head up and down slowly. "All of these people here think you're so innocent, but I know you've got a little devil on your shoulder. And I also know that you've got a certain love interest in town named—"

"On second thought," Homer blurted out, his face red. "I'll take that information to my grave."

Amy smiled triumphantly. "How's that for bribery?"

I didn't know what they were talking about. While mildly curious, I wanted to search the spot where the Lexus had been parked, so I asked Susan if they had located it.

"Yeah, it's over here." Susan waved for us to follow, and she led the way about a dozen yards from where her Tahoe was parked. She pointed to a set of peel-out marks that began on the grass of the northern shoulder and continued through the shells. "It looks like he sped off from here, and then headed for Cypress Highway."

I studied the ground around the peel-out marks, searching for anything that might've fallen from the Lexus. I wasn't much concerned with anything that Jerome would've dropped. Instead, I wanted to see if the real killer had left anything behind.

"We photographed and searched the area around the tracks," Amy said when she walked up. "It hasn't rained in a while, and with the ground as hard as it is, we weren't able to find any shoe impressions."

I nodded and glanced around. "Any evidence of a second vehicle?"

Susan shook her head. "Not so far, but we had just started branching out from the tracks when y'all drove up."

"Homer and I will take that side of the road," I said, pointing toward the southern shoulder. I then told Homer to head west while I headed east. "We're looking for anything that's out of place. A driver's license or a birth certificate of the suspect would be great."

Homer snickered and began walking slowly away from me, heading back toward the main highway while I headed farther down the road.

It was approaching noon and the sun was high in the sky. It was a warm and dry day, and sweat was soon pouring down my face and into my eyes. I blinked repeatedly, as the salty moisture blurred my vision. A few times along my walk I thought I saw something of interest in the weeds of the adjoining ditch, but when I'd wipe my eyes, I'd see that it was either an old Styrofoam cup or some other piece of outdated trash.

Always one to detest litter and those who left it, I gathered up the trash while I walked my assignment. When my hands would get full, I'd leave the trash in a neat pile on the shoulder so I could return for it. By the time I'd searched 100 yards of roadway, I'd left eight piles in my wake.

Susan was on the opposite side of the road and walking in the same direction as me. Takecia had returned to her shift, and Amy had headed west on Susan's side of the road. I looked back a few times to check on Homer's progress, and I noticed that Amy was keeping pace with him. Since I knew her well, I was sure she was either harassing him about his new love interest, or bestowing upon him her investigative wisdom.

I laughed to myself, and said, "Probably a little bit of both."

"What's that?" Susan asked from her side of the road.

"Nothing serious," I said. "I was just wondering what kinds of things Amy might be telling Homer."

"Oh, I guarantee you she's ribbing him about Remi," she said. "She saw Homer walking back from the elevators with her at the hospital, and she said they looked like a couple of teenagers who got caught kissing under the stadium."

"Is Remi that new reporter?" I asked, feeling a little out of the loop. "The one who's about his age?"

Susan nodded.

I remembered seeing her with Ali at the hospital, but I'd had no clue she and Homer were an item, so I asked, "How long have they been dating?"

"Oh, they're not...yet," Susan said. "They just met yesterday."

"What kind of person is she?"

"From what I can gather, she's a good girl," Susan said. "I know her mom, and she's good people. Amy was going to pull her aside and interrogate her, but Baylor asked her not—"

"Hey!" called a voice from some distance away. "Hey!"

I turned to see Amy a half mile down the road, and fifty, or so, yards in the middle of a grassy field to the north. Her blonde hair was dancing on the wind, and she was waving her arms frantically about like she was going into labor. She was saying something, but I could only hear a word here and a word there. She was excited about something, and whatever it was, I didn't think it was good.

At around the same time, I caught a flash of movement to the left in my peripheral vision. When I looked, I saw Homer sprinting across the road and jumping the ditch. It was clear that he also thought Amy was in trouble.

"Damn, that kid's fast," Susan said, breaking into a run. "They're gonna love him at the police academy."

I nodded, and joined Susan as she sprinted the half mile up the street. She had always been in better shape than me, thanks to all the time she spent in her custom gym. Her dad had been a professional boxer, and he had instilled within her a lifelong love for the fight game. Training was a major part of fighting, and she did it religiously.

I never took my eyes off of Amy as we ran. She didn't appear to be in distress, but she kept waving her hands and saying something that we couldn't hear. Finally, she dropped one hand to her hip and the other to her belly and just stood there waiting for us to reach her.

It appeared that she was breathing hard. Her legs were spread a little, and it looked like she might've been doing so for balance. There was no way she was going into labor, as she wasn't even close to giving birth. If she was having pains, then that wouldn't be a good sign. It was possible that she was out of breath from the heat, or jogging across the uneven ground. Everything was harder when a woman was pregnant, and the field was rough and unyielding.

And that's when it occurred to me. She might've found something—something that had excited her enough to start screaming at us and waving her hands and...

"Oh, shit!" I said, running faster.

"What is it?" Susan asked, matching my pace. "Do you see something?"

"I bet she found Wess Griffin!" I said. "I bet he's dead!"

CHAPTER 35

When Susan and I were parallel to Amy and Homer, we quickly jumped the ditch and raced across the field, dodging potholes here and clumps of earth there. Homer had long since reached Amy, and they were both standing around looking down at something on the ground.

I couldn't tell by their demeanor if the news was good or bad, but I feared the worse. Whoever had killed Ann had abandoned the Lexus in that area, and it stood to reason that we might find Wess there as well. If Amy had found the boy, and he had been killed and abandoned there, then I could only think of one reason for the kidnapping. It made me sick to my stomach and about as angry as I'd ever been.

"What did you find?" I hollered when we were still a dozen yards from Amy and Homer. "Is it him?"

"What?" Amy called, raising a hand to shield her eyes from the sun.

"What did you find?" I asked again, my voice shaking with the pounding of my boots.

"A piece of paper," Amy said, her bottom lip jutting out in frustration. "The wind picked it up and I had to chase it all the way over here before it—"

"What in the hell?" I blurted out, and lurched to a stop. "You…found…a piece of…paper?"

I bent forward and rested my hands on my knees. I took several deep breaths, thanking God out loud as I did so. My legs were weak, and it wasn't from running. I had already been going over the conversation I thought I'd be having with Thad Griffin in the coming hours, and nothing about it was pleasant. In my mind's eye, I had been envisioning all the horrible things that Wess might've endured, and in that short time, it had taken a lot out of me.

I straightened only after my heart had slowed to a more manageable rate. Amy had a look of confusion on her face.

"Are you pregnant, too?" she asked. "Why are you so flustered and out of breath?"

"I thought you found the boy," I said through heaves in my breathing. "I thought Wess Griffin was dead."

"Oh, shit!" Amy's eyes widened. "I'm so sorry!"

I waved her off and started to close the remaining distance between us. Susan was already there, and she was bending over to see the small white sliver of paper stuck to the thorns of a thistle plant.

"Those are good eating," Homer was telling Amy, pointing to the weed. "You just peel off the thorns and skin and snack down on it."

Amy scrunched up her face. "You do know we've got grocery stores around here right?"

Homer laughed, but turned serious when I reached them.

"Damn, Ames," Susan said. "I think you might've found something!"

"What'd she find?" I asked, squatting next to my wife. "A social security card?"

"No, a receipt," Susan said, squinting to try and read it. "It's hard to see what it says."

"You screamed and jumped around just for a receipt?" I asked, finally able to speak in a normal tone. "You scared the shit out of me."

"I was yelling for one of y'all to bring some gloves and an evidence envelope, but I guess none of y'all were paying attention," Amy said with a grumble. "I wasn't about to carry my pregnant ass all the way back across this bumpy field. I'm lucky I didn't break a leg in one of those crawfish holes."

"Amy, did you see where this receipt is from?" Susan asked, her voice taking on a strange tone.

"No, but it looked fresh, so I wanted to recover it," Amy said. "It couldn't have been here more than a day, so I thought it might be significant."

Susan straightened and looked from Amy, to Homer, and then to me. "It's from Copper Head, Tennessee."

"No shit!" Amy and I said in unison.

"What's Copper Head, Tennessee?" Homer asked.

"That's where Thad Griffin is from," I said, quickly dropping to my knees to get a closer look at the details of the receipt. "This is *not* a coincidence!"

I had knelt right in a patch of pickers, but I didn't care. I was too focused on trying to read the tiny, purplish print. Although I was nearing forty, my eyes were still sharp, but I could barely read what was on it.

"I know what you can do," Susan said. "Take a picture with your cell phone and enlarge it."

I nodded and did what she said. Once I'd figured out the perfect angle and adjusted the zoom, I took the picture and pulled the screen to my face. It was a great idea, and I said so as I began reading every word that was printed on the tiny document.

The relevant parts told me that the transaction had been made two weeks earlier—the twenty-ninth of April, which would've been a Saturday—at a service station called Copper Head Gas and Stuff. The customer used pump #03, purchased 15.558 gallons of fuel for a total of $77.77, and paid with cash.

"Damn it!" I shook my head and tilted the phone so Susan could see the line indicating that cash had been used. "Of course they paid with cash. They couldn't have made it easy for us."

"What time did they pump the gas?" Amy asked.

I checked the photo on my screen. "One minute before noon."

"If they used cash," she continued, "they would've walked inside to pay the teller. Find out who was working on that day and at that time, and you'll have your witness."

I nodded and glanced back at the receipt. According to the information printed at the top of the document, the gas station was located at 1818 Old Highway 12 in Copper Head, Tennessee. A phone number was also listed, but I had no intentions of calling it. At that very moment, I decided Susan and I were driving to Tennessee. If our killer had come from Copper Head, the chances were good that he had returned there, and there was no other place I'd rather be at that moment. It also explained why we hadn't been able to locate him or Wess Griffin anywhere in town.

"Go home and pack your bags, Sue," I said as I headed for my Tahoe to retrieve an evidence bag. "We're going to Copper Head."

"Today? Right now?" She sounded surprised, and more than a little skeptical. "Are you serious?"

"Just as soon as I talk to the famous author," I called over my shoulder. "There's something he's not telling us, and I want to know what it is."

CHAPTER 36

After recovering the receipt from the thistle plant, I dropped Homer off at the police department to get some sleep so he could work his night shift later, and then I headed toward Tiger Plantation Boulevard. Meanwhile, Susan had gone home to ensure that her mom could watch Grace and Isaiah overnight, and she had also planned on packing our bags.

I didn't know how long it would take to reinterview Thad Griffin, but even if it was brief, I wasn't leaving town until Grace got home from school and I got to tell her goodbye. Although we'd celebrated her fifth birthday on Sunday and it had been a joyous time, she was set to graduate from Pre-K the following week and I wanted her to know how proud I was of her. I didn't know what dangers we might face on our trip, and I would hate to leave this world without her knowing how I felt about her accomplishments thus far.

When I reached the end of the street, I parked in front of the neighbor's house and knocked on the door. I had barely returned my fist to my side when the door burst open and Thad was standing there.

"Did you find him?" His eyes were swollen and bloodshot, and his clothes disheveled. He looked like he had been on a three-day bender before being run through a trash compactor and then getting pieced back together by a group of elementary students. "Did you find my boy?"

"I'm sorry to say, we haven't," I began slowly, and sincerely. "But there's been a development, and I'd like you to come down to the police department so we can talk about it."

"Sure," he said without hesitation. "I'm ready."

"Before we go, I have to ask you something."

He nodded. "Anything."

"Have you received a ransom demand?"

"No." He blinked, obviously confused. "Do you think this was a kidnapping for ransom? Do...do you think they're holding Wess? If so, that's a good thing, right?"

"I don't know exactly what to think at the moment," I admitted. "I just had to ask, and I need you to be completely honest with me. If you received a ransom demand and they told you not to notify the police, you need to defy that order. You understand that, right?"

"Absolutely," he said. "I've done enough research on the subject to know better than to handle that kind of thing alone."

I studied him for a long moment. Finally, I stood aside and gestured for him to walk ahead of me. He seemed to be sincere, but I had to keep reminding myself he wrote believable lies for a living. While he walked around to the passenger's side, I slipped into the driver's seat, but kept a wary eye on him. I surveyed his waistline through his shirt as he walked, looking for any bulges that might indicate a weapon. I didn't notice any.

Once he settled in and fastened his seatbelt, I drove to the police department and led him to the first interview room. Homer had taken up residency in the second one, so I tried not to make any noise while we were out in the hallway.

"So, what's this all about?" Thad asked when I was seated across from him. "You said there was a development."

I nodded and described everything that had happened since we'd last spoken, only providing enough detail to give him a rough picture of the events that had transpired. He interrupted me several times to ask questions, but he nearly fell out when I mentioned we had recovered the Lexus and Wess wasn't inside.

"What do you mean he wasn't there?" he echoed loudly. "How can that be?"

I went on to explain how Homer had captured Jerome Folse, what he had said, and how we had located a receipt in the field to the north of where Jerome had found the Lexus.

"Wait a minute," he interrupted again. "Are you telling me that you actually believe what this criminal said?"

"Most of it," I said with a nod. "And it's our working theory that the suspect either had an accomplice who drove him away, or he stashed a getaway car where he dumped the Lexus. We don't know if it's a man or a woman, but we—"

"Look, I'm no detective, but I've interviewed a lot of them and, as you know, it's my job to write about them," he began. "I have to say, this is the biggest load of crap I've ever heard. This criminal asshole is playing you for a fool. He killed my wife, he stole her car, and he kidnapped my son—and the proof is right in front of you! For God's sake, he killed two more people and almost killed your officer. What more proof do you want?"

"Well, the problem is, this fellow, Jerome Folse, is originally from New Orleans. He's lived there and in surrounding parishes his whole life." I accessed the photo of the receipt on my cell phone and turned it so he could see. "This is the receipt we found in the field where the Lexus was abandoned. As you can see, it's from Copper Head, Tennessee."

Thad's face grew paler than it already was. He opened his mouth to speak, but no words came out. After a few failed attempts, he gave up altogether and clamped it shut.

"I see I've got your attention now," I said, lowering my phone and leaning back in my chair. "My question to you is this; who in Copper Head, Tennessee hates you so much that they'd drive more than 600 miles to Mechant Loup, Louisiana just to murder your wife and kidnap your son?"

Thad didn't answer right away. I could see that his mind was racing, so I let the silence linger. I wanted him to feel so uncomfortable that he would blurt something out. I figured he knew exactly who had attacked his family, and I wanted him to tell me.

"That's...that's impossible," he finally said after a full minute of keeping his mouth shut. "It can't be anyone from there."

"Oh, it's definitely someone from there." I showed him the date on the receipt. "They must've shown up here within the last two weeks."

"Maybe it's just someone on vacation." His eyes were darting around the room as though he were looking for a place to hide. "I run into people from Tennessee all the time who are visiting this area. It's very common."

"And they just so happened to lose a receipt from Copper Head, the town in which you were born, right next to where your stolen Lexus was found?" I shook my head. "Nice try, but no, this is not a coincidence."

"What do you mean by saying it's a nice try?"

"Well, it seems like you're trying to divert my attention away from Copper Head, but it won't work," I explained. "The key to this case is in Tennessee. Like it or not, that's where the evidence is leading us. Hell, your son's most likely over there. I would think you'd want to do everything you could to help me find him."

At the mention of his son, Thad's tear ducts sprung a leak, and he began bawling. I let him cry for a while. After all, I had some time before Grace got out of school, so there was still no rush.

CHAPTER 37

"Come on, Thad," I finally said after he'd cried for a while. "Tell me who hates you enough to do this to your family. Help me bring Wess back home to you. I'm sure he's scared and lonely, and he has to miss you."

Wiping a rivulet of tears from his face, the despondent author shook his head slowly. "I…I have no idea who it could be! I swear to God! I've never done anything to anyone that would warrant this kind of behavior. I…I've got no enemies. I've never pissed anyone off to this extent. I'm…I'm at a total loss as to who it could be!"

"Let's start with the people you pissed off a little bit." I leaned forward and rested my forearms on the desk. "There has to be someone. Shit, I could talk all day about the people I've pissed off in my lifetime. If someone ever comes after me, you'd have to write a book as long as the Bible to allow your characters to sift through the suspects."

"I swear, I don't have any enemies." Thad shook his head vigorously from side to side for emphasis. "I've never been in a fistfight before. I don't even know what it feels like to be punched in the face. I have to do a lot of research and interview a lot of people to figure out how to write my fight scenes. If someone ever attacked me in real life, I wouldn't know what to do."

I stared in awe at him. "Are you serious? You've never been punched in the face?"

He shook his head again.

I wanted to ask if he'd let me change that for him. I could tell that he was withholding crucial information from me, and I figured it might do some good to knock a little sense into him. While I would never just up and punch a witness or suspect without being legally justified to do so, I *might* consider doing it if they requested it…and I'd make sure to get it in writing.

I blinked the thought away and settled back in my chair. "Mr. Griffin, I know you're lying to me."

"Excuse me?" He tried to feign shock. "I'm the victim here! Why on earth would I be lying?"

"I don't know why you're lying," I insisted, "but I know you're withholding information from me."

"No!" His tone had lost some of its initial conviction. "I'm not lying! I don't know who did this. Don't you think I would tell you everything I knew if I thought it would bring my son back?"

I found his choice of words interesting. "Is that why you're not telling me the truth?"

He blinked. "What do you mean?"

"Are you keeping it from me because you don't believe it'll bring your son back?"

"That…that's not it at all."

I nodded slowly, studying him carefully. He was fidgeting in his chair, and his face had turned ashen. If I were a betting man, I'd put money on him losing whatever food he had in his stomach at some point. I was just hoping he'd wait until he was out of my sight.

"Okay, you say you've never been in a fight before," I finally said. "What about an argument?"

"I mean, sure, I've had arguments in my life, but nothing that would make someone want to attack me or my family." He sighed heavily. "Look, I still think this has something to do with my books. I think I might've written something that offended someone."

"Like what?" I asked.

"I don't know! I mean, it could also be somebody who's jealous of me because of my fame. It could even be a fellow writer who never made it big. Like, one of my competitors. You can maybe check out the authors who are in the same genre as me, and see which one of them lives around here. I know of at least one other author who writes alligator books. He's originally from Louisiana, so maybe he's mad that I'm having more success than him and I'm not even from here?"

"I don't know." I drummed my ink pen on the desk. "It's not like you're James Patterson or something. I mean, no offense, but I've never heard of you, and I only live a few miles down the road. And I hardly think authors are competitors. While it's true that authors need readers to succeed, there are plenty enough readers to go around. I don't see mystery writers offing each other to get ahead."

"It *has* to be because of my books!" Thad said in a wailing tone. "There's no other reason."

The way he said it piqued my curiosity, and I made a mental note to check on Lindsey to see what she had learned from his writings. Susan had told me earlier that Lindsey had spent the night at work, reading well into the morning hours. She had stopped for an hour to sleep, and then got back to it. Maybe she had found something useful.

"I don't know," I pressed. "I think it's something more personal, and I think you have an idea what it might be."

"Are you calling me a liar?"

"I just said it in plain English." I shook my head. "Look at it any way you like, but I think you're not telling me everything."

"That's offensive!" He jumped to his feet. "I demand to see my attorney immediately! I have a Constitutional right to have one present during questioning!"

"Those rights don't apply to you," I said in a calm voice.

It shook him that I wasn't moved by his outrage. He swallowed hard and sat down. "What do you mean?"

"You're not in custody, so you don't have a right to shit." I shot a thumb toward the door. "You can leave whenever you want. I just have to say, though, that it would look highly suspicious if the husband of a murdered wife and the father of a kidnapped son suddenly stopped cooperating with the investigation. That would lead me to believe there was a lot more to his story—like, maybe he was involved."

"I didn't do this!" He shouted the words so loud that his voice turned shrill. "It wasn't me!"

"You're lying about your past, so why should I believe you about the present?"

"I've never been in a fight," he moaned. "I swear it! I've got no enemies."

"What if you have an enemy you don't know about?" I offered. "Maybe you did something evil in your past—perhaps something that's too embarrassing to mention now that you're famous—and no one knew about it until recently. And maybe the person who found out is the one who came after your family."

"What kind of person do you think I am?" He spat the words. "I've never done anything evil in my life!"

"Have you ever had an affair with a married woman?" I asked.

"Maybe the woman kept your secret for all this time, and then somehow her husband found out. If y'all were both married at the time of the affair, it would've been in both of y'all's interest to keep things quiet, but if she got divorced, maybe she started talking. Even though he's now divorced from her, I could see her ex-husband getting mad enough to come after you. Of course, I imagine he would've killed you, and not your wife. A better scenario would be if a woman left her husband for you, and she took her kids with her. That would make more sense. He would then try to take from you everything that he lost because of you."

"I've never had an affair with a married woman," Thad said heatedly. "And I'm really not liking this line of questioning."

"I don't expect you to," I said. "Somebody murdered your wife and kidnapped your son, and you know exactly why they did it. I think you feel responsible, and that's why you're lying to me."

"I already told you, I'm *not* lying—" Thad suddenly clamped his mouth shut and took a deep breath. He let it out forcefully. "I'm not in custody, right?"

"That's correct."

"Then I can leave whenever I want?"

"That's also correct."

Without saying another word, Thad jumped up and headed for the door, mumbling something under his breath as he did so.

"I can give you a ride home," I called after him as he stormed out of the room. "It's hot outside."

"No thanks," he spat back. "I'd rather walk through hell than put up with another minute of this abuse."

"Suit yourself," I said and stood lazily to my feet.

As I headed for the dispatcher's station, I said a silent prayer that Lindsey would have something I could use.

As it currently stood, our only lead was a receipt from a small town gas station, and we were two weeks behind the suspect. In my experience, the retention period for many surveillance systems utilized by convenience stores and gas stations was anywhere from several days to several weeks. If we were lucky, Copper Head Gas and Stuff would fall into the latter category. If not, our best hope for solving the case would be the memory of whichever attendant was working that day.

And if the gas station was a popular spot and cash was king in Copper Head, the attendant might have a hard time remembering which person had come in at exactly one minute before noon to buy $77.17 worth of premium fuel.

CHAPTER 38

When I entered the dispatcher's station, I found Beth Gandy at the controls.

"Hey, Beth," I said cheerfully. "Have you seen Lindsey?"

"Yeah, she's reading in Susan's office." Beth finished jotting something down in the day logs and spun around to face me. "It's so sad about Deputy Richmond. He had a wife and three kids. They had just moved here from Florida. They joined my church and I got to be friends with Patty. I just can't imagine what she's going through right now."

I frowned. Beth had lost a son, so it was my guess that she knew full well what Patty was going through. When I didn't comment, Beth turned and snatched something off the desk.

"Susan asked me to pass these around," she explained, turning and handing me a mourning band for my badge. "She also asked me to get someone to put the flag at half-staff out of respect for Deputy Richmond."

"Thank you," I said, and immediately put the band around my badge. "I'll take care of the flag."

It was her turn to thank me, and I hurried away to meet with Lindsey. The door to Susan's office was closed, so I knocked lightly on it in case Lindsey was napping.

"It's your office, Chief," Lindsey called out. "You don't have to knock on my account."

When I opened the door, she turned to face me and started in the chair. "Oh, wow, Clint, I wasn't expecting to see you there."

I nodded, and indicated the reading device in her hands. "Are you getting anywhere with our author friend's books?"

"I'm on the last book in the Atlanta detective series," she said with a shake of her head. "I haven't found anything that's remotely similar to what happened at his house, and he doesn't write about any controversial topics. I even found a dozen, or so, short stories online that he wrote, and they're all very tame."

I dropped to the chair opposite her and considered what she'd said. Although he kept trying to push the investigation in that direction, it was quite possible it had nothing to do with his books. He had gotten very defensive when I'd started asking about his past, so I thought there was something to it. I decided to tell Lindsey about the interview to see what she thought.

She listened intently, hanging on my every word. She nodded at times, scrunched up her face at others, and even laughed when I told her how he had stormed out of the interview room.

"He walked all the way to his house?" she asked, still laughing.

I shrugged. "I don't know. I never went to check on him. If he didn't get a ride, then he should still be walking."

"He must be hiding something," she agreed. "He's smart enough to know that any husband would be a suspect—I mean, he even wrote about it in one of his books—so it seems he would cooperate fully so you wouldn't have to waste valuable time trying to clear him. If I had a son and he was kidnapped, I'd do anything you asked of me to help find him."

"What reason might he have not to cooperate?" I asked. "What kind of secret would it have to be for you to risk your son never being found again?"

Lindsey mulled it over for a full minute. Finally, her eyes lit up. "He definitely killed his wife!"

"Huh?"

"He must've done it," she insisted. "The only reason he wouldn't cooperate was if he were guilty. And if he is guilty, then he's not worried about his son, because he knows he's safe."

The more I thought about it, the more I liked the idea. The only physical evidence we had pointed to Copper Head, and that was where he was from. He had connections there. He could've easily gotten someone to come to Mechant Loup and murder his wife while he was upstairs establishing an alibi defense for himself. The killer would've needed the Lexus to pick up Wess from the bus stop, so the auto theft had to be a part of the plot. After getting Wess, the killer would've dropped the car off at the park, and gotten the hell out of town. By the time Thad went downstairs and "noticed" his wife dead in the driveway, the killer and Wess would've been long gone. While I had casually suspected Thad earlier than that moment, the receipt from Copper Head made things seem real.

Of course, Thad was insisting that the attack on his family had been because of his books. While part of me thought it might be a smokescreen, I was also growing increasingly suspicious that he had an underlying reason for pointing me in that direction. Maybe he *had* done something evil in his past that had brought about his difficulties, and maybe it was hidden between the pages of his published works. It might be too embarrassing for him to admit, so maybe he wanted us to find it on our own.

"I like it, Lindsey." I nodded for emphasis. "It's the best working theory we've had thus far, but keep looking for anything he might've written that could've made him a target."

She smiled and picked up the reading device. I figured it was my hint that she had to get back to work, but I indicated the device.

"It looks like you're getting pretty cozy with that thing," I said. "Where'd you get it?"

"I borrowed it from my mom," she said. "I hate to admit it, but it's pretty darned cool."

I nodded, not knowing one way or the other. "How many more of Thad's books do you have left to read?"

"Well, this is the last one that's been published," she said with a sly wink, "but Amy printed out the one he's working on now, and I'm about to dive into it."

It was then that I noticed the thick stack of paper on the desk next to Lindsey. I leaned over and grabbed it. I thumbed through the first few pages, reading a few passages here and there.

"How many books does he have to his credit?" I asked idly, as I glanced at the last page of the book. It pertained to some fight with an alligator, and I remembered him saying in his first interview that he had been doing research for the scene. I grunted, no longer wanting to believe him.

"He's written six books in the Atlanta series and three in the Gator Haven one," Lindsey was saying. "So, nine all together, not counting the one he's working on now. He barely sold any of the Atlanta books back then, and they're still not doing well. You would think the people who started reading his Gator Haven series would go back and read the other stuff he wrote, but his recent success hasn't translated to sales of his older stuff."

"Yeah, I wouldn't know about any of that." I put down the stack of papers and thanked her for the hard work. "You're the best."

She smiled and turned back to the electronic reading device, while I headed outdoors to lower the American flag that flew proudly over the police department. I thought about the events that had transpired over the previous day and night, and I felt terrible for the families who had been adversely impacted by the actions of one idiot.

I wasn't sure if God honored such prayers, but I sure prayed that Jerome Folse would get more than he had coming to him for all the sins he had committed in our little town.

CHAPTER 39

"When will y'all be back?" Grace asked when Susan and I sat her down to tell her we were leaving for a work trip.

"We should be back in a couple of days," I said as I cradled Isaiah in one arm and fed him a bottle with the other. "Maybe three at the longest."

"Three days is too long," she said. "Isaiah is gonna miss y'all."

"What about you?" Susan asked, giving her a peck on the forehead. "You won't miss us?"

"I'm too big," she said. "When you grow up, you don't miss your mommy and daddy anymore."

"That's not true," Susan said. "I miss my mom when I don't see her for a long time."

"Yeah, and you're not grown up yet," I said. "When you grow up, you'll have to move out the house, and I'm not ready for that."

Grace walked closer and wrapped her small arms around me. "Daddy, I'll never move out of your house," she said with pouted lips. "I'll live with you forever!"

"Promise?"

She nodded her head emphatically up and down.

"After I'm done with Isaiah," I explained, "I'll write it on a piece of paper and have you sign it."

"Why, Daddy?" She scrunched up her face inquisitively. "Why you gotta write it down?"

"I need proof that you promised to live with me forever," I said. "That way, if you ever try to move out, I can hire a lawyer and sue you for breach of contract."

I heard Susan's mom burst out laughing from the living room, but I didn't crack a smile. Grace turned excitedly to Susan.

"Mommy, do we really get to go to the beach when y'all come back?"

I didn't know how she got that from "breach of contract", but the idea of going to the beach sure got her excited. She jumped up and down, her curls bouncing each time she did.

Susan rubbed her head. "Sure, Honey, but first you have to be good and watch over Isaiah while we're gone."

Grace leaned close to Isaiah and told him all about the trip we would be taking to the beach, and she told him he would have to be good if he wanted to go, too.

After a while, I reluctantly handed Isaiah to Susan's mom, and kissed him and Grace goodbye. When I hugged them, it was especially tight. Next, I called Achilles and Coco over. Achilles lifted himself from the rug in the living room and sauntered to me. Coco didn't even open her eyes. I rubbed Achilles' ears and whispered for him to take care of Grace and Isaiah.

Like Beth Gandy, I had been through some trying times and suffered more than my share of loss. I also knew what Thad was feeling—or I thought I did. My daughter had been taken before, and it had terrified me. If Thad had orchestrated the kidnapping of his son and the murder of his wife, I would make him pay dearly for it.

Once Susan and I were in my personal truck and heading down the road, she punched in the address to the gas station and then began combing through the mountain of paperwork Lindsey had printed up on Thad Griffin.

In between reading his published books, Lindsey had taken a deep dive into his social media accounts and his website, and she had printed up every post he'd ever written, every bio she could find, and every exchange he'd ever had with his readers. Lindsey had intended on reading through everything herself, but Susan had taken a copy along to ease some of her burden.

Also in her possession, Susan had an external hard drive that contained a copy of every file, document, and image from Thad's laptop and computer. The hard drive had been copied when she and Amy had executed the search warrant for the author's residence, and a subsequent search warrant had given them permission to search through the hard drive. Susan had planned on doing that, too, but she thought she might have more luck with the public information—especially if Thad was targeted because of something he had written.

It was a little after three in the afternoon and we were more than nine hours away from Copper Head, so Susan and I would have lots of time to go through the information. Besides, some of the smaller towns in Tennessee turned in early for the night, so there was no guarantee that Copper Head Gas and Stuff would be open when we arrived. Thus, we had booked a room in Gadsden, Alabama for the night, so that would give us even more time to sift through the millions of words contained in the paperwork. We planned on arriving at the gas station early on Wednesday morning, and we would hopefully be well versed on the author.

"Lindsey pulled up the address for his mom," Susan said after I'd been driving in silence for about thirty minutes. "Plain Ridge is about an hour south of Copper Head. Should we pay her a visit first?"

"Absolutely," I said. "We might find Wess there."

"God, I wish." Susan looked up from something she had been reading. "Wouldn't that be the best case scenario? That Thad's family was involved and Wess is safe and sound with them?"

"Yeah, and I think it's possible," I said. "Thad is originally from Copper Head. Even though his mom moved to Plain Ridge, I bet he still has family in Tennessee."

"He does," Susan agreed. "Lindsey ran a search of all relatives, and I remember seeing at least a couple of addresses in Copper Head."

I was thoughtful for a moment. Finally, I said, "It would suck for the boy, because his dad would spend the rest of his life in prison, but at least he'd be alive."

"That's true."

As I considered what we might find in Plain Ridge and Copper Head, I thought about how we might approach things from that end. I knew it wouldn't be as simple as showing up at Thad's mom's house and looking around for Wess. If it had been a staged kidnapping and she was involved, she would certainly hide the boy once we showed up. I had decided to take my personal truck so we wouldn't be readily identified as cops, and that meant we couldn't contact the local sheriff's office until we had gotten a good look around. We would also have to come up with a good reason for knocking on her door and introducing ourselves.

Susan had apparently been thinking about the same thing at the same time, because she suddenly said, "Why don't you park your truck down the street from her house?"

"Thad's mom?"

"Yeah." She nodded excitedly. "We can walk up and pretend to be new neighbors. I searched her address and did a street view on the map. She lives in a subdivision a few miles outside of town, so it would be perfectly believable that we were new to the area. Especially with your accent."

"*My* accent?" I feigned offense. "What's wrong with the way I talk?"

"Nothing. I love the sound of your voice." She leaned over and rubbed her soft hand across my face. "But when you open your mouth to speak, you'll stick out like a twelve-foot alligator on the streets of downtown Gatlinburg."

I laughed and switched my blinker on to access the interstate. We were only thirty minutes into our journey, and my stomach was already grumbling. It didn't help that Susan mentioned buying a chocolate cake for Thad's mom.

"We have to make it look legit," she said. "And no southerner would show up without food of some kind."

I nodded and suggested that we stop at Spahr's on our way out of Louisiana.

"It might be the last real seafood we see for a few days," I complained, remembering past trips out of town. Aside from a restaurant called Cajun Lady Seafood in Ocoee, Tennessee, where a real Cajun woman served authentic Louisiana seafood, I hadn't been impressed by much of what I'd found out of state. Hell, there were even some restaurants in Louisiana that didn't measure up to my idea of real Cajun food.

"I'm not interested in starving to death," I continued. "We've got kids to raise."

"Uh-huh," Susan said idly, and then mumbled something I couldn't understand.

I glanced over and realized that I had been talking to myself, because my wife had once again buried her face in the files.

CHAPTER 40

Lafourche Parish, Louisiana

While Clint drove, Susan continued to scour the pages upon pages of information that Lindsey had printed. She read all of the biographical sketches Thad Griffin had listed in various places, and they all pretty much said the same things, with slight variations. Most of them stated that he was from a small town in East Tennessee, that he had worked as a farm hand while attending school, and his love for storytelling began as a little boy while listening to his great grandpa spin tall yarns about the old days.

Only one of the bios had him living in Copper Head, Tennessee, while the others had him residing in Plain Ridge, Georgia. The bio that listed Copper Head as his residence didn't mention a relationship status. The older ones from Plain Ridge stated he lived with his fiancé, Ann. Subsequent ones had Ann listed as his wife, and even later ones mentioned a son, but it didn't provide a name.

Susan sighed as she put away the biographical sketches. They didn't offer any reasons why someone might want to attack Thad's family, and they didn't help figure out why he might want to orchestrate this himself.

Next, she began looking through the printouts from his website. He had a more detailed bio on the About page, but it offered nothing in the way of leads. He had a webpage that listed a number of short stories. It appeared that some of the stories had clickable links. Curious, she pulled out her cell phone and accessed the website. She navigated to the Short Stories page and began clicking on the live links. Although Lindsey had read most of the stories, she decided to give a few of them a try.

"If this dude's first series of books is as boring as his short stories, then I can see why they didn't sell." She shook her head. "They're listed as mysteries, but there's nothing mysterious about them. You know who the bad guy is right away."

Clint glanced at her and nodded. She didn't think he fully appreciated how bad they were, so she read a few of them to him. Finally, he begged her to stop.

"Told you," she said with a triumphant nod. "They really suck. He said in his bio that his love for storytelling began when he was a little boy. It sounds like that's when he wrote these stories."

Clint chuckled and then got serious. "We're almost at Spahr's," he said. "You hungry?"

Susan glanced at the clock on the dash. It wasn't quite five o'clock yet, but she hadn't eaten lunch, so she nodded and said, "I'll research while I eat."

The parking lot was nearly full when they drove up, and Clint barely found an open spot. Susan tucked away her cell phone and shoved some of the printouts in a file folder. When she was ready, she walked inside with Clint. They were shown a table at the back of the room in the far corner, where the large windows overlooked the swamps. Normally, she would've loved looking out at the pelicans, egrets, and occasional bald eagles gliding on the wind, and the alligators lounging about, but she was on a mission.

"Here, let me take some of those," Clint offered, extending a hand. "If we're both reading, it'll go faster."

"Good idea." Susan split the stack she had gathered up and handed one section to her husband. She then turned her attention back to Thad's website on her cell phone.

The layout was professional enough, but it was simple in design and function. There were but a few pages. After backing out of the *Short Stories* page, she clicked on *Bio* to see if there were any clickable links on that page. There weren't. She navigated back to the *Home* page and perused that one.

After reading every word on *Home*, she clicked on the *Novels* page just to see what it was all about. She had no intention of reading any of his books, but when she saw that there were links to purchase the books on Amazon, she decided to click on them to see if she could read the first few pages. She was in luck. When she reached the landing page on Amazon for his first Gator Haven book, she was able to access the *Look Inside* feature and see the first dozen or so pages.

Susan scrolled to the first page and found the publication information. Thad was listed as the publisher, it gave the standard disclaimer about everything being fictitious, and a short excerpt credited Ann for the cover art. When she scrolled to the *Acknowledgments* page, she turned her cell phone so Clint could see.

"He dedicated it to his 'supportive wife' and 'wonderful son'," she said. "You think he meant it?"

"Even if he did kill her, he could've meant it at the time," he offered. "And just because he thought she was supportive, it doesn't mean he loved her."

"True." Susan backed out of the first book and navigated to the next two. Each of them was dedicated to his wife and son, and the wording was verbatim. She smirked. "Either this dude's got no other friends, or his wife didn't let him mention anyone else, because all of his books are dedicated to his wife and kid."

"If I was a writer, I'd dedicate all of my books to you and the kids," Clint said. "Outside of the three of y'all, nothing else matters."

Susan felt her face flush. Before she could respond, a friendly waitress walked up and asked what they wanted to drink.

"We actually know what we want to eat, if that's okay," Clint said. "We're heading to Tennessee, so we need to get back on the road."

"Absolutely," the waitress said. "What can I get for y'all?"

As he always did, Clint gave Susan a nod to go first, and she ordered a seafood gumbo, half a shrimp poboy, and a glass of water. Clint ordered crawfish etouffee, fried jumbo shrimp, and a house salad.

"And a drink for you?" the waitress asked.

Clint hesitated. Susan knew he wanted a Dr. Pepper, but after a few seconds, he sighed and ordered a glass of water.

As soon as the waitress was gone, Susan turned back to the Amazon page and clicked on Thad's name. The next page she landed on was his author profile, where all of his titles were listed. She clicked on the first book in the Atlanta detective series, and searched for the dedication page. She shook her head when she saw that it was also dedicated to Ann and Wess. While the thought might've been nice, it also seemed redundant

"Maybe if he would've dedicated the first book and then left the others blank it would've made more sense," she said out loud.

Clint looked up from the page he had been reading.

"What'd you say?" he asked. "Were you talking to me?"

"That's not important," she said idly, suddenly having a thought. "But this might be. He had a publisher for his first series. It's a small one called Crossbow Press."

"He actually had a publisher?" Clint asked. "For the series that flopped?"

"Yep." Susan accessed the search bar on her cell phone and typed in the publisher's name. "You know what publishers do as part of their marketing campaigns?"

Clint was thoughtful for a few seconds, and then asked, "They build an author page on their website to help promote the book?"

"Yeah, and they usually post an author interview or a FAQ page, so readers can become familiar with their authors."

After a quick search, Susan found that there was only one publisher by the name of Crossbow Press, and they had several dozen authors in their stables. She quickly ran down the alphabetical list and located Thad Griffin's name.

"Found him!" She quickly clicked on his name and scanned the webpage that had popped up. Almost instantly, she saw a clickable link on the right-hand side of the page. "And they do have an author interview!"

Clint had stopped reading through his documents, and leaned closer to see what she had found.

"But how much good can an author interview do?" he asked. "It's not like he's going to say he'll murder his wife in the future."

"I'm not looking for a confession," Susan said. "I'm looking for a lead. A great detective once told me that every interview should lead to another interview, and every piece of evidence should lead to another."

"I don't know if I would listen to that dude," Clint said dryly. "He sounds like an asshole and an idiot."

Susan laughed so unexpectedly that she snorted, but then she grew serious and began reading the questions and answers with interest. She paid particular attention to Thad's answers, searching for the tiniest bit of information that might be helpful.

After some time, Susan read an answer that stopped her short. She mouthed, "Holy shit!"

"What is it?" Clint asked, craning his neck to see. "What'd you find?"

"I might've just found our next lead!"

CHAPTER 41

Interview with Author Thad Griffin:

INTERVIEWER: Do you recall how your interest in writing began?

THAD: When I was a little boy, I would go visit my papaw and he would tell me stories about all the things he did as a kid growing up. They were hunting stories mostly, and they were very exciting. The more I listened to him, the more I wanted to tell my own stories. Only, nothing interesting or exciting ever happened to me.

One day, while a couple of my friends and I were playing in the river, I decided to make up a story about an adventure I would've experienced the previous week. I took one of my papaw's real stories about a coon hunt he had gone on as a boy, and I inserted myself into the story. I changed some of the details to fit my own situation and location, and I made it a little more harrowing. Wouldn't you know, three boys who couldn't sit still through a single schoolhouse lunch break sat spellbound the entire time I told the story. They hung on my every word. It was an amazing and empowering feeling.

The next time we met on the river, I told another one of my made-up stories, and I got the same reaction. Before long, every time we got together they would beg me to tell them one of my stories. I think they knew deep down that I was lying, but they loved the stories I told so much that they wouldn't be denied. Sometimes, I wouldn't feel like telling one, but they would beg me until I gave in. They even began bribing me when I didn't feel like telling a story. One friend gave me his prized knife. The other a radio. One friend even gave me a gold coin that his meemaw had given him. I still have that coin.

INTERVIEWER: Wow, that's an interesting fact about you, and it illustrates the power that authors wield over their potential readers. Wouldn't you agree that authors have a responsibility to play fair with their readers, especially in the mystery genre?

THAD: Oh, absolutely. I believe you should give readers an opportunity to solve the crime before it's revealed at the end of the book, but you shouldn't make it too easy on them. You want them to work for it.

INTERVIEWER: And speaking of "working for it," I understand that this isn't your first attempt at writing.

THAD: That's correct. This is actually my second attempt, and it's been a long road to get here. When I first wrote *Back Alley in the ATL: A Detective Braxton Mystery*, I queried every agent I could find that represented mysteries. Oh, I must've sent out 150 query letters, maybe more. I think I only heard back from five or six of them, but they were just standard rejection letters. None of them ever asked for a sample, which was very frustrating.

Anyway, after about two years of failed attempts, I decided to start querying publishers directly. I hit up all the big ones first, but they never responded. I later realized that most of them don't accept un-agented queries, so the months spent contacting them and sending manuscripts had been a colossal waste of time and money. Finally, I got my hands on a copy of the latest *Novel and Short Story Writer's Market* and I started to learn a little about the querying process. I also compiled a list of publishers who accepted un-agented submissions. That's how I found you guys. The rest, as they say, is history.

INTERVIEWER: When you queried the agents, was that for *Back Alley in the ATL,* or was that for your first novel?

THAD: It was for *Back Alley.*

INTERVIEWER: Do you plan on letting Crossbow Press have a look at your first attempt?

THAD: Oh, no, that one was written under a pseudonym when I was twenty-one, and it was a horrible attempt at a first novel. I hadn't taken any classes on writing and I hadn't done any research, but I was so desperate to get published that I paid a vanity press about $1,000 to print twenty-five copies.

INTERVIEWER: $1,000 for twenty-five copies? That's highway robbery.

THAD: Well, they said most of the cost went toward the cover and editing services. Still, it was an embarrassing moment in my writing life, and I'm happy to report that only one or two copies sold, and the rest were destroyed in a flood.

CHAPTER 42

Des Allemands, Louisiana

Susan pointed to the last line in Thad's interview, where he mentioned that only one or two copies of his first book had been sold.

"We need to find one of them," she told Clint after the waitress had delivered their appetizer, drinks, and Clint's salad. "Lindsey has read everything else he's ever written, and she couldn't find anything worthy of murder and kidnapping. Maybe the key to it all is in his first book."

Clint nodded thoughtfully as he began attacking his salad. Susan took a piece of crawfish bread and went back to the interview, hoping to find the name of the book. It was nowhere to be found. After swallowing her food, she worked her thumb across the screen of her cell phone and called Amy.

"Hey, sister," she said when Amy answered, "I might've found something."

"If it doesn't pay off my house and let me stay home with my baby," Amy began with a huff, "I don't want to hear about it."

"If it turns into something, it might be better than all of that," Susan said, explaining what she had found in the interview. "If we can find that book, maybe it'll provide some clues. I'll send you a screenshot of the interview so you'll know what I'm talking about."

"Do y'all really think his books are the key to all of this?" Amy sounded skeptical. "I think he screwed somebody over at some point in his life, and they're coming back for revenge. Or maybe his wife's the one who screwed up. I just don't see how somebody would target you just for writing lies."

"Clint said he keeps insisting that it's about his books," Susan explained. "It's to the point that Clint thinks he's being subliminal."

"Huh." Amy was silent for a second. "Okay, what do you need me to do?"

"Can you go find him and ask him about his very first book?" Susan asked. "He wrote it under a pseudonym. We need to know who he wrote it under, what the title is, and if he has a copy. It was written when he was twenty-one, so that would've been before he met Ann. If you can find out who he was dating at the time, that would also be great. No one can shed more light into a person's habits than an ex."

"Especially a disgruntled ex." There was movement in the background, and Amy said, "I'll head that way now."

"Oh, and take Melvin with you," Susan said quickly. "Just in case he gets—"

"Yeah, yeah, I've got it, Mother."

Susan laughed and ended the call. The waitress brought their meal shortly after her conversation with Amy, and she and Clint ate while reading through some of the other files. Once they were done eating, had paid the bill, and were back in Clint's truck, she started going back over his short stories and writing down the names of every character he listed. Once she was done collecting the names, she searched for authors by those names, hoping he had used one of his characters for his pseudonym. She had no such luck.

She was about to move on to something else when Amy called to say she had interviewed Thad. Susan put the call on speaker, so Clint could be kept in the loop.

"He wasn't happy to see me, but I softened him up a little," Amy said. "Anyway, he says his Atlanta detective novels were the first books he's ever written. I pressed him on it for a while, and he insisted that he had never written another novel. He seemed a bit defensive, too. It was weird. He was acting more like a suspect than the husband and father of two victims. Anyway, I showed him the interview and asked him to explain it."

"Oh, yeah, how'd he take that?"

"First, he demanded to know where I had gotten it," she said. "When I told him we'd found it online, he said Crossbow Press had folded, and that the website was supposed to have been taken down. I explained to him that websites can remain online for years, depending on when the domain name and hosting are set to expire."

Amy took a breath before continuing. "At that point, he said the interview did help to jog his memory, and that he does remember writing another novel, but he can't remember anything about it. When I asked for the title, he said he couldn't remember it. He claims it was over twenty years ago, and that he hardly remembers what he ate for breakfast."

"Bullshit," Susan said. "There's no way he forgot the title of the first book he ever wrote."

"That's what I said." Amy took another breath. "He asked to see the interview again, so he could see if he mentioned the title or if it would jog his memory. I let him read it, and then I asked who bought the few copies that were sold. He said he doesn't remember that either. When I asked what happened to the rest of the copies, he said he had stored them in his grandpa's barn when he got married and moved in with Ann, and everything got destroyed when the barn flooded."

"He remembers nothing about these books, but he remembers losing almost twenty copies to a flood?" Susan asked incredulously. "That's more bullshit."

"Yeah, I called him on it, but he insisted that's all he could remember," Amy said. "He even said he knows it looks bad, but that he has a horrible memory. He said his mind is so filled with stories that are begging to come out, that he can hardly keep up with what's real and what's fiction."

Susan shook her head and stared out the windshield, trying to think of a way around Thad's lies. She and Clint had entered Mississippi, and the traffic had thinned out. Before she could say anything, Amy spoke up.

"Oh, and he wanted to know where Clint was."

"What?"

"Yeah, he grew kind of suspicious at one point, and he asked if Clint was out of town," Amy explained. "When I asked why he cared, he said it was just weird that Clint wasn't questioning him. He said he had dealt with Clint throughout the entire investigation, and suddenly someone new had shown up. He even asked if Clint was going to Copper Head."

Clint's head jerked around. "What's that?"

Amy repeated what she'd said. "For some reason, he thinks you're headed to Copper Head, and he didn't look happy about it."

"Damn it," Clint said. "He's definitely hiding something!"

"Absolutely," Amy agreed. "Do you want me to take him in and interrogate him? Baylor and I are still in front of his house."

"Do it," Clint said. "Try to make him tell you the name of that book, and try to get your hands on a copy. If he got defensive about it, there's something in it that he doesn't want us to see."

"We searched his entire house," Susan said. "He's got several bookshelves with tons of books by various authors, but all of the names were recognizable. He did have one small shelf where he kept a print copy of his own published books, but they were all in his name."

She saw Clint mutter a curse and shake his head.

"I'll see what I can do," Amy said. "Meanwhile, y'all be good. That's a work trip, not a honeymoon."

Susan chuckled and ended the call. She glanced at Clint. He was staring intently ahead, his mind seemingly racing. After a few long moments, he turned slowly to look at her.

"Don't you have a copy of everything on his computer?" he asked, his brow furrowed.

"Yeah," she said. "We downloaded everything to a hard drive, but Amy and I went through his writing folder and didn't find any strange manuscripts."

"Did the search warrant cover his emails?"

Susan nodded slowly, not sure what he had in mind.

"In his interview," Clint continued, "he said he had queried a bunch of agents for his Atlanta book. Maybe he did the same for his first book? If you can find where he emailed some agents, you might find the title of the book."

"I mean, I wouldn't know where to start looking," Susan said. "We searched through the email accounts that were open on his desktop, and we took screenshots of a lot of them, but we didn't go back twenty years. He also didn't give us his passwords and user names, so I wouldn't be able to go back into them now."

Clint took a breath and exhaled forcefully, looking straight ahead as he continued driving.

While he mulled it over, Susan decided to pull out the hard drive and plug it into her laptop. Within seconds, she was perusing his files, searching for anything that seemed even remotely related to writing. She didn't know how long she dug through his writing life, but at one point, she noticed street lights flashing by, and that was how she knew it had gotten dark outside.

Clint stopped once for gas, but Susan didn't stop what she was doing to get out. She had stumbled upon a file of old documents and screenshots that had been buried in a folder titled *Pre-Published*, and she was thinking she might stumble upon something related to the first book. She was wrong.

Clint had finished pumping gas and they were back on the road by the time she had opened every document in that folder. There had been dozens of screenshots of emailed queries that Thad had sent to agents and publishers relating to his Atlanta series, but nothing on the first book. Nothing was dated more than a dozen years earlier, and Susan was starting to think she wouldn't find anything.

She had been about to try something different when her cell phone rang. She glanced at the screen and saw that it was Amy.

"Hey, what's up?" she said, exhausted from a lack of success. "Please tell me you broke the bastard and he spilled everything."

"Sorry to disappoint." Amy huffed. "This prick did the same thing to us that he did to Clint. He jumped up and stormed out of the interview room. He also threatened to sue us for questioning him and calling him a liar. I explained that he could only sue for false arrest, not false questions. He didn't like that and left."

"Did he walk home again?"

"Yeah, unless he got hit by a car. In that case, he would've only walked part of the way home." Amy paused, and then asked if Susan had gotten anywhere with her search for the book title.

"No," Susan said. "I searched every file and document I could find in his writing folder, but I didn't find anything pertaining to that ghost book. I was about to search his other folders to see if maybe he hid it there, but..."

Something suddenly occurred to Susan, and she allowed her voice to trail off. She could feel Clint glancing sideways at her.

"What's going on, Sue?" Amy asked after a few seconds. "Did you find something."

Susan didn't answer right away. She opened a file folder, slid the cursor to *View*, and clicked on the selection that read *Show Hidden Items*. Once she'd made her selection, she returned to Thad's writing folder and clicked on the folder that contained his novels.

"No way!" she said breathlessly.

CHAPTER 43

"What did you find?" Amy asked impatiently. "Did you find proof that the bastard killed his own wife?"

"No," Susan finally answered. "I found a hidden folder titled, *Gunther Foxwell*."

The folder had been invisible earlier, but was now present, if only a shade lighter than the other folders. Not knowing what she should hope for, Susan clicked on it. "Shit!"

"What is it?" Clint asked.

"It's empty." Susan backed out of the folder and typed *Gunther Foxwell* into the search bar. She clicked the *Enter* key and waited. The search returned zero results.

"Is that the title of the book, or his pseudonym?" Amy asked. "It sounds more like a name to me."

"Yeah," Susan agreed. "It sounds like a name, but it could be a name of anything."

"Want me to find Thad and ask him about it?" Amy offered. "I'm sure he hasn't made it off of Washington yet."

Susan told her to go for it, and then ended the call. Next, she did an Internet search for the name. Nothing came up. She tried four different search engines, several book websites, and called Lindsey to run a name inquiry. While she waited, she asked Lindsey if she had found anything within Thad Griffin's writings.

"I've read just about everything he's written, but nothing seems off," Lindsey said. "I can't find anything that seems controversial or that fits the circumstances of his wife's murder."

Susan relayed the information to Clint, and waited for her to finish running the name inquiry.

After a minute or two, Lindsey said, "This is odd. The name Gunther Foxwell doesn't exist. I mean, there's not a single entry. That's never happened to me before. It must be a fictitious name that Thad made up."

Susan gave Lindsey an update on their location and thanked her for running the name. When she ended the call, she sank back in her seat and stared at her husband.

"I really thought we had something," she said. "Why hide a folder if there's nothing in it?"

"I agree," Clint said. "Maybe it's the name of the main character in his first book."

"Could be." Susan stared out the windshield for a long moment, trying to figure out what the name could mean. It was quite possible it was Thad's pseudonym, but it would do them no good if they couldn't get their hands on a copy of the book.

Finally, she decided to continue searching through the external hard drive. She decided that once she finished looking through the writing folder, she would check each of the other folders. Perhaps Thad had hidden the manuscript somewhere else and under a nondescript name. She was searching through one that contained dozens of character photographs when Amy called back to say she had located Thad Griffin.

"I asked him about the name Gunther Foxwell, and he got real pale," she said. "You can ask Baylor, he was so freaked out that he was almost translucent. Still, he wouldn't say anything. He just turned and continued walking down the road like a petulant child."

"We've got nothing, Clint," Susan said after tossing her cell phone to the center console. "If the gas station doesn't pan out, we're done…finished."

"His mom might know something about the book," Clint suggested. "When we visit her, maybe we can turn the conversation to writing. You know she'll want to brag on her son. If we get her talking, we might be able to get her to mention his first book. Hell, she's probably the one who bought one of the copies."

Susan nodded her agreement. "Let's hope so."

Clint drove in silence for a few miles, and then he said they should probably go straight to Thad's mom's house and skip the hotel altogether.

"Thad's growing suspicious about my whereabouts," he said. "If he thinks I'm heading to Copper Head, he might also think I'm going to Plain Ridge. If his mom's involved, he'll definitely call her and warn her not to say anything. And if Wess is with her, Thad might tell her to get him the hell out of there. If we can get there during the night and watch the house, we might catch her in the act of trying to move the kid."

Susan agreed with that assessment and said so. "We're still picking up a cake, though," she added. "If she doesn't take it, I'll eat it."

CHAPTER 44

Wednesday, May 17

It was a little after two in the morning when Susan and I cruised into Esther Griffin's neighborhood. We located her house easily enough. It was an old white wooden house with green shutters. The place was in desperate need of a paint job. There was a faded wooden fence that stretched the entire width of the property, and four red and black signs warned us to beware of the dog. The fence was too short to keep in a large dog, the spaces between the three boards were too wide to keep in a small one, and there was a wide opening to allow cars to access the property, so I figured the signage was a bluff.

"They could have one of those invisible fences," Susan offered. "The ones with the buried wire and the sensors."

"You could be right," I muttered as I drove slowly past the house. The only visible light around the house was over the front porch. Other than that, the place seemed to be dead. We had driven down Church Street from the east, and when we reached the end, we turned and headed back from whence we'd come.

It was too early to be knocking on doors, so we decided to park and stake out the area. I had seen an abandoned house that was for sale when we'd first turned onto the street, and it was there that I headed. There was a sign from Peace of Mountain Real Estate planted in the front yard, and I backed my truck up right next to it.

If anyone would stop to challenge us, we would simply say that we had driven up from Louisiana to see the house, and we had gotten there earlier than expected, so we had decided to wait there for our agent. It seemed perfectly reasonable to me for potential buyers to wait in the driveway of their future home rather than paying for a hotel stay. However, I never got to find out if anyone else would agree, because nary a single car drove by.

We passed the night without incident, and saw our first car around five in the morning. It appeared to be someone from the neighborhood leaving for work, and the man didn't even glance in our direction.

"This must be a good neighborhood," Susan observed. "He didn't care enough to look at a strange car parked in the driveway of an empty house."

I nodded, but didn't say anything. I was staring intently toward Thad's mother's house. Just like we had on the drive into Plain Ridge, Susan and I had taken turns sleeping and watching the house throughout the stakeout, but there had been no movement during the night. If Esther Griffin was involved in the kidnapping of Wess, and if Wess was inside her home, they hadn't been alerted to the possibility that the law from Louisiana might be closing in on them.

We remained where we were, and it wasn't until daybreak that we saw the first movement from the house. It came when the porch light turned off and the front screen door opened to allow a small fluffy dog to step out and do its business. I laughed out loud. Although we were some distance from the house, I could tell that it was about the size of a large bowl of popcorn, only much whiter.

"That looks like a deadly ball of fur," I said, still snickering. "The signs make sense now."

"It's a bichon frisé," Susan said. "The only way you'd have to beware of one of those is if they had a bomb strapped to their collar."

I nodded my agreement, realizing the signs had probably been installed during a time when a larger dog occupied the residence. I craned my neck to try and see the person who had let the dog out, but it was too dark in the shadows of the screened-in porch. I asked Susan if she could see the person, but she could not.

I took a breath. "Well, are we going for it?"

"I guess so." She twisted around in the seat and grabbed the cake from the back floorboard. We had picked it up at a grocery store on the drive in. It wasn't impressive, but it would do.

I shoved my pistol under my shirt and stepped out of my truck behind Susan. She put on her best smile—which was stunning—and we began walking down the street hand in hand. We were still about ten yards from the Griffin residence when the screen door opened wider and a woman stuck her head out. She said something to the dog, but it didn't respond. She clapped her hands and called louder. I couldn't hear what the command was, but the dog broke into a run, heading straight for the street.

"Linus!" cried the woman. "Get your ass back over here!"

Her cries did nothing to slow down her dog. In fact, it seemed to spur him on. As soon as he made it to the sidewalk, he hooked a right and headed straight for us.

"You got him?" Susan asked, shifting the cake to her left hand. "Or should I?"

"I've got the little cotton swab." I kept my eyes straight ahead, acting like I didn't see the dog. It looked like he was doing the same, and within a few seconds, he would be right beside me.

"Linus!" The woman was wrapped in a green terrycloth robe that flapped in the breeze as she sprinted across her front yard, heading for the sidewalk. "Stop, Linus! Stay!"

Linus was still two steps from me when I quickly bent over and swooped him from the ground. Just as I was bringing him to my chest, he twisted his head around and bit me on the hand. His teeth were sharp and he snarled in determination as he buried them into my flesh, but I wasn't about to let him go.

"It's okay, Linus," I coaxed. "I'm bringing you to your momma."

"Linus, no!" the woman said when she reached me. There were deep wrinkles in her face, but she was an attractive woman. She also appeared fairly fit, and feisty. "If you don't stop biting that nice man, I'm going to bite you!"

I smiled to let her know it was okay, and handed Linus to her. Several drops of blood appeared on the top of my hand, but I brushed it on my jeans.

"He doesn't have rabies, right?" I asked with a smile.

"Oh, I don't know," said the woman. "He hasn't been vaccinated in…oh, ten or eleven years, I guess? And he has been acting strange lately."

I saw a look of concern come over Susan's face, and I felt my knees grow a little weak. While I thought it was a long shot that the little dog had rabies, I also knew I could have terrible luck at times, and I wasn't interested in getting preventative shots to my stomach.

I guess the woman noticed I was no longer smiling, because she quickly laughed and said, "I'm just kidding! He gets vaccinated every year. Come on in. I'll show you his papers, and I'll give you some disinfectant."

I glanced at Susan. She indicated the cake and raised her

eyebrows, as though she didn't know what to do with it anymore. I shrugged. I had no clue what to do with it either, except to eat it later. Thanks to this fortunate turn of events, we had an opening into the woman's house, and it had only cost me a few drops of blood.

"Thank you so much for catching him," the woman said, as she held the screen door open for us to enter. "When he decides to run, he usually makes it around the entire block, and I don't have time for that right now."

Once we were in the lighted kitchen, I was able to get a better look at the woman. I frowned. There seemed to be deep sorrow to her expression, and her eyes were a bit glassy. I decided to dispense with the charade.

"Mrs. Griffin, my name is Clint Wolf," I said as she reached above the sink to open a cabinet door. "And this is my wife Susan. We work for the Mechant Loup Police Department."

I saw her body stiffen. She turned slowly and looked from me to Susan. Had I removed my face and revealed that I was an alien, I think she would've been less shocked.

CHAPTER 45

"Is...is this about my grandson?" Esther Griffin finally asked after taking several shaking breaths.

"Yes, ma'am," I said with a nod.

She clutched frantically at the front of her robe. Terror filled her face, and I knew right then that she had nothing to do with her grandson's disappearance.

"Did...did you guys find him?" She seemed almost too afraid to get the question out. Not because she was afraid to talk to us, but because she was terrified of the answer.

"No, ma'am," I said in a soothing voice. "We're still looking for him, and that's why we're here."

She seemed confused. "What...why...do...do you think he's here? In Plain Ridge?"

"We're not sure where he is," I explained, "but we have reason to believe the kidnapper was in Copper Head a couple of weeks ago. We're trying to backtrack this person and hopefully find some clues as to Wess' whereabouts."

Mrs. Griffin thought about that for a long moment, her chin trembling uncontrollably. Finally, she asked, "Then why are you here? Do you think they're coming after me, too?"

"Oh, no, ma'am." I waved my hand dismissively. "We were just hoping you might be able to give us some insight into Thad's younger years. We believe this crime is either related to his writing career or something from his past. We were hoping you might be able to remember an incident or situation where someone would've been angry enough at Thad to have held a grudge over all these years. Maybe a neighborhood bully, or an enemy from school, or anything like that."

"Thad never had any enemies." She shook her head slowly. "He's never even been in a fight. He was a good boy. He hated conflict. I…I have no idea who did this to him. I talked to him for over an hour yesterday, and he keeps saying it's got to do with his writing career. He said it has to be someone who's jealous of what he's become. He's attained quite a bit of fame from his work, you know? I mean, everyone in Plain Ridge knows who he is now, but before his alligator books came out, he was just another man on the street. Now, people stop him in the grocery store to ask him to sign his books. Well, that was before he moved away."

Mrs. Griffin's frown deepened. "I…I begged him not to go. I know he had to move for his work, but I had a bad feeling about it. Now, I know it was the Lord trying to warn him."

"What about stalkers?" I asked. "Do you know of anyone who started showing an unhealthy interest in him after he became famous?"

"Everyone around here showed an unhealthy interest in him, if you ask me. They put him on a pedestal. They treated him like he was some kind of big shot. They wrote about him in the newspapers. They talked about him on all the local news stations. The libraries and bookstores from here to Atlanta wanted him to do book signings and talks." She sighed heavily and tears welled up in her eyes. "I was afraid it would swell his head. I kept telling him that pride comes before a fall, and for him to remain humble and to give thanks to Jesus for his success. I…I keep wondering if this was a result of him letting pride creep into his life."

I stepped forward and put a hand on her forearm. "Ma'am, this is the actions of an evil person—pure and simple. It's not Thad's fault."

"But you asked if he did something bad in his past, so you must think it's his fault."

"Nothing in his past gives anyone the right to do what they did," I explained. "The only reason we ask about it is to find someone with a motive. And even if he did have enemies, it doesn't necessarily mean it was them who did this. We're just trying to look at every possibility."

She nodded her understanding and wiped her eyes. "Well, I've been racking my brains trying to figure out who attacked Ann and took Wess, but I can't come up with anything."

I pursed my lips and glanced at Susan. She shook her head, equally discouraged. If Thad didn't have any enemies or stalkers, I didn't know where to go to find his killer. Our only hope at that point would be the gas station in Copper Head. If that was a dead end, we'd have no choice but to head home in defeat.

Wess had been entered into the National Crime Information Center's (NCIC) database, and we would have to pray that some law enforcement agency somewhere ran across him and his captor or captors before it was too late for the kid.

"Ma'am, has Thad had any relationships that ended badly?" Susan asked after I'd gone silent for too long. "Has he broken any hearts in his youth?"

Mrs. Griffin shook her head. "He hasn't had many girlfriends that I know of. He dated casually in high school, but never anything serious."

"What about after high school?" Susan asked. "Did he have many girlfriends after graduating, and do you know of any problems he's had with girls?"

"Oh, he never talked about his girl problems. And he moved out right after high school, so I don't know a lot about who he dated. I mean, he would bring some girls around every now and then, but it always seemed to be someone new. It was sad, really. He only lived a few miles away, but he didn't visit often. I worried so much about him back then, especially when…"

Her voice trailed off, and Susan asked if she would elaborate.

"Well, he moved out of a town for a couple of years not long after graduating, and I never heard from him." Mrs. Griffin shuddered inwardly. "I…I didn't know if he was alive or dead. He never really talked about that part of his life, but I don't believe he had any enemies even then."

Mrs. Griffin paused and touched a hand to her face. "I don't think he dated anyone while he was gone either. He was definitely single when he moved back. I…I was so worried that he would never find true love. I prayed so hard that God would bring him the perfect girl. And then, one day, he showed up with Ann. I knew right away that God had heard my prayers. She was perfect for him, and she was good for our family. She encouraged him to visit more often, and she and I became close. I loved her so much—like a daughter, in fact. I…I can't believe she's gone. It just doesn't seem real. Who on earth would want to hurt her?"

Mrs. Griffin's dam burst and she sank to her knees and wept. Susan dropped on the floor beside her while I searched around the room for some tissues. I didn't see any in the kitchen, so I walked through the living room and down a hall in search of a bathroom. I located one at the end of the hall, and I found a box of tissues inside. I grabbed it and headed back toward the kitchen.

On my return trip, I looked in every open door, visually examined every corner of each room, and studied every picture frame on the wall. Other than a dozen photos of Wess, there was no sign of him anywhere. I didn't even see any boys' toys scattered around. It didn't mean there weren't any in the house for the young boy to play with when he came to visit. It just could've been that they were picked up in one of the rooms with the doors closed.

I handed Susan the box of tissues. While she continued consoling Mrs. Griffin, I continued my visual inspection of the parts of the house that were in plain view. As hard as I looked, I could see nothing that would indicate Thad's mother was involved in the kidnapping. And if her behavior was any indication, she was as innocent as they came.

Now that I knew Mrs. Griffin wasn't involved in any way, and since she couldn't provide us with any helpful information, I was in a hurry to leave. We were burning daylight, and the killer and kidnapper might be out there somewhere putting more miles between us and him. Or her. Although most of the criminals I encountered were men, I never ruled out women.

I stepped outside and called Amy to see if anything was happening back in town.

"It's quiet here," she said. "Melvin is heading up the ground search for the boy. He's got about a dozen sheriff's deputies assigned to him. They're searching the woods behind the Griffin residence and all the backroads in the surrounding area. I've been to every hotel and motel in the parish trying to see if anyone from Georgia or Tennessee has checked in within the past few weeks."

"Any luck?" I asked. "It isn't tourism season, so I can't imagine there were many."

"There were exactly four of them," she said. "Two were from the Nashville area, one was from Atlanta, and the fourth was from Memphis. All of them were here to work the boats, and they're all still offshore."

I shook my head in frustration, and wondered if Susan and I were doing the right thing. A lot of times, investigative work boiled down to intuition and hunches. Sure, the biggest piece of evidence we'd uncovered had pointed us to Copper Head, but there was no guarantee that our suspect had returned to that area. There was no way to know if we had wasted valuable time making the trip to Georgia and Tennessee. If I was wrong, it could prove to be a crucial mistake.

Hell, for all we knew, the suspect was still holding Wess in Southeast Louisiana. If so, I felt confident that Amy, Melvin, and the rest of our crew would be able to find them. However, if he had taken Wess somewhere else—like south toward the border—it would take a miracle for the kid to ever be seen again. As it stood at that moment, we didn't know if he was alive or dead, and that terrified me.

"Clint, are you still there?" Amy asked. "Is everything okay?"

I told her where we were and how we had made contact with Esther Griffin.

"The poor woman doesn't know anything," I said in conclusion, "and she wasn't able to add anything to the investigation."

"So, you got bit for nothing?"

"That about sums it up." I heard some noise from the screened-in porch and looked to see Susan approaching. "I have to go, Ames. We're heading to that gas station next. Call if anything comes up."

Amy told me to do the same, and ended the call.

Susan held up her cell phone when she drew near. "Mrs. Griffin pulled out the few photographs she had of Thad and other girls, and she let me copy them."

As we walked back to my truck, she showed me the photographs. There were five in all, and three were of Thad and the same girl. Susan had snapped shots of the backs of the photographs, and all of them bore the date, Thad's name, and the name of the girl. The girl in the three pictures was named Mia. The other two girls were Mona and Sonja.

"Any last names?" I asked.

"Mona Hickman, Sonja Kittles, and Mia McJunkin." Susan stopped walking and turned to me when we reached my truck. "Those were the only three girls she knew for sure that he dated after high school, but she knew of no problems with any of them. I asked if the girls had ex-boyfriends who might've been mad at Thad, but she said he never mentioned it."

I nodded and jumped in my truck. While I would have to check my notes to be certain, all of the names sounded familiar, and I was pretty sure Thad had mentioned all of them when I'd asked about prior lovers.

When Susan was sitting beside me, I asked if Mrs. Griffin knew anything about Thad's earlier book and if the name Gunther Foxwell meant anything to her.

"No on both accounts," Susan said. "She's never heard of the name, and she thought Thad's first book was about the detective in Atlanta. She seemed shocked to learn he had written something under a penname. Hurt, even. She was genuinely offended."

"I would be, too." I drove away and was thoughtful for a long moment. Finally, I said, "I know how easy it can happen."

"What's that?"

"Moving out and forgetting about your parents sounds really familiar." I shook my head. "I was like Thad. I moved on and got so busy with life that I didn't keep in touch with my parents like I should have."

"But you had good reason," Susan countered. "You had just lost everything."

"In those times, I should've turned to my family." I shook my head. "I just hope Grace and Isaiah never run off and lose contact with us—even for a week. Lord knows I would deserve it, but I hope He spares me."

CHAPTER 46

Susan and I had grabbed some breakfast from a small diner before we'd headed to Esther Griffin's house, and we were getting hungry again by the time the sign for Copper Head came into view. We drove by a restaurant that looked to serve hamburgers, and Susan pointed it out.

"That looks like a cool dive," she said. "Let's eat there after we check out the gas station."

I only nodded, as I was searching for the sign to Copper Head Gas and Stuff. According to my map, we were only a mile away, and it should've been coming up. From what I recalled of the map I'd studied earlier, we would drive past a cheap motel, a Piggly Wiggly, and a bank, and then it would be on the right.

"There it is!" Susan said, pointing ahead. "I see the sign."

I slowed and put on my blinker. Surprisingly, the parking lot was busy, and I had to wait for a red truck to leave before I could find a spot.

"Well, here goes nothing." I shut off the engine and took a look around before stepping out of my truck. I indicated the several people milling about with a nod of my head. "Any one of these people could be the killer."

"Or none of them." Susan pointed toward the eaves of the building. "And I don't see any cameras, so I think we're shit out of luck."

"Let's hope the workers here have great memories." I stepped out and waited for Susan to walk around to my side. When she had caught up to me, we strolled toward the front door together.

I scanned every face that walked out of the gas station, but it was impossible to find a suspect when we didn't know for whom we were looking. I held the door to let a skinny girl slip out of the store and then followed my wife inside.

There were two people at the counter, and we had to wait about three minutes for them to finish making their purchases. When it was finally our turn to step up to the cashier, I pulled out my badge and put on my best smile.

"Hello, ma'am," I greeted. "My name is Clint and this is Susan. We're officers with the Mechant Loup Police Department in Louisiana. We need to speak with a manager about a case we're working."

"I'm the manager." The lady's name tag told me she was Silvia, and her expression told me she was skeptical. "Did you say y'all are police from Louisiana?"

"Yes, ma'am."

"We don't have a police department anymore." She looked from me to Susan, her eyes lingering on Susan for a long moment. When she looked back at me, she scowled. "The sheriff's department handles cases out here. Maybe I should give them a call. I don't feel comfortable giving out information to strangers."

"Fair enough." I gave a nod. "We can wait."

She reached for the phone, but hesitated. "What should I tell them y'all need?"

I pulled out a photocopy of the receipt and slid it across the counter. "We need to know who was working the day shift on April twenty-ninth," I said. "And we need to ask them if they remember this transaction, which took place at 11:59."

Silvia glanced at a calendar that hung on the wall. Her eyes widened just a little.

"Um, I worked that day," she said hesitantly. "What's this all about?"

"Do you remember this transaction?" I asked, ignoring her question. "They paid in cash. Does that happen often?"

"It happens more than you would think. It's checks we rarely see anymore." Silvia took up the receipt and pulled it close to her face. She squinted as she studied the details of the transaction. When she looked up, I could see that we were out of luck. She asked, "Do you know what kind of car it was, or what the person looked like?"

I shook my head.

She frowned. "I really don't remember. We get so many customers in here every day, especially the weekends, that it would be impossible for anyone to remember a single customer. If you had some kind of description…"

She let her voice trail off, as she stared again from me to Susan. "I mean, I would love to help, but I just can't remember."

"Are there any hidden surveillance cameras here?" I asked, taking another glance at the ceilings and walls. My earlier examination had revealed nothing.

She shook her head. "The boss can't afford it."

I looked up when a customer approached. Sighing, I stepped out of the way to let Silvia check him out. I didn't know where else to go with the questioning. She either remembered the transaction or not. It was really that simple. And seeing how robotically she handled each customer, I wasn't surprised she didn't remember. In fact, I was certain if someone asked her later in the day if two plainclothes cops had gone into the store late that morning, she would stare at them blankly and shake her head.

Once the other customer was done, I sidled back up to the counter, and asked, "Say, do you know Thad Griffin?"

"Oh, my God!" Her eyes lit up. "Of course, I know Thad! I went to school with him! He's famous around here. He's Copper Head's Stephen King, only he writes mystery books."

"What can you tell me about him?" I leaned on the counter, ready to hang on her every word. We had before us someone who knew him in his youth, and that someone wasn't biased like a mother would be.

"Oh, not much." She was thoughtful. "I remember him mostly from high school, because we were on the yearbook team together. I know we were in the same grade all through elementary and middle school, but we didn't really associate back then. We ran in different circles. He was kind of a nerd, and I was a cheerleader."

"Did you ever know of him to get into trouble?"

"Not at all." She shoved an elbow on the counter and scrunched up her brow. "How can I say this nicely? He was kind of a wuss, if you know what I mean? That's what I heard anyway. Not back then, but after he became famous. My brother said he never wanted to play contact sports or ride broncs or anything. All he ever wanted to do was show cows and act in the plays. Don't get me wrong, my brother showed cows, too, but he also competed in the local rodeos and he played football three of his four years of high school."

"They showed cows?" I asked. "What's that?"

"Oh, they were in AG in school," she explained. "They would go around showing cows. I went to a few shows to watch my brother, but I don't remember seeing Thad there. I guess I was only paying attention to my brother. Anyway, they just go around the arena with the cows and make them start and stop and stand up a certain way. It's kind of crazy, if you ask me, that they can teach a cow to walk around like a dog and follow commands."

As I nodded, my hopes of learning more about Thad were quickly fading. His mom was right. He was a good kid, which meant he was probably mostly invisible.

"Did he have any girlfriends in high school?" I asked, wondering if she knew the girls who were in the pictures.

"I mean, I'm sure he did." She shrugged. "Every boy has a girlfriend in high school, right? I mean, like the Kenny Rogers song goes, 'there's someone for everyone.' But I wouldn't know who they were."

I gave Susan a nod, and she pulled out her cell phone to show Silvia the photos of Thad and his three girlfriends.

"Oh, wow, I didn't know he dated Mona. She actually married a boy from the city. He's a chiropractor now. Sonja has three kids and lives in Knoxville now. Mia…hmm, I think Mia moved to Florida. I know she's on her second marriage. I think she's with a real estate agent. She had a kid with her first husband, but I don't think she has any with the new man. She used to go to my mom's church when she was married the first time." She looked up with a wicked grin. "I know all of them are kicking themselves in the ass right now for not staying with Thad. I mean, he's literally a town hero. He put this place on the map. And you know he's got money—lots of it!"

I raised an eyebrow. "Is he really a town hero?"

"Oh, yeah." Her head bobbed up and down. "People drive through here all the time saying they heard that this was the hometown of Thad Griffin, the famous author. Businesses that were about to shut down because of lack of tourism dollars are now thriving. You see all this traffic?"

I glanced up when Silvia waved a hand around to indicate the crowded store.

"We didn't have this much business before he became famous." She nodded. "People around here love him now."

"While people might love him now, do you know if any of them hated him before he became famous?" I pressed. "Did he have any enemies in high school, or later? Now that he's famous, I'm sure his enemies are really talking."

"Like I said, we didn't really run in the same circles, but I never knew of him to have problems with anyone, and I never heard anything bad about him lately." She shot a thumb toward a pink cell phone that was resting on the counter. "I can call my brother and ask him what he remembers."

I glanced at Susan, and she nodded.

"Please," I said and turned to survey the customers in the store while waiting for her to make the call. No one seemed to be paying any attention to us, but I was sure trying to read the minds of everyone in that place. Someone around that town must know something, and it was our job to try and figure out who they were.

CHAPTER 47

Silvia spent about ten minutes on the phone with her brother, stopping often to tend to her customers. She never missed a beat, either in the conversation or in her job. She was definitely a pro at what she did.

As she worked and talked, I made a mental note of how many people paid with cash, and how many people swiped a credit card. More than half used cash, which surprised me. I pointed it out to Susan.

"Yeah, if you asked me to identify the first person who walked in and paid with cash, I wouldn't be able to do it," she said. "Sometimes we ask a lot more of our witnesses than we could give ourselves."

She had a point, and I nodded my agreement.

When Silvia ended the call, she turned and waved for us to get closer. When we did, she said, "He remembers Thad from AG, but he said they lost touch after high school. He said he was always quiet, and he wasn't very smooth with the girls. My brother, he had the pick of the show girls, so I guess Thad got the ones he didn't want. Now, my brother did say some of the boys in school made fun of Thad because he showed cows."

"Why'd they make fun of him about that?" I asked, genuinely confused. "I thought being a farmer was cool around here."

"Well, most of the high school boys we grew up with liked to ride bulls, play football, and race dirt bikes. Since it was mostly girls who showed cows, the rodeo boys thought it was a girls' sport, and they made fun of most of the boys who participated."

"Did they make fun of your brother?" I asked.

"Oh, hell no! They knew better than to mess with him." She seemed to suddenly have a thought, and let out an evil giggle. "You know what's really funny? Nearly all the boys who showed cows in AG grew up to own their own farms and ranches, while the boys who teased them ended up working for them."

Susan and I both snickered at that tidbit. It was funny how life worked sometimes. I grew serious again as I considered Thad's plight. Had he done something horrible in his past to warrant karma paying him such a nasty visit? If so, I doubted we would find out at Copper Head Gas and Stuff.

I asked Silvia a few more questions about Thad, his past, and the girls in the photographs, but she didn't know more than she had already told us.

When I was done, I turned to my wife and asked if she had any questions for Silvia.

"Yeah," she said with a nod, "have you ever heard of Gunther Foxwell?"

I wanted to punch myself in the nose for forgetting all about Thad Griffin's pseudonym. I shot a quick glance at Silvia to see her reaction, but her expression didn't change.

"No," she said. "Who's that?"

"He's another author from around here," Susan explained. "Are you sure you haven't heard about him? He would've written a book about twenty years back."

Silvia thought about it some more, but finally shook her head. "No, that name doesn't ring any bells. What did he write?"

"I don't really know," Susan admitted. "I just know he was from Copper Head and he wrote a book that didn't sell well."

"Oh, that's probably why I never heard of him," she said. "I didn't read a lot back then, so it would have to have been something really good."

"Have you read Thad's Gator Haven books?" Susan wanted to know.

"Every single one of them, and they're good, too! I never thought books about alligators could be so interesting." Silvia leaned forward conspiratorially. "Are any of those stories based on actual cases? Do alligators really hunt people down and kill them?"

Susan chuckled and shook her head. "No, it's all fiction."

"Aww, shucks." Silvia seemed disappointed. "I was hoping some of them were true."

After asking a few more questions, Susan glanced over at me and raised an eyebrow to see if I was done. I nodded, and we both thanked her before heading out to the parking lot.

The wind had picked up and some clouds had gathered. Not only did it look like rain, but it also smelled like it. My gauge had been reading low for the past fifty miles, so I decided to pull my truck around to an open pump and fuel up before the downpour began. While I filled up the tank, Susan ambled around the parking lot, no doubt checking out each of the patrons while also taking in the beautiful mountains in the distance. We both loved East Tennessee. In Louisiana, the biggest mountain I'd ever seen was this giant ant pile that had formed behind—

"Hey, Clint, get over here," Susan suddenly called. "Come check this out."

I replaced the nozzle and walked to the edge of the parking lot where she was standing. She pointed to a clump of trees off in the distance. They grew along the road that passed behind the gas station, but there didn't seem to be anything remarkable about them.

"What is it?" I asked. "What am I looking at?"

"You see that sign next to those trees?"

I squinted to get a better look. Sure enough, there was a white wooden sign with faded blue letters that read, *Copper Head Public Library*.

"Yeah, I see it," I said, still not sure what she was driving at. "What about it?"

"Where's the first place authors go when they publish their books?" Although she phrased it as a question, she didn't wait for me to answer. "Their local library."

I wasted no time in heading back to my truck.

CHAPTER 48

When Susan and I walked into the library, the first thing we saw was a section with a large sign that read, *Local Author Thad Griffin.* We traded glances.

"He can't be much of a hero around here," Susan whispered. "They've only got two of his books on the shelf."

"Can I help you all?" asked an elderly woman from behind the counter. She had a name tag that read *T. Ball*, and she looked friendly enough.

"I was interested in Thad Griffin's books," Susan said, "but I see you don't have many of them."

Miss Ball smiled warmly. "It's because they keep flying off the shelves. He's written nine books in all, and we've got five copies of each. As you can see, only two of them are currently available. And if you wait until this afternoon to check them out, those will be gone, too."

Susan nodded, as though impressed. "Do y'all have any books by other local authors?"

"Oh, yes, dear, we've got about a dozen of them." Miss Ball pointed to another display that was to the right of the entrance. "That whole wall is dedicated to our locals."

Susan and I approached the wall. She began on one side, and I began on the other. We worked our way toward each other, reading the author's name on the spine of every book. I didn't find anything by Gunther Foxwell, and neither did she.

I had begun to think we had struck out again, when Susan headed back to the front counter and asked Miss Ball if she'd ever heard of an author named Gunther Foxwell.

"He's supposed to be from Copper Head," Susan said, "but we can't find him on the shelf dedicated to locals."

"Foxwell?" Miss Ball's wrinkled face scrunched up. "I've lived here my whole life, but I've never heard that family name. Are you sure he's from Copper Head?"

"That's what I heard."

"Hmm…" Miss Ball seemed to think about it for a long moment. Finally, she said, "Let me look it up in our system. If it ever came through here, we'll have a record of it."

While Susan leaned against the counter and waited, I began perusing the library, searching for the author's name in each of the different sections. I hadn't made it down one side of the building when I heard some excited whispering from the front counter. A few seconds later, my wife came hurrying down the aisle.

"She found the book!" Susan was carrying a sliver of paper and waving excitedly for me to follow her. "She said it should be at the back of the room in the crime section, and on the very top shelf. The title is Blood On The Pavement."

I followed Susan to the back of the room and began scanning the top shelf as soon as it came into view. We were still a dozen feet away from it when I spotted the author's name on the spine.

"There!" I said. "It's the black and red book to the right of that thick green one."

Susan gave a nod and headed straight for it. When she pulled it down from the shelf, she cradled it in her hands as though it were a stick of unstable dynamite. There was a layer of dust on the cover. She wiped it off and settled down at a nearby desk. I sat beside her and leaned close.

It was surreal to see the pseudonym in print. We hadn't been sure it was the right name, and even if it was, we never dreamed we'd actually get our hands on a copy of the book. I couldn't help but wonder how Thad would feel if he knew where we were and what we were doing, and I also couldn't wait to find out if he had, indeed, been keeping any secrets.

The first thing Susan did was turn over Blood On The Pavement to read the description printed on the back cover. As I read along, my heart began to beat faster in my chest.

"You've got to be kidding me!" Susan sounded out of breath, and she was in phenomenal shape. "This book is about someone who murders a man's wife."

"How was the wife murdered?"

Susan began flipping through the pages. She was reading and flipping faster than I could, so I settled back into my chair and waited. It didn't take her long to find the answer. When she looked at me with her startled eyes, I already knew what she would say.

"She was run over with her own car," she said, "which makes perfect sense considering the title. And you know what else?"

"He had a son who was kidnapped?" I guessed.

"Close. He had a daughter who was kidnapped, but she was taken from the back yard."

"What about the dad?" I asked. "Was he an author?"

"I don't think so." She turned her attention back to the book and began searching for more answers. After a while, she said, "The husband was at work at the factory during the murder. According to what he told police, he found his wife dead when he pulled into the driveway. The little girl was last seen playing in the back yard by a neighbor."

My mind was racing as Susan continued reading. There was no way Thad hadn't thought about his old plotline as things were unfolding at his house. In fact, I was certain it was the first thing he'd thought about. I couldn't for the life of me think of why he might conceal that fact, unless, of course, he had committed the crime himself.

Susan was flipping through the book furiously now, stopping here and there to read for a few long seconds before moving on. When she finally looked up again, she was frowning deeply.

"Clint, the little girl was found dead three days after the kidnapping." My wife's usually tanned face was pale. "If this case plays out like the book, then that means…"

She didn't need to finish her thought. I knew what she was about to say, and it terrified both of us. If Ann's killer was following the plot of the book, then Wess was running out of time—and so were we. The following afternoon at roughly three o'clock would mark the third day since the boy's kidnapping, and I didn't like our chances of finding the killer before then.

I pointed to the book. "Is there a library card that can tell us who checked it out last?"

"Oh, that's a great idea!" She quickly flipped to the front flap and pulled out the card. She turned it so I could see the front. "It's blank. Not a single person checked it out."

"When was it published?" I asked.

She flipped to the copyright page. "Twenty-one years ago."

"Damn, and no one checked it out in all that time?" I leaned back against my chair. I was about to voice a thought when Susan flipped the page and sucked in a breath.

"Hey, Thad—or Gunther—dedicated this book to a girl named Daphne!" She handed it to me. "That name hasn't come up yet, right? I wonder if she could be a lead?"

"He never mentioned her when I asked about former girlfriends." I squinted to see the inscription on the dedication page. It read: *To Daphne, my one true love.* "Oh, he's definitely hiding something. And, of course, there's no last name. I wonder if I should have Amy bring him back in. He's been lying his ass off, but I just don't know why. We need to confront him about it."

I paused and handed the book back to Susan. "But even if we confront him," I continued, "there's no guarantee he'll tell us about the girl. I guess I could have Lindsey search for everyone in this area with the first name of Daphne."

"I have a better idea," Susan said. "Let's go back to the gas station and ask Silvia. She seems to know everyone around here."

I nodded and followed Susan to the counter, where she asked Miss Ball if we could borrow the book.

"You would have to sign up for a membership first." Miss Ball slid the application form across the counter with one hand, while fingering the book suspiciously with the other. "What is it about this book that interests you?"

Susan shrugged, handed Miss Ball her driver's license, and began filling out the form.

"Oh, you're from out of state," Miss Ball said apologetically. "I'll have to charge you for the card."

Susan smiled. "That's no problem."

CHAPTER 49

When Susan and I left the library, it was raining. We jogged for my truck and headed straight for Copper Head Gas and Stuff. We were able to park under the eave and avoid most of the rain. When we slipped into the store, we found Silvia in the same place, working just as hard. She glanced over at us, smiled, and mouthed that she would be with us in a second.

We stood near a rack of chips while we waited, and I could feel my stomach growl. It was way past lunchtime, and I didn't even know if the diner up the road would still be open. Some places closed after lunch, and reopened for dinner, and I was hoping that wasn't one of them.

"Hey, come on over," Silvia called when the last of her customers walked out. "What can I do for y'all?"

Susan opened the book to the dedication page and showed it to Silvia. "Do you know anyone by the name of Daphne who dated Thad?"

Silvia looked at the dedication, and then glanced at the cover of the book.

"This is that Gunther Foxwell author you were asking about earlier." A puzzled expression fell over her. "Is this guy also Thad Griffin?"

"We think so, but we're not positive," Susan acknowledged. "Do you know if Thad dated anyone named Daphne?"

"I know a girl named Daphne, but I don't know if she dated Thad." Silvia took a sip from a bottle of Diet Coke on the counter near her. "Her last name was Haley. She did go to school with us, but she was one of the popular girls. I couldn't see her dating Thad."

Susan glanced at me, and then back at Silvia. "Was she the only Daphne in your school?"

"Yes, ma'am."

"What about any other girls around town by that name?" asked Susan.

"She's the only Daphne I ever heard of."

"Does she still live around here?" Susan wanted to know.

"I'm really not sure. I think her family moved away not long after graduation." Silvia was thoughtful. "You know, one of her brothers was the same age as mine. They graduated together. He might know what happened to their family. Want me to call him and ask?"

"Please." Susan backed away from the counter and we waited while Silvia placed the call.

In the meantime, I called Amy and told her everything we'd found out thus far. I kept my voice low so as not to give anything away to Silvia.

"You've got to be shitting me!" Amy bellowed. "This case is going down just like a book he wrote?"

"That's what it looks like," I whispered. "He needs to be questioned again. We need to know who Daphne was to him, and we need to know why he didn't tell us about this book."

"I'm on it." She took a breath. "Anything else?"

"Yeah, have Melvin or Takecia go out there with you," I said. "And ask Lindsey to run the name Daphne Haley up and down and sideways. We need to know where she's currently living, what she drives, and what she had for breakfast this morning. If she dated Thad while he was writing this book, she might know if he had enemies at the time. If it's not an enemy from back then, someone must've gotten their hands on the book and they're living out the plotline."

Amy agreed to take someone along, and she said she would pass the message to Lindsey. I begged her to be careful, and she told me to stop acting like I was her dad.

"Lord knows you're old enough," she said with a playful sneer, "but last I checked, we're not related."

I laughed when she signed off, and afterward stood there lost in my own thoughts. Mostly, I was worried about Wess. Would we find him before the deadline came and went? Was the timeline even relevant? What if someone had initially set out to follow Thad's script, but then realized he couldn't bring himself to kill a child?

And then there was the idea that we might be dealing with a

female. If Thad had screwed Daphne over royally, she would be a viable suspect. But wouldn't she have murdered Thad? As I tried to rectify this latest wrinkle, I found myself going back to the author.

What if he had orchestrated all of it? He could've planted the receipt in the fields to lead us to Copper Head, where he might've figured we'd discover his book. After all, the library where one of the only living copies existed was directly behind the gas station from whence the receipt had come. But how could he predict we'd take the trip to his hometown?

I rubbed my face and tried to focus on what was right in front of us. At the moment, it was Daphne Haley. She was our next lead. We needed to get something to eat, and we needed to find her. With luck, Silvia would lead us right to the woman, and she would lead us to the killer.

After another five minutes, Silvia hung up the phone and told us that her brother thought Daphne had moved to the country. "He hasn't seen hide nor hair of her since high school," she said. "He didn't know she went with Thad. He thought he heard that she got married, but he didn't know to whom. Could it have been Thad?"

Susan and I traded glances.

"We have no clue," Susan said. "The first we've ever heard of her was this inscription in Blood On The Pavement."

After asking a few more questions of Silvia, we thanked her and left. The rain was coming down in sheets, and I was relieved to learn that Susan had packed our rain gear.

"What would I do without you?" I asked once I'd slipped into mine.

"Get wet," she said with a smirk.

"That, too."

I drove to the diner we'd first seen upon rolling into town, and I began making calls while waiting for our food to arrive. Susan said she had skipped around a lot in the book, and she wanted to read more of it to get a better feel for the plot.

"It's a bit disjointed," she had complained on the drive to the diner. "I can see why no one would publish it. I read the last few pages, and still don't know who killed the wife and daughter. It must be buried earlier in the book."

"What if it's one of those serial books?" I'd offered. "Like the streaming shows nowadays? You know, the plot drags on and on, and everything is revealed in the last book in the series."

"Love, this book was written more than twenty years ago." She had leaned over to pat my face. "Streaming shows weren't available back then."

The first call I made was to Sheriff Turner. I wanted to find out how Deputy Richmond's family was holding up. I also wanted to know when the funeral would be, because there was no way we were missing it.

After I had finished with him, I called Amy to find out if she'd spoken with Thad again. She sounded out of breath when she answered, and it was a quick second before she could get the words out.

"We can't find the prick," she said. "His neighbors said he left a few minutes ago."

"What?" I sat up straighter. "Where'd he go?"

"They said he ran to his house, got into his truck, and left out of there spinning his tires like he thought the devil was on his ass," she explained. "They said he showed up on foot earlier complaining about the way we were treating him. He told them we thought he was lying about something, but he wouldn't tell them what that something was. After about an hour of him pacing the floors and mumbling to himself, he asked them what day it was. When they told him it was Wednesday, he took off. We found his garage wide open and his house doors unlocked, so we searched the house for him. He's nowhere to be found."

CHAPTER 50

After getting off the phone with Amy, I received a call from Lindsey.

"Hey, Clint, this is Lindsey," she began. "Amy said you wanted me to search for a Daphne Haley from Copper Head, Tennessee."

"Yeah, were you able to find anything on her?"

"No. I've been looking her up all kinds of ways, and I can't find anything at all on that name."

"Of course," I said. "She's the one person who just *might* be able to give us some insight into who Thad Griffin was at the time he wrote his killer's blueprint, and now you tell me she's a ghost."

"Wait...what book?" Lindsey sounded befuddled. "Did you find another book by him?"

I quickly explained about the pseudonym, how we had come to locate Blood On The Pavement, and the fact that he had dedicated it to a girl named Daphne.

She listened in silence for all of it, except for when I mentioned how we had found Daphne's name.

"Wait a minute!" she shrieked. "I know her last name!"

"How?" I asked, but only heard a thump indicating she had dropped the receiver. I waited for almost a full minute before she was back.

"Thad Griffin named one of his characters after his old girlfriend!" she exclaimed. "It's not Haley. It's Potter!"

"Potter?" I glanced at Susan, who was watching me over her book. "Daphne Potter?"

"Yes, she's the wife in his Atlanta detective series." I could hear

Lindsey's fingers working furiously over the keys. "The main female character in the second book he wrote is named Daphne, and he dedicates his very first book to a Daphne? It can't be a coincidence, right?"

I had to agree with her. I was wondering if Silvia's Daphne was the same person Thad had mentioned, when Lindsey provided the answer.

"Daphne Haley Potter!" There was triumph in her voice. "She lives at 108-A Squatter's Lane in Devil's Gap, Tennessee! It looks like she used to be married to a man named Brayden Potter, but that was a while back. This address hasn't been updated in two years, so she may not be living there anymore."

"Lindsey, you're brilliant!" I pulled out a pen and scribbled the address on a napkin. "What else can you tell me about her?"

"That's all I have on this end," she said. "I'll start digging some more. I might be able to find her on social media."

I thanked her and pressed the red button on my cell phone. Susan had heard my end of the brief conversation, so I started to fill her in on the rest, keeping my voice low. I didn't know who in that establishment might be familiar with this Daphne Potter and who mightn't. I quit talking altogether and smiled when the waitress walked up with our food. When she was gone, I resumed.

Susan immediately went to work on her own phone, and soon turned it to show me a map with directions.

"It's forty minutes from here on some back country roads," she said. "We need to go now while it's still light outside."

I nodded my agreement and waved for the waitress. When she returned to our table, I asked if we could have bags to go, and I handed her fifty dollars.

"Will this cover it?" I asked, unsure anymore, thanks to the cost of food rising so much in recent years.

"It's more than enough," she said. "It'll be about half this."

"Just keep the rest."

She thanked me and hurried away to get the bags. She was a perceptive one, and she knew my phone call had been urgent and that we were now in a hurry.

CHAPTER 51

Susan continued reading the book while I drove, and we were soon lost in the network of winding roads that made up most of Tennessee's back country. Even on a stormy day, it was all beautiful to behold. We passed rolling fields, crossed raging creeks, and drove through thick forestlands.

I took a bite here and there from my burger as I drove, but I never shifted my eyes from the curvy roads. I also maintained the limit of thirty-five miles per hour. Roads with blind curves were not the place to violate speeding laws. One never knew what would be hiding around the next bend in the road, and we encountered more than our share of obstructions within the first few miles of our travels.

In addition to a Mennonite family in a buggy, we came upon a young man on a slow-moving scooter, two dogs, and a shepherd herding his sheep from one side of the road to the other. It appeared the field from which he was transferring them had started to flood, and he was moving them to higher ground.

I was going to get out and offer to help, but Susan told me I'd probably scare them into the flooded waters and cause them to drown. Out of the corner of my mouth, I thanked her for the vote of confidence, and I remained in my seat.

Twice during the drive, my cell phone rang, but no one was there when Susan tried to pick up. She saw that it was the police station. She tried to call back, but to no avail.

"The service here is spotty," she said. "I feel like we're back in the swamps."

My satellite phone was in my Tahoe back in Louisiana, where it did us absolutely no good. I hadn't thought to bring it. I asked Susan if she had one in her bag of tricks, but she had frowned and shook her head. She hadn't talked much on the drive. Her cute nose had been stuck between the pages of Blood On The Pavement, and every now and then she would share what she had learned. None of it seemed to get us closer to our killer, but still she plodded on, intent on finding the solution to the mystery.

"He's trying hard to make us think it's this one person," she had said earlier when she'd looked up at the shepherd, "but I don't think it's him."

The map on my cell phone indicated that we were three miles from our destination. We had taken so many left and right turns onto different back roads, that I figured I'd never find my way back. Something suddenly occurred to me.

"Sue, how in the hell are we gonna get out of here?"

She looked up from the book. "What do you mean?"

"We have no cell service, so how are we gonna punch in the address to the town?" I pointed to my phone. "We looked up Daphne's address before we entered the Twilight Zone. What in the hell are we supposed to do once we get there?"

A smile played across her face. "That's a good question. I've been reading, so I haven't paid attention to the route. Maybe stop and ask someone?"

I glanced in my rearview mirror. All I saw were thick trees and a road that curved like it had a severe case of scoliosis. When I looked ahead again, it was all the same. I hadn't seen a house in miles. Had it not been for the built-in compass on my dash, I wouldn't even know in what direction we were heading. Even that changed every hundred yards or so as the road curved sharply one way or the other. Several times, we even came upon switchbacks that had us heading in the exact opposite direction, with a mountain rising to one side and a steep drop off on the other.

Still, it was beautiful country, and a nice drive through the country with my bride. I could almost forget we were on a mission...almost.

Finally, the map told us the house was several hundred feet ahead and to the right. I slowed and glanced at Susan. She hadn't looked up. Her face was buried intently in the book, and her mouth slowly fell open.

"Holy shit!" she whispered. "The dad did it all!"

"What?"

"It was the dad all along!" She looked up from the book, stunned.

"The dad murdered his wife and kidnapped the daughter to make it look like it was someone else. He then murdered his own daughter, but he never got caught. He pinned it on somebody else. That's why someone else is in jail at the end."

I slowed and put on my blinker. "Who'd he pin it on?"

"The guy his wife was screwing," she said. "He had been following his wife for a while and learned her pattern. It seems she would pick the dude up at the same grocery store a few times a week. He would leave his truck parked behind the store, and then drive the woman's car to a desolate park, where they would have sex. The husband knew the man's DNA would be on the steering wheel of the wife's car, so he wore gloves and used it as the murder weapon. And it worked! The detectives found his DNA on the steering wheel, the shift, and the keys. They also found a single print on the rearview mirror that matched his right thumb."

My mind raced as I absently turned onto the narrow gravel driveway that connected to the road we had been on. A sign told us that it was *Squatter's Lane*. Trees hung low over the drive, and several branches slid across the top of my truck as I creeped forward. There had been several *No Trespassing* signs nailed to the trees at the edge of the road, and I wasn't sure if I should've proceeded. We might've been inviting trouble. However, I wanted to speak with Daphne.

"How'd the husband frame the dude for the murder of the girl?" I asked, squinting to see through the sheets of rain that bounced off the windshield. My wipers were struggling to keep up with the torrential downpour.

"The wife's lover was a smoker, and he would toss his cigarettes out the window after having sex with the woman," Susan explained. "The husband swooped in and collected one of the butts the night before he planned to frame the man. When he dumped the daughter's body in the same park where they would have sex, he placed the cigarette butt on the ground near her body."

I shook my head in disbelief. "But why would he kill his own daughter? I mean, I get why he killed the wife, but what in the hell did the daughter do?"

"She knew about the affair and never told her dad."

"No way!"

"Yes way." Susan nodded her confirmation. "She had even gone with her mom to meet the lover dude a few times. According to the book, they didn't have sex those times, but they had a little picnic at one of the tables and acted like a family."

212 | BJ Bourg

About half a mile down the lane, we came to a locked gate, so I stopped my truck. I was trying to recount every single word Thad Griffin had spoken during our interviews, searching for the slightest hint he might've given to suggest he had murdered his son. If it had been there, I had missed it. And because of it, we were now hundreds of miles away on a wild goose chase, when we should be back home interrogating the shit out of the clever author.

"Clint, do you see that sign?" Susan asked, pointing toward the gate.

I leaned forward to see better. The rain had slacked off a little, which enabled me to see the ominous warning:

If you'uns friendly, call 555-0101.
If not, call 911—cuz you'uns gone need 'em!

Another sign told us to beware of the attack Dobermans, while still a third told us that if we could read the sign, then we were already in range. I laughed.

"I love it," I said, peering past the gate and toward the house. It looked like the driveway rose gradually to the top of a hill. Through the narrow opening in the trees, I could see an aging white house nestled at the center of a grassy clearing. It had grown much darker than when we'd first embarked on the long drive, and an occasional flash of lightning helped to illuminate the area.

I tried to push Thad from my thoughts and come up with a solution to the current problem. We had already come that far, so we were definitely going to make contact with Daphne Potter to see what she could tell us about Thad. For all we knew, the two of them were in cahoots. It could be that they had reconnected at a book signing or other public event, and they might've planned to get rid of Ann and Wess so they could be together. At that point, anything was possible, and no one was free from suspicion.

Although I wanted very much to interview Daphne, I wasn't about to trespass onto private property. If they did have dogs and those dogs attacked us, I wouldn't have the right to fight them, considering we weren't supposed to be there.

Intent on calling the number to the house, I grabbed my cell phone and checked for bars. I had none.

"I don't have service either," Susan said. "Maybe try blowing your horn."

It was a good idea, so I tried it. I waited for a few long seconds, and then blew it again.

"Look," Susan said, leaning forward and pointing up the driveway. "Check out the second floor window."

I focused on the window to which she referred, but it was too dark to see anything.

"What is it?" I asked.

"I think I saw movement when the lightning flashed the last time," she said. "Where are your binoculars?"

I twisted around in my seat and dug in my tactical backpack for a bit until I came up with them. Since it had been her idea, I handed them over and waited for her to zero in on the window.

With my naked eyes, I could see that the exterior of the house was covered in old-fashioned slate siding. There were obvious cracks in some of the sections, and the awning over the porch seemed to sag in places. The lone upstairs window was above the awning, and it was cloaked in darkness.

"See anything?" I asked after twenty or thirty seconds.

"I need to get out." So saying, she dropped from the passenger's side and tromped up to the gate.

I followed and watched as she pulled the hood on her raincoat over the binoculars to block out most of the rain.

Suddenly, there was a flash of lightning, and I heard Susan suck in a violent breath. The lightning was followed almost immediately by a booming chorus of thunder that seemed to shake the earth. The noise was so loud that it nearly deafened me, but it didn't drown out my wife's string of expletives.

"What is it?" I asked.

"I think I see movement," she said. "I think it's a small boy!"

CHAPTER 52

Mechant Loup

Homer Verdin toweled off after his shower and quickly slipped into some jeans. He hesitated before pulling on his T-shirt. He buried his nose in the fabric and sniffed.

"That smell," he murmured. "Where's it coming from?"

Ever since he had tried to save Lisa Grant two days earlier, he couldn't get the smell of burning human flesh out of his nostrils. He now knew that he was only imagining it, but it still seemed very real. On the previous evening, when he and Baylor had stopped for supper at a local diner, a waitress walked by their table with a sizzling steak and he'd almost hurled.

Baylor had noticed and asked what was wrong. When he'd told his training officer what was happening, Baylor had explained that it was the aftereffects of battle.

"Smells, sounds, and things you see will sometimes take you back to a place you don't want to go," Baylor had said somberly. "It's normal. Just reassure yourself that you did all you could do, and move on. Leave it where you left it. Don't dwell on it. If you do, it'll drive you crazy."

Homer had nodded and tried his best to push the horrible incident from his mind. It hadn't been easy. He had dreamed about her for two nights straight. In his most recent dream, he was inside the blazing vehicle and all he had to do was unsnap the seatbelt and Lisa would've been saved, but he had been too afraid to act. His hands wouldn't move. She had been screaming and begging for him to remove her seatbelt, but he had only knelt there petrified. He'd tried to tell his hands to move, but they wouldn't.

He had awakened with a start, covered in sweat and trembling. His arms and back had seemed to be on fire, and it took him a second to remember his wounds and how they had occurred. When he'd opened his eyes, the sun's rays through the crack in the curtains had blinded him. He had been disoriented. It had taken him a few more seconds to remember he was at Baylor's house.

As he had lain there, he had started to remember how he had come to be there. Early on in their shift, he had decided not to take the long boat ride back home and was going to rent a motel room, but Baylor had insisted he crash at their place. He and Baylor would not normally be due back to work until Friday, but Baylor had said that there was a good chance they would be called out to assist with the search for the missing boy, so it was best to remain close by and to stand ready.

"I don't want to impose," Homer had protested when Baylor had made the offer.

"Nonsense," Baylor had said. "Amy will be at work. You can sleep in the room we've fixed up for the baby. It's got its own bathroom, so you'll have your privacy."

As he'd recounted that conversation in his head, he had suddenly remembered running into Remi Walton in the parking lot at the police department as he and Baylor had knocked off of shift. She had stopped there to check on him—on *him*—and to see if he was okay. They had spent the better part of an hour locked in conversation while Baylor waited patiently in the office.

As Homer had lain there in Baylor's unborn son's room going over every word that had been spoken and every gesture that had been made, he had suddenly remembered telling Remi how much he enjoyed talking to her.

Red faced and fidgeting, Remi had casually commented that she would be free around lunchtime, and Homer had blurted out an invitation to meet at a Thai restaurant in Central Chateau. Remi had readily accepted, and he had walked away light-headed and giddy—until he'd slipped into Baylor's truck and remembered he didn't own a vehicle. Hell, he didn't own much of anything, so why would Remi ever get serious about him? There was the tribal truck that stayed parked at the boat launch, but he would never use it for personal reasons.

When he had mentioned his dilemma to his training officer, Baylor had immediately offered to let Homer use his truck. Once again, Homer hadn't wanted to impose, but Baylor had insisted.

"You're family now, kid," Baylor had said. "Amy and I have adopted you. You're stuck with us."

It had felt good to hear that, and he was constantly trying to think of ways to pay them back for their generosity. Now, as he pulled on his shirt, he tried to convince himself that the burnt smell was stuck in his nostrils, and that his shirt didn't stink. The last thing he needed was for Remi to get a bad impression of him on their first date.

After getting ready, he had a brief conversation with Baylor, where he repeatedly thanked his training officer for loaning him the truck.

"Forget it," Baylor said. "Oh, and grab one of those umbrellas by the door. It's raining outside."

"What's an umbrella?" Homer asked with a chuckle. "I thought you were a man."

"It's not for you." Baylor arched an eyebrow, as though to tell Homer to keep up.

"Oh, right!" Homer slapped his forehead. "I'm not good at this."

"I wasn't either," Baylor said. "Back where I was from, the guys who did all the talking seemed to get all the girls. I'm glad it worked out that way, because I was available when I moved here and met Amy."

Homer nodded thoughtfully, wondering if he could ever be so lucky as to start dating Remi. After a moment, he blinked and snapped out of it. He thanked Baylor one last time and headed for the door, grabbing an umbrella on the way out.

During the entire drive to the restaurant, he wrestled with himself about whether or not he could call what was about to happen a *date*. He hadn't used that word when asking Remi if she wanted to go eat. She had simply said she was free for lunch, and he had asked if she'd wanted to meet up. It wasn't until he finally pulled up to the restaurant that he resolved the question within himself.

"It's not a real date," he said aloud as he parked Baylor's truck in front of the restaurant and shut off the engine. "It's just lunch."

CHAPTER 53

Homer didn't think for one second that a girl like Remi would care about money or material things, so he wasn't worried about her finding out that he was just some poor kid from the swamps. He simply didn't think someone as amazing as she was could be interested in someone like him—especially if she ever found out what he had done to that terrorist named Spider. She seemed too sweet to ever condone or forgive such behavior.

It had rained a little during the entire drive to the restaurant, but the rain was currently falling in sheets. Homer couldn't see anything with the wipers off, so he cranked up the engine again and began searching the parking lot for Remi. He didn't know what she drove, so he tried to see through the windows of every car that pulled up. Finally, he saw her pull up in a red Jeep Wrangler.

It looked like Remi was also searching for him, and she parked right beside Baylor's truck. Homer grabbed the umbrella and quickly slipped out of the truck with it. As he walked around to meet Remi, he fumbled with the button to get it open. He'd never used an umbrella in his life, but it turned out to be pretty easy to figure out, and he was soon holding the canopy above the driver's door to Remi's Jeep.

Remi smiled warmly through the window as she opened the door. She grabbed her purse and dropped to the ground next to Homer. She paused for a second to look up at him. She was so close that he could smell the spearmint on her breath when she talked.

"Thank you," she said. "You're such a gentleman."

"It was Baylor's idea," he blurted without thinking. "I didn't even know it was raining outside."

"You're also honest." She smiled and touched a hand to her chest. "I like it."

Homer could feel himself blushing, as he escorted Remi through the rain and into the restaurant. He shook off the umbrella and placed it in the corner near the door.

"Have you ever eaten here?" he asked.

Remi shook her head. "I've driven by it a hundred times, but I haven't been here since it was a Pizza Hut."

The hostess walked up with menus and asked them to follow her. Once they were seated, they continued talking while figuring out what they wanted to eat. From there, time seemed to fly by. Before Homer knew it, they had placed their order, the food had come, and then it was gone. During that entire time, they never stopped talking. He had never met someone so easy to get along with. They agreed on most topics, and she seemed to like his darker humor. She was also very funny, and Homer couldn't remember a time when he'd laughed so much.

When it seemed like they had stayed there too long, Remi mentioned that she'd have to get back to work.

"Oh, I'm sorry," Homer said. "I'm technically off until Friday, but Baylor thinks we might be called out later on. I guess I've just been babbling without thinking about the time."

Remi's eyes were glassy as she smiled across the table at him. "I don't mind. It's been a lot of fun. I can't remember the last—"

"Remi?" called an authoritative voice from across the room. "Remington Walton, is that you?"

Homer noticed Remi cringe a little. He turned toward the sound, and saw a tall deputy walking toward them. He was flanked by two other deputies. Homer remembered seeing the first one at the foot chase scene on the previous day. He had been one of the deputies who had stopped at the edge of the water, and who hadn't pursued the suspect any farther. When he got closer, Homer saw that his nametag read, *J. Morvant*.

"Josh," Remi said, glancing up and giving a curt nod. "How are you?"

"What...what're you doing here?" Josh asked, glancing from Remi to Homer.

"Isn't it obvious?" she asked.

The nonresponse seemed to anger the deputy, and he turned his beady eyes on Homer. "Aren't you that crazy kid who jumped in the water?"

Homer smiled easily. "That would be me."

"That was a pretty stupid move." The deputy shook his head and glanced over his left shoulder. "This is the fool I was telling y'all about. He decided to play hero after we lost Stan."

Homer frowned. "I'm real sorry about your friend."

One of the deputies smirked, but the other one didn't seem amused by Josh's attitude. He leaned past Josh and said, "Thanks for catching the bastard that killed Stan."

Before Homer could say anything, his cell phone began ringing. He pulled it out and saw that Baylor was calling.

"Oh, it's my training officer," he said quickly, and answered.

"Homer, we need to go to work," Baylor said. "Someone's climbing a radio tower in town. The caller thinks he might jump."

"On my way." Homer looked up at Remi. "I need to go. There's a situation in town."

"They must need someone to direct traffic while the men do the real police work," Josh said. "You go do that. I'll take care of Remi."

"You're not taking care of anything," Remi said heatedly.

Homer ignored Josh and fished for his wallet. "I'll pay on our way out."

Remi nodded and gathered her purse to stand. Josh started to move in front of her as though he wanted to block her path, but Homer had anticipated the move. He stepped on Josh's toe and the deputy stumbled forward and fell into some tables across the way.

Homer stood and reached for Remi's hand. Smirking, she took it and stood to her feet.

Josh had righted himself and turned angrily toward them. "You're not going anywhere! You assaulted an officer of the law!"

Homer laughed and guided Remi around Josh. As he pushed past Josh, the deputy grabbed his shoulder.

Homer stopped and looked coolly at him. He didn't want to have to hurt the deputy—especially in a restaurant while Josh was in uniform—so he decided to be diplomatic.

"Look, I know it's been a rough couple of days for you and your agency, and tensions are high. I'm sorry about your friend. I wasn't trying to show off or anything. I just wanted to catch the bad guy—same as you." Homer paused, and nodded. "We all want the same thing. We're on the same side. So, if you don't mind, I need to go direct some traffic."

The deputy who had thanked Homer chuckled and grabbed Josh's arm. "Leave him alone, Josh," he said. "The kid's okay in my book."

Josh hesitated a moment longer. Finally, and begrudgingly, he stepped aside.

Homer allowed Remi to go first, and then he followed her to the counter to pay for their meal. After escorting her to her Jeep with the umbrella, he hurried to Baylor's truck and backed out of his parking spot. He glanced in the rearview mirror once as he was about to drive away, and he saw Josh standing in the rain talking to Remi. He was waving his hands as though he were angry.

Homer was about to whip the truck around, but he saw the taillights on Remi's Jeep come on, and she backed out quickly, with no regard to the man standing beside her.

Homer chuckled as he drove off, but a part of him wondered what the fuss had been about. It was obvious that Josh and Remi knew each other, and Josh had seemed surprised to see her with Homer. Could it be that they were dating? Was that why he had acted the way he had? After all, Remi had never said she was single, so there was that possibility.

As Homer headed south at a high rate of speed, he continued to wonder if Remi was dating that asshole. The very thought of it turned his stomach. She deserved better—much better. Although he didn't consider himself to be better than anyone, he knew he would never approach her the way Josh had, and he would never speak to her in that manner.

Homer shook his head. After seeing the way Josh had waved his hands and seemingly yelled at Remi near her Jeep, he regretted deeply not laying him on his ass in the restaurant. While he wouldn't have wanted to start a fight in front of Remi, there were times when a body just had to take out the trash.

CHAPTER 54

Homer was still wondering if Remi was single thirty minutes later when he and Baylor were standing with Melvin, Takecia, Amy, and a half dozen deputies at the base of the radio tower. The rain continued to fall in sheets and fog had rolled into the area, making it hard to see the top of the tower.

"It's definitely Thad Griffin's truck," Amy said, "so it's got to be him up there."

"Can y'all still see him?" Melvin asked, cupping his hands over his face to shield his eyes from the rain. "He climbed the step bolts on the eastern leg. It looks like he's in the damned clouds now."

"I see a shadowy figure, but it's over the western leg," Amy said. "I think he accessed the crossbeam to get to the other side. It's too hazy to know for sure, but it's got to be him. It has to be Thad."

"Other than suicide, what would his reason be for going up there?" Melvin wiped the rivulets of rain from his face and looked around at the other officers. "If he does want to kill himself, what in the hell is he waiting for? He's plenty high enough, and he's been up there for nearly half an hour."

"Maybe he wants attention," Amy offered.

"Well, he's got it." Baylor indicated the string of cars that had stopped alongside the highway to watch what was happening in the field near the tower. "I don't know how the word spread so fast."

"Social media." Amy snorted, and pulled the cap on her raincoat higher on her head. "So, who's going up there after him? I'll take a guess that having a pregnant woman climb a radio tower is frowned upon in present company, so who will it be?"

"I'll go up," Homer said quickly. Out of all the officers there, he had the least to lose. Takecia had a new love interest, Amy and Baylor had a child on the way, and Melvin already had a family. "I've been climbing tall trees since I was old enough to walk, and this thing has all kinds of hand and foot holds."

Melvin backed a few yards from the base of the tower and looked up again. "Homer, that tower's at least 300 feet tall. The bolts are wet. It's hard to see. I say we let him kill himself."

"He has to have some information about his kid's disappearance," Amy pressed. "We need to find out what he knows. Clint and Susan are trying to locate the boy, and we need to drain every bit of information we can from that asshole before he jumps."

"Have you spoken with Clint or Susan lately?" Melvin asked, still looking up toward the heavens. "Maybe they already found the boy. Maybe that's why he's up there. If he had something to do with the murder of his wife and his son's kidnapping, someone might've gotten word back to him that they found Wess. If he thinks it's the end of the road, he might see this as his only option."

"I've called a dozen times, but both of their phones go straight to voicemail," Amy said, answering his initial question. "The last thing Clint said was to find Thad and interrogate him. I think we need to follow through with that order until told otherwise."

Homer watched the back and forth between Melvin and Amy in silence. While he wasn't itching to scale the slick metal structure in that weather, he would do it if necessary. Especially if it meant helping to save a small boy.

Finally, Melvin turned to him. "Are you sure you want to do this?"

"Yes, sir," Homer said, but then quickly winced. "Sorry. I mean, yes."

Melvin sighed and headed for his truck. "Let me get my climbing gear," he called over his shoulder. "You're not going up there without a rope."

Homer wasn't wearing a slicker suit. When he had arrived at Baylor's house, he had just tossed Baylor the keys to the truck and jumped in the marked Charger. Thus, his clothes were saturated, and his T-shirt clung to him like wet toilet paper. He figured it might hinder his movements, so he peeled it off. He leaned against the concrete pillar at the base of one of the tower legs and pulled off his boots, too. His feet were calloused from a lifetime of tromping through the brambles and cypress knees, and he figured he could get a better grip on the bolts barefooted than with the rubber soles of his boots.

When Melvin returned, he handed Homer a harness and a bag of clips. As he helped Homer into the harness, Melvin offered a crash course on clipping, and he explained the dangers of back clipping.

"I want you to clip in every ten bolts or so," Melvin concluded. "As long as you go straight up, there won't be any problems. And don't clip into the bolts. The carabiner could slide off the end. I want you clipping in to any crossbar you can find."

Homer nodded and attached the bag of clips to his harness.

"I'll be down here belaying," Melvin continued. "Don't worry, I'll put on the brakes if you fall. You might drop a few feet and get banged up a little, depending on how much slack there is in the rope when you fall, but you'll be okay."

Melvin paused and Homer saw him look over the bandages on his bare arms and torso. "Are you sure you're up for this? Your bandages are getting wet, and the doctor specifically said that shouldn't happen."

"My mom used to say that raindrops were God's tears," Homer replied with a grin. "If that's true, they'll probably help my burns heal faster."

Melvin didn't smile. He only gave a somber nod. "Be careful and don't do anything heroic. We just need to get as much information as we can from Griffin about his little boy's whereabouts before he jumps. As soon as you make contact, get him talking about the boy. His name is Wess and he's eight. Tell him we're concerned about the kid, and we want to get him back safely. Let him know the boy needs him and misses him."

While Melvin turned to Baylor and Takecia to discuss how they would handle things on the ground, and where each of them would be stationed, Amy walked up to Homer and began feeding him the questions she wanted him asking Thad Griffin. She also handed him a small device and a police radio.

"This is a digital recorder," she explained about the small device. "It's already recording. Put it in your pocket and don't touch it. I want every word on record. And this radio is keyed up. We need to know what's going on at all times, so we can make sure to keep you safe. If you see a gun, tell us." She shot a thumb over her shoulder. "One of them will have a rifle, and they'll shoot Thad's ass right off that tower if he threatens you."

Homer nodded his understanding, and lithely mounted the large concrete pillar at the base of the eastern leg. He then began making his way up the metal pipe, scaling the step bolts with ease. As Melvin had instructed, he attached the clips to the crossbars, and then fastened the rope to the clips. He looked up intermittently, but each time he did, the rain pelted his eyeballs and distorted his vision.

When he had climbed for about five minutes, he heard Amy holler from below that he was more than halfway to the top, and that Thad was above him and to the left.

"Ten-four," he said, and glanced up in that direction. He could see Thad Griffin standing on a crossbar about twenty feet above him. He was clutching one of the step bolts that was attached to the western leg with his right hand, while his left hand dangled against his side.

Homer clipped in for the last time, and climbed several more of the bolts. When he was almost level with the author, he slipped out onto one of the crossbars and moved a step closer. The man wasn't looking in his direction, and he didn't seem to notice that someone else had joined him up in the clouds.

"Hey, Mr. Griffin," Homer began softly, "how's it going?"

Thad Griffin jerked around so hard that he almost slipped and fell from the crossbar. He let out a screech and wrapped his arms around the radio tower leg nearest him.

"What…what…who are you?" His eyes were wild, and it was clear to Homer that he hadn't gotten much sleep in the days since his wife had been murdered and his son kidnapped.

"I'm Homer," he said with a friendly grin. He wanted to keep his tone light. "Homer Verdin."

"Are you some kind of cop?"

"Nah, I'm no cop." Homer shook his head from side to side. "I'm supposed to be in training, but I don't know if I'm cut out for this. I hear you're a famous author."

Thad didn't react to the comment. Instead, he began turning so he would be facing the ground on the outskirts of the tower, rather than the middle of it.

Rain continued to pelt Homer's head and shoulders, and he brushed his wet hair out of his eyes.

"I wanted to come up here to talk about your son," Homer began again. "Wess is his name, right?"

Thad hesitated. "What…what do you know about Wess?"

"We want to bring him home safe and sound," Homer said. "If there's anything you can tell us to help make that happen, we'd appreciate it."

"It's too late." Thad leaned forward and looked toward the ground. "There's nothing anybody can do now."

"That's not true." Homer tried to keep the uneasiness from his voice. Amy had told him to be careful when he dropped the impending bomb, because she said it might make him jump. "You can help us bring Wess home. We just need you to tell us what you know about Daphne Potter and your first book, Blood On The Pavement."

Thad's head jerked up and around in Homer's direction. "Who in the hell are you? How do you know about that?"

"I'm a rookie in training," Homer explained. "I was sent here to talk to you about your first book and Daphne Potter."

"Who told you about that?"

"Does it really matter?" Homer asked. "If it can help bring your son home, wouldn't you want to share that information with us?"

Thad hesitated for a long moment. Homer could tell he was thinking about jumping, so he quickly brought up Wess again.

"Detective Wolf is close to finding Wess," he said with more confidence than he felt. "Once he does, your son will need you more than ever. He's already lost his mom, so it would destroy him if he lost his dad, too."

"It's too late to save him." Thad's shoulders slumped. "He's already gone."

An icy chill came over Homer. "What do you mean?"

"I...I've done a horrible thing." Thad wiped his eyes and glanced down at the ground again. "There's no coming back from it. There's no salvation. It's...it's over."

"Tell me about it." Homer remembered Amy saying for him to do whatever he could to keep Thad talking. "We've all done something horrible. No one's perfect. The people down there, they can help you."

"No." Thad shook his head from side to side. "No one can help me now."

After he made that statement, Thad Griffin squatted deeply. Before Homer could utter a word in protest, the author jumped.

CHAPTER 55

108-A Squatter's Lane, Devil's Gap, Tennessee

"Do you want to take my truck and head back up the road?" I asked Susan after looking through the binoculars myself. "Maybe you can find cell service and get some help. I'll keep watch over here."

She nodded and hurried off. The lane was too narrow to whip the truck around, so I knew she would have to go backwards up the half-mile lane, and that would cut into her time. I returned my attention to the house. I rotated the dial to the highest magnification and zeroed in on the window again.

"Come on," I said, hoping for more lightning. "Show yourself."

I waited for almost two minutes. While there was an almost constant rumble in the sky, there were no more flashes. As I stood there, I started to get an uneasy feeling. Could someone be watching me? What if they had heard the truck horn and were creeping up at that very moment?

I pulled my eyes from the binoculars and took a slow look around. Everything was wet and dark. In addition to the thunder overhead, the driving rain made lots of noise as it pelted the trees and ground all around me, and I would've never heard anyone sneaking up.

When I was satisfied no one was about to pounce on me, I peered through the binoculars once more. I was sure there was movement in the window, but I couldn't make out any details. Maybe if I got closer? There were no dogs visible, and I figured I could venture several yards beyond the gate without being noticed.

After thinking about it for another minute, I slung the binoculars around my neck and reached for the top of the tube gate. I already owed a farmer one gate, and I was hoping I wouldn't damage that one as I braced my foot against the bottom crossbar. I was about to pull myself up when I suddenly heard what sounded like sharp claps of thunder, only I knew better.

"That's not thunder," I muttered aloud. "Those are gunshots!"

I quickly took cover behind a tree and studied the house. I didn't remember drawing my pistol, but it was there in my hand. I had been about to trespass, so I couldn't return fire. Sure, it wasn't legal to shoot trespassers, but I certainly couldn't shoot back after making that attempt.

After a brief pause, there were more gunshots. I frowned. There was no movement from the house or anywhere on the property, and the bullets weren't impacting the area around me. So, where could the shots be coming from?

That's when it hit me—the shots hadn't originated from the house, and they weren't directed at me!

"Susan!" I whipped around and began running up the lane. The two-month-old injury in my leg ached as I ran, but I ignored it. Water had gathered in several potholes, and I tried to avoid those as I raced through the loose gravel. Gunshots continued to reverberate loudly through the trees, and I could tell they were rifle shots.

Fear rose up and gripped me around the throat when I got far enough up the driveway to see the road. There, parked sideways in the intersection, was my truck. The windshield was peppered with bullet holes, and I could see where a few had skidded across the hood. I couldn't see Susan, and I couldn't hear return gunfire from her pistol. Every shot that was being fired was coming from up the road to my right and out of view, and they were relentless.

It was never a good thing to shoot what one couldn't see or identify, but I was desperate. I snapped off two quick shots, aiming through the trees toward where I could hear the gunfire originating. I knew it was impossible to hit the bad guys, but my shots had the desired effect. There was a momentary pause in the attack on Susan, and I could hear voices hollering back and forth. There were at least two of them. I couldn't make out what they were saying, but it was obvious they were angry and they were making plans.

I hadn't taken two more steps when bullets began whizzing past me. One struck an evergreen that grew on the edge of the road, and splinters from it speckled my face. I cursed, ducked low, and kept charging ahead. I saw more bullets hitting the windshield of my truck, and I knew that they hadn't abandoned their attack on Susan. They had simply divided their efforts.

There was a slight pause from my attacker, and I realized immediately that he was reloading. Taking a chance, I veered to my right and bolted through the trees, heading straight toward the source of the shots. I dipped and ducked and circled through the thick woods. At one point, I had to cover my face with my arms and push through a wall of thick branches, and by the time I squirted out the other end, bullets began whizzing in my direction again.

I dove behind a large rock that jutted up from the ground, and landed with a thud against it. I was much closer to the gunfire at that point, and the suspect must've seen me, because he narrowed his focus to the piece of cover I'd chosen. Chunks of rock exploded into the air with each shot that found its mark, and I tried to burrow as deeply in the ground as I could.

"I've got the bastard pinned down!" hollered a rough-sounding voice in a country accent. "Circle that sumbitch and take him out! He's behind that rock!"

I rolled quickly to my back and brought my pistol to my chest. I had fired two shots from the eight-shot magazine. Counting the one in the chamber, that left me with seven rounds in the gun, and one fully loaded magazine in my pocket. Not nearly enough to take on two men with rifles. From the sounds of the gunfire, they had semi-automatic weapons, and my guess would've been cheap SKS carbines, which would've accounted for the length of time it took for my suspect to reload. If only both of them could run out at the same time!

Bullets began to kick up the earth directly to my right as I lay on my back, while others impacted the rock above me and the trees to my left. It became readily apparent that the second suspect was circling me, because his bullets began to get closer and closer. As my hiding spot shrunk, so did my chances of survival.

If there was one thing that gave me comfort, it was that they had taken their attention off of my wife. I didn't know what her condition was, but I was praying for the best. I was also hoping I'd be able to take out both riflemen with my pistol and the few rounds I possessed. Even if they got me in the end, if I could just take them out and save my wife, I would feel like my death was a good one.

As the bullets continued to inch closer to my right side, I realized the first suspect had paused. I figured he must be reloading, so I quickly rolled to that side of the rock and steadied my pistol. It was a colossal mistake. The suspect was kneeling behind his own rock, and he had his rifle trained on my exact location, no doubt waiting for me to try to run from his comrade's bullets.

A wicked grin spread across his face as he pulled the trigger. To my surprise, his bullet went wide and struck a branch above me. That's when I noticed his face was twisted in pain and he was biting down hard with his stained teeth. I took advantage of whatever had happened and aimed two shots toward center mass. His jaw went slack and he disappeared behind the rock.

I heard a burst of gunfire that was unlike the others I'd been hearing, and the second man cried out in pain. I raised up to my knees and peered cautiously over the rock behind which I'd been hiding. I was just in time to see Susan approaching the second man at a crouching sprint, my AR-10 pressed firmly to her shoulder.

The man was big and burly, and I could see that the front of his overalls was covered in blood. Although he was leaning precariously against a tree, he still held the rifle in both hands, and he was trying to bring it to bear. Susan was hollering commands at the man, but he ignored her. She stopped running and widened her stance. She gave one last command, and when he didn't heed her warning, she shot him dead.

CHAPTER 56

I half slid down the side of the mountain in my haste to reach Susan. When I made it to level ground, I paused long enough to shoot a glance at the suspects. They were separated by a few dozen feet. It was obvious that the one Susan had shot didn't pose a danger to anyone, but the one I'd sent two bullets into seemed to still be alive. Keeping a wary eye on him, I turned to Susan.

"Are you okay?" I put my hands to her face and tilted it so I could examine the specs of blood on her perfect cheek. "Are you hit?"

"No, it's only glass fragments," she explained. "They opened up on me as soon as I backed into the road. I didn't realize they were there until the windshield began exploding."

"How'd you not get hit?" I asked as I continued to check her for bullet holes.

"I dropped down and ate the floor mats," she said. "It wasn't until you got their attention that I was able to crawl over the seat, grab your AR-10, and go to work."

"This is the second time in as many months that you've had to save my ass. Let's not make it a habit." I smiled and kissed her on the forehead before rushing to the suspect who was writhing in pain on the side of the mountain.

"What's your name?" I asked, kicking away his rifle as I did so.

"Stump Haley," he called through gritted teeth. "Please help me! I'm bleeding out! Call an ambulance! I…I'm dying!"

"Not before you tell me where I can find Wess Griffin," I said. "And if you lie, I'll let natural selection run its course."

The large man hesitated for a brief moment, but then nodded sullenly. "I'll tell you, but it's already too late for the boy."

"What do you mean?" My heart sank to the earth. "Why is it too late for him?"

"He's already gone."

"How?" I asked heatedly. "Who?"

Stump glanced at the other man, who was so similar in appearance that they had to be brothers. "It...it was Gideon."

"Is he your brother?"

Stump nodded. "Gideon...he did it. I didn't have the heart."

I cursed under my breath. Blood was oozing from his chest and I knew he didn't have long. I didn't have long either. I needed to check the house for Wess. If Susan saw a child moving inside, then maybe he was okay.

"Did he also kill Ann Griffin?" I asked, pulling out my cell phone to record what would probably amount to a dying declaration.

"No." He took a pained breath and shifted his position to make himself more comfortable. "Please get me some help."

"Only if you tell me what y'all did. If I think for a second that you're lying..." I let my voice trail off and shook my head. When he didn't say anything, I asked, "Did you kill her?"

He hesitated for a long second, but then nodded.

"How'd you do it?"

He moved again, but winced and froze in place. His breath was coming in gasps at that point. "I need an ambulance. I...I feel myself slipping away. I'm getting lightheaded."

"Tell me what you did!" The command came out more forcefully than I'd intended, but it seemed to spur him on.

"Okay!" he said. "I killed her."

"How'd it happen?"

"Ran her over."

"I need details," I insisted. "All of it!"

"We...we watched them for two weeks. They never even knew we were there. Rich people living in rich neighborhoods all think they're invincible." There was contempt in his voice, and that seemed to energize him a bit. "They didn't lock their doors and they left the keys in their cars. Thad's wife would follow the same routine every day. She would sit on the front porch talking on the phone, and then she would go get her kid at the bus stop. Sometimes she would come back home, and other times she would go shopping."

"What'd you do?"

"Well, the...um...the plan was for me to sneak into the garage and kidnap her when she left to get the boy."

"But that's not what happened, is it?" I asked when he paused for a breath.

"No. I got into the garage and was inside the car trying to figure it out, and I accidentally pressed the start button. The engine fired up, and it was loud." He shook his head. "I had no choice at that point. I knew they would hear the car, and I knew I had to get out of there. I pressed the remote for the garage door. As soon as it opened, I backed out of there. I left in such a hurry that I didn't even realize she had come to the back of the car. By the time I saw her in the rearview mirror, it was too late. I felt the tires go up and down, and I knew I'd hit her."

"What'd you do next?"

"I closed the garage door and headed up the street."

"Did anyone see you?" I asked, figuring I already knew the answer to that question.

"Their house is way in the back and they have trees blocking the view of their place from the rest of the neighbors, so I didn't think anyone had seen anything. I know I didn't see anyone anywhere on the street when I hauled ass to the front. I...I called Gabriel and told him what happened."

"What'd he say?"

"He said to stick with the plan and get the boy, so I did." His face scrunched up in pain. "Can you...please...please call that ambulance now. I...I told you everything."

"Why'd you target Thad's family?" I pressed. "And how'd you take the boy from the bus stop?"

Stump opened his mouth to speak, but before he could utter another word, he looked past me and his eyes widened in horror. I glanced over my shoulder, but nothing was there. I couldn't be sure, but it seemed like he was peering right through the gates of hell, and the devil was probably wagging him forward with a crooked finger.

"Where's Daphne?" I demanded quickly, knowing I was running out of time. "Who else is in the house? And what did Gideon do to Wess? Come on, man, redeem yourself! Tell me about the boy!"

As he stared straight ahead, the muscles in his face slowly relaxed and his expression faded to one of emptiness. His head slumped to his left shoulder, and his eyes glazed over.

I shook him violently. "Who else is in the house?"

When he didn't respond, I stretched him out and pounded on his chest. That brought about a sucking reaction from him, but after opening his eyes wide and letting out a rattling gasp, he relaxed once again and sank back onto the earth. He was gone.

I shook my head.

"The devil's got him now," I muttered to Susan, "and he ain't letting go."

CHAPTER 57

After shoving my cell phone in my pocket and standing, I replaced the partially empty magazine in my pistol and turned to my wife. "Could it be a kid that you saw in the window? Maybe Wess Griffin?"

"It's possible."

"You heard what Stump said about Gideon killing him, right?"

She nodded and said, "That's why we need to hurry."

After rushing to my truck, Susan returned with a fresh magazine for the AR-10 and a can of pepper spray. I knew without asking that she had brought the spray for the dogs. We both loved dogs, and we wouldn't want to shoot one unless it was an absolute last resort. As it turned out, it wasn't necessary, because there were no killer Dobermans on the property. In fact, there were no dogs at all.

We made our way to the uneven front porch without being challenged. We weren't sure where Daphne was or if there were more bad guys lurking around, so we had moved one at a time while the other provided cover. Although it was still raining, it was brighter in the clearing on top of the hill, and we were able to survey our surroundings with relative ease.

Still holding my AR-10 at the ready, Susan whispered, "I'll cover the back."

I nodded and waited for her to disappear around the corner to the left. Once I'd given her enough time to set up around back, I stepped gingerly onto the wooden porch. The boards creaked under my weight, and I paused for a second to see if there would be a reaction from inside. There was none, so I stepped closer to the wall. Taking up a position to the right side of a porch swing and using the corner wall as cover, I did a quick-peek to see if the back door was clear.

In that brief instance, I saw that the exterior door was metal with two large panes of glass, while the main door was wooden. The main door had a pane of glass covering the top half, but a thick curtain kept me from seeing inside.

I hesitated while studying the situation. If I were to step out and approach the door, I would leave myself exposed. I didn't see any vehicles in the yard and I hadn't heard any movement from inside, so it was quite possible Wess was in there alone. While Stump hadn't mentioned anyone else being involved in their crimes, he'd died before he could tell me where to find Daphne, so it was also possible that there was an army of bad guys hiding inside the house just waiting to pounce.

And what of Wess? Had Gabriel really done him in? Or was there a chance that the boy was still alive? I hoped desperately for the latter, and I knew I had to take some risks to check on him. Thus, I stepped out into the open.

Taking one careful step at a time and keeping my pistol trained on the window, I drew closer and closer to the door. When I had reached it, I squatted low and knocked softly on the glass to see if I'd get a reaction from inside. Almost instantly, I heard a *thump* from somewhere above me. I grew instantly hopeful.

I waited, but there was no other sound. I was within reach of the handle on the storm door, so I slowly extended my arm and pressed the thumb release. I felt the door come free, and I swung it toward me. The hinges squealed, but that was the only sound I heard. Once the storm door was open, I was able to see that the main door was padlocked from the outside.

I pulled out my cell phone and glanced at the top of the screen. Still no bars. We possessed no legal authority in Tennessee and we had no way to call local law enforcement. What we did have, though, was a confession from one of our murder suspects, which included his statement that the boy was inside and possibly injured or dead. That made my decision easy.

In one swift motion, I shot the heel of my right boot toward the right side of the doorframe. There was a satisfying crunch as wood splintered and the door crashed inward from the force of my kick. I heard some shuffling sounds above me, but that was it.

"Wess!" I called as I stepped into a musky and moldy kitchen. "Wess Griffin, are you here?"

A quick scan of the kitchen and the adjacent living room area told me there were no occupants. That was the good news. The bad news was that there was an open container of antifreeze on the table next to a jug of orange juice and a box of oatmeal. I sucked in a breath.

"Wess!" I yelled as loud as I could. "Don't drink the orange juice!"

I made my way rapidly toward a set of wooden stairs that led to an upper level. Before I reached it, the back door burst open and Susan appeared there, ready for battle.

I indicated the stairs with a nod of my head and continued for it. She nodded and set out to search the lower level.

"Wess, it's the police," I called as I scanned the stairwell above me. "Don't drink the orange juice!"

I had just hit the landing when I heard a frail voice call from somewhere to my right.

"Help! Help me! I'm stuck in here!"

My heart swelled and I felt a lump in my throat as I rushed toward the sound. I came to a bedroom door that was also locked from the outside.

"Stand back, Wess!" I prayed silently to God that he hadn't drunk the poison. If he had, it might already be too late. "I'm gonna break down this door!"

As soon as I heard his footsteps retreat, I quickly kicked the door open. It took a second for my eyes to adjust to the darkness. When I was able to make out the shapes inside the musty room, I saw a young and frightened boy standing there brandishing a chair leg in both hands. The boy's hair was unkempt, there were dark tear-stained smudges on his cheeks, and his clothes were tattered, but he otherwise looked to be in good health. He looked just like the pictures that Thad had given us of his son.

I scanned the interior of the room and sighed when my eyes came upon a small table with a glass of liquid and a bowl of food. It appeared that nothing had been touched.

"Did you drink the orange juice?" I asked, holstering my pistol at the same time.

He shook his head slowly, seemingly confused.

"We're here to rescue you and bring you back to your family," I said. "I'm from Mechant Loup."

Wess let out a screech and dropped the chair leg. With a jolt, he lunged forward and threw himself at me. I caught the boy in midair and lifted him off of his feet. He was big for eight, but I carried him down the stairs like he was Grace's age. As I made my descent, I ran into Susan coming up.

"The house is clear," she said. "There's no one else here."

"There were two bad men," Wess said bravely. "One of them stole me from the bus stop. I want to go home! I want to see my mom and dad again!"

I groaned inwardly and set him down on the floor. Of course he didn't know about his mom. Unless the killers had told him, how could he? One thing was certain...I wasn't going to be the one to break the news to him.

"How did they take you from the bus stop?" I asked while Susan left to check the exterior of the house.

"When I got in my mom's car at the bus stop, I put on my seat belt and asked for ice cream like I always do. I didn't even look to see who was driving." Wess swallowed hard. "We took off fast and went toward the town, and that's when I realized a man with sunglasses and a hat was driving. At first, I thought it was my dad, but when he told me to shut up, I knew it was somebody else."

"Where'd y'all go?"

Wess shrugged. "I don't know. He drove to a cornfield or something, and he dragged me out of the car and put me in the back seat of a truck. Another man was driving the truck, and the first man got in the back seat with me. They told me if I screamed or did anything stupid, they would kill my mom and dad."

Although he must've been frightened, Wess remained composed.

"Do you know where y'all went after that?" I asked.

"We drove far away. It got dark and then it was daylight again, and we were still driving. I slept for a long time, I think. When I woke up, we were here." Wess waved his hand to indicate the house. "When they were driving, they made me lay down on the floor in the back seat. They said they didn't want anybody seeing me."

"Did they hurt you at all?" I asked, fearing the answer.

To my relief, he shook his head.

"No, sir, they just didn't give me a lot of food, and they left me locked in that room upstairs for a long time."

"Are you sure you didn't drink the orange juice?"

Wess bobbed his head up and down. "I was about to, but I heard a knock on the door and I got scared, so I grabbed a stick to protect myself. And...and that's when you came in."

I removed my slicker top and handed it to him. "Well, we've got you now. You're safe. You'll be home before you know it."

A minute later, Susan appeared and said the coast was clear. Once the three of us were outside, I grabbed Wess by the hand.

"Come on, big man," I said. "We need to get out of here right away."

"Will they come back and get me?" he asked, his eyes wide with fright.

"No," I said with confidence. "Those two are never coming back."

That seemed to satisfy him, and he walked bravely beside me. Susan walked ahead of us with the rifle, and I kept my right hand on my pistol. I didn't know where Daphne was or what her involvement might have been, but we weren't taking any chances. We had found Wess alive and well, and we were not about to let anything bad happen to him now.

Looking over my shoulder often, I followed Susan up the long driveway and to my truck. We didn't meet any resistance. Once at my truck, I made sure to keep Wess' attention away from the two dead men at the edge of the mountain, and we tried to get my truck started. We had no such luck. After I'd gathered up what gear I could carry, we secured my truck as best we could, and then I made a quick search of the Haley brothers' truck.

I found a crate of ammunition, a Desert Eagle pistol, and Wess' school bag in plain view. I grabbed the pistol and the school bag and was about to back out of the truck when something caught my eye. It was the corner of a book, and it was sticking out from under the front passenger seat.

I retrieved it and saw that it was a faded copy of Thad's first book, Blood On The Pavement. The front cover was bent back to reveal the first page, where a handwritten note was inscribed. I read it with increasing interest. As I did so, a deep anger began to burn in my chest.

When I was done, I handed the book to Susan and grabbed Wess' hand to begin the long journey back to civilization.

CHAPTER 58

Mechant Loup, Louisiana

Amy watched in disbelief as Thad Griffin squatted low in preparation for his leap from the radio tower.

"No!" she yelled, sprinting forward and waving her arms wildly. "Don't do it! Think about Wess!"

Thad hadn't given them any useful information, so if he died now, they might never know what had happened to his son or his wife.

Amy had only taken three or four steps when Thad leapt from the crossbar upon which he had been standing. What happened next played out in slow motion through her eyes. Thad's body shot upward and outward from the radio tower. As he reached the apex of his trajectory, he seemed to pause in midair. Even through the rain and mist, Amy could see his eyes. They were frantic. It seemed clear that he instantly regretted his decision.

Homer was several feet away and a little lower than Thad. He had been watching the author intently, and it appeared to Amy that he had anticipated the move, because he never hesitated. He sprang from the step bolts and launched himself directly at Thad.

Amy gasped, and someone screamed Homer's name from the highway. There was nothing Amy could do but watch in horror as their newest deputy did exactly what Melvin had warned him not to do: try something heroic.

Homer's arms and legs were spread wide as he sprang through the air, giving the impression of a squirrel leaping from one branch to another. As soon as he collided with Thad, Homer's arms and legs instantly coiled around him like a python smothering its prey. Homer's left arm had caught Thad across the throat, while his right arm had hooked under the author's right armpit. Homer's legs closed in around the gut line, wrapping Thad in a body triangle.

In her peripheral vision, Amy noticed that the slack in Homer's rope was rapidly being taken up as he plunged toward the earth. The last time he had clicked in had been a dozen feet lower than where he had jumped, so he fell a little more than twenty feet before the rope came taut. When that happened, Amy heard an audible grunt from Thad and Homer, while Melvin cursed out loud as he was sent sailing through the air.

When Melvin left the ground, Homer and Thad dropped several more feet, but they were brought up short when Takecia dove on top of Melvin and added her weight to the mix. At that point, Homer and Thad were slammed violently into the sides of the radio tower, and Homer lost his grip on Thad's throat and armpit.

Thad's upper torso bent in half, and he let out a bloodcurdling scream as his head slammed forward into one of his own knees. Amy was certain the man thought he had hit the ground and died. Homer grabbed a handful of Thad's hair and pulled the man back into his clutches, while Baylor rushed forward to held Takecia keep Melvin grounded.

"Hold tight, Homer!" Melvin called in a strained voice. "I'm letting y'all down slowly."

As Amy watched, Homer and Thad began to glide slowly toward the earth.

"Shit, that was too close!" Amy muttered to herself as she leaned back against the nearest vehicle she could find.

"You're telling me!" said a feminine voice to her right. "I haven't even kissed him yet."

Amy glanced over to see Remi Walton standing there soaked from head to toe, looking up toward Homer with frightened eyes. She wasn't even trying to keep the rain off her face, nor could she hide her feelings for the daredevil cop.

By the time Amy looked back toward the radio tower, Homer's feet were just touching the ground and he was releasing his hold on Thad, who fell in a heap.

Amy turned back toward Remi. "What're you waiting for?"

Remi opened her mouth to speak, but clamped it shut. After taking a deep breath, she stomped forward through the sopping ground and pushed her way through Melvin, Baylor, and Takecia.

When she stopped in front of Homer, she paused and looked up at him. Her breasts were heaving and her eyes were fluttering. For a brief moment, Amy thought she would chicken out, but then she grabbed him by the face and pulled his mouth to hers.

"What in the hell is going on?" Takecia asked when Amy joined the group.

"I don't know," Amy admitted, as she watched a shirtless and dripping wet Homer wrap his sinewy arms around Remi. "But I guarantee you this—that boy ain't never been kissed like that before, and that girl ain't never done anything that crazy."

CHAPTER 59

Homer didn't know what caused his heart to beat harder, nearly falling to his death, or feeling Remi's soft lips pressed firmly against his mouth. When she pulled away from him, he nearly fell over from the rush of blood and adrenalin.

"What...what was that for?" he asked as he looked down into her sparkling eyes. Although he could see Melvin and Amy taking Thad into custody in his peripheral vision, it seemed like they were miles away. In fact, it seemed like he and Remi were alone on an island, where no one could hear or see them.

"You seem to have the life expectancy of an adult mayfly," Remi said breathlessly, "so I needed to do that while I was still able."

Homer didn't know what a mayfly was, and he didn't care at that moment. "But...but I thought maybe..."

Homer hesitated, and his voice trailed off.

"What did you think?" There was genuine curiosity in Remi's eyes. "Go on, say it."

"The way that Josh dude was acting," Homer continued, "I thought maybe he was your boyfriend."

"Oh, God, no!" Rain shot from Remi's hair as she shook her head violently from side to side. "He tries to strike up conversations everywhere he sees me, and he keeps begging me to go out with him. I think he's even lied to some of his buddies and said that we're together. I told him it'll never happen and that I don't date cops. He's like a used car salesman who can't take no for an answer, so he keeps pestering me every time he sees me." She paused and giggled. "I guess he was a little confused when he saw us together, with you being a cop and all."

Homer nodded at first, thinking she was letting him know that their lunch hadn't been a date, but then he scowled. "If you don't date cops, then why'd you just kiss me?"

Remi's smile was radiant. "For a smart boy, you sure are clueless."

"What's that mean?"

"It means you're the exception to the rule, Homer Verdin." Her expression grew serious as she rubbed his face and studied his eyes. "No one has ever made my heart flutter the way it did when you first looked at me."

Homer licked his lips. He wanted desperately to kiss Remi again, but he felt the eyes of his companions on them. "I need to get dried off and get dressed," he finally said, as the rain continued to drip down his face, neck, and torso. "Can we finish this later?"

Remi smiled. "Promise?"

"Oh, hell yeah, I promise!"

She raised up to kiss him one last time, and then she returned to her Jeep, which was parked along the road with several other cars. As Homer watched her walk away, he saw a cluster of sheriff's deputies milling about, and he instantly recognized one of them as Josh Morvant. The large deputy stood there glowering at Homer with his feet spread and his arms crossed.

Homer shook his head and went to retrieve his shirt and boots. Once he was back in Baylor's cruiser, his training officer asked if he wanted to sit in on Amy's interrogation of Thad Griffin.

"Since you were in the last interview with Clint and Thad, Amy thinks it'll be good to have you in there."

"Sure, I'll do whatever y'all need me to do," Homer said, but his mind was far from the case. He could still feel Remi's mouth on his, and his heart was still pounding with excitement.

Within minutes, they had reached the office and Homer had changed into some dry clothes he'd borrowed from Baylor. He then met with Amy in the dispatcher's station, and the two of them headed for the interview room. By that time, he had managed to turn his focus back to the job at hand, but Remi was still at the edge of his thoughts.

"Hello, Mr. Griffin," Amy said with a nod. "This is Officr Homer Verdin. You two met earlier on the radio tower."

Thad looked up and gave Homer a sincere nod of appreciat' but he didn't say anything.

"Sir, we need to talk to you about Daphne Potter, and ho

might fit into the attack on your family," Amy began. "I know it's a touchy subject, but it's important that you tell us everything you know. Earlier, you asked about Detective Wolf's whereabouts. Well, he's in Copper Head, Tennessee looking for Wess."

Homer studied Thad's expression as Amy questioned the man. He had no idea what kind of reaction she was looking for, but he did notice the man's face soften when she mentioned his son. His lower lip even began to tremble, and Homer thought he might start crying.

"They...they won't find him," Thad said. "It's too late. He's already gone."

"How could you possibly know that?"

When Thad didn't answer, Amy leaned forward and placed a hand on his forearm. "Please, Mr. Griffin, help us understand what's going on. A lot has happened over the past few days. Your wife and two other people have lost their lives, and you and Officer Verdin here could've also died. If you know anything, I think you owe it to yourself and to the rest of us to say what it is."

Homer gulped silently when Amy mentioned he could've lost his life. He hadn't thought that was the case for even a second. He had put his full and complete trust in Melvin and the rope, and he never thought he was in any danger. If what she said was true, then that was a sobering prospect.

"I...I don't know for sure who did this," Thad began slowly. "I do know that they're using the first book I ever wrote as a blueprint for their actions."

"The one that Officer Verdin mentioned?" Amy asked. "Blood On The Pavement?"

"Yes, ma'am." Thad took a breath. "In...in the book, a child is kidnapped, and that child is murdered three days later. I...I believe whoever killed Ann has also killed Wess. If he isn't dead already, they'll kill him today."

Thad stopped talking and lowered his head to weep silently for a moment. Finally, he looked up and continued. "I...I don't want to accuse anyone falsely, but I might know who's responsible."

"Daphne?" Amy asked.

Homer watched as Thad shook his head slowly from side to side.

"Daphne's dead," he said. "She killed herself a few months ago. Right before we moved here. In fact..."

"Yes?" Amy asked after he allowed his voice to trail off.

"That's the real reason we moved," Thad finally said. "I was at a book signing in Plain Ridge one day, and one of Daphne's brothers approached me with a copy of my first book. It was the one I had given to Daphne. He...he told me she had committed suicide after she found out about my fame and fortune. He also said...um...he threatened me and my family."

"How?" Amy asked. "What did he say?"

Homer found himself leaning forward, hanging on the author's every word. He was fascinated by the interrogation, and although he wasn't allowed to speak during the process, he was happy to be there.

"He said the same thing that happened in the book would happen to me and my family." Thad shifted in his chair. "He...he's been known to start trouble with people, so I took him at his word. I...that's when I decided to move my family far away from there. I had no idea they would follow us here."

"Who do you mean when you say *they*?" Amy asked.

"Him and his brother," Thad explained. "There're two of them. Gideon and Stump."

Homer watched Amy nod slowly. She remained quiet for a long moment, and it seemed to make Thad more and more uneasy.

"Daphne killed herself because of you, didn't she?" Amy suddenly asked.

Thad jerked as though he'd been slapped. "What did you say?"

"You heard me," Amy said coolly. "Please answer the question, and understand that there will be no judgment from me or Officer Verdin. We're only concerned with bringing Wess back home safely—nothing more."

Thad glanced at Homer, and Homer felt it appropriate to nod, so he did so.

"God forgive me," Thad whispered, and then sat in silence for another long moment.

Finally, Thad began telling his story, and it appeared to Homer's untrained eye that he became more and more relaxed as he talked. He was reminded of a scripture his mom had quoted on more than one occasion as he was growing up:

"Then said Jesus to those Jews which believed on him, 'If ye continue in my word, then are ye my disciples indeed;

"And ye shall know the truth, and the truth shall make you free."

Homer had always known his mom was a smart woman, but he was still amazed every time something she used to say to him as a child came to pass in the present. As he watched Thad Griffin make his statement, he knew everything the man was saying was the truth, because it seemed to make him free.

CHAPTER 60

Interview Room #2

Amy tried to remain emotionless as Thad Griffin told his story, but the more he talked, the more she began to seethe.

"When Daphne—she was a Haley back then—and I first started dating, things were hectic but nice. I worked two shit jobs while writing my first book, and so did Daphne. Since we didn't have much spare time, we wanted to spend all of it together, and that didn't allow much time for anything else. We lost touch with family and friends."

"Did you stop her from seeing her people?" Amy asked. "Or was it her choice?"

"It wasn't really a choice," Thad said. "We were just so busy that we didn't have time for anyone but each other. I...I went almost two years without talking to my mom during that period of my life. She later told me that she didn't know if I was alive or dead, and it nearly killed her."

"You didn't talk to your mom for *two years*?"

"Yes, ma'am." Thad sighed. "Anyway, when the book was done, I tried to get an agent, but that didn't work out. I eventually decided to go through a vanity press just to get it out into the world. I thought once people started reading it they would love it, but I couldn't get anybody to give it a shot."

He paused and took a deep breath. "I have to admit, I got depressed and downright ornery when I couldn't sell a single copy. Well, I take that back. I did sell two copies—one to the local library, and one to Daphne. She wanted to buy the first copy of the first book I ever wrote, so I let her do it with her own money. After that, I couldn't even give them away."

"That must've been rough," Amy agreed. "Did that negatively affect your relationship?"

Thad nodded. "I…I started drinking a lot to drown the depression, and I became a little aggressive at times. I remember this one night in particular. We had gotten into a really bad argument, and she had rushed up to me like she was going to hit me. I don't even remember what we were arguing about, but I kicked her in the privates a few times and…and she fell down the stairs. I…I wasn't trying to hurt her. I was only trying to stop her from attacking me, but I used too much force. She was hurt pretty bad, and it took more than a month to heal."

Amy stared down at her notes for a long moment, trying to control the anger that was burning in her chest.

"Did she tell the doctors what happened?" Amy finally asked. She needed Thad to continue talking, so she was extra careful not to grit her teeth. "Did they suspect that she had been abused?"

"She refused to go to the doctor. I…I think she was too afraid of me to go." He lowered his eyes in shame. "We stayed together for a few months after that night. I promised her I'd get help for my drinking—and I did—but I messed up one weekend. The Falcons were losing to the Saints for the second time that season, but they were coming back at the end of the game. Well, our quarterback threw an interception right when Daphne walked in the living room, and I kind of snapped. I threw my beer can at her and it hit her in the face."

"Hold up." Amy leaned close to Thad. When she spoke again, her voice was laced with contempt. "You blamed Daphne because your team's quarterback threw an interception? You thought Daphne—who was in her living room a million miles away from the stadium—caused your team to lose the game?"

"I know it's stupid," Thad admitted. "I was a different man when I was drinking."

Amy wanted to vehemently call bullshit, and she also wanted to rip his throat out, but she couldn't. She was bound by the law she served. So, instead, she settled back into her chair and forced herself to ask him what happened after that incident.

"She left me one day while I was working," he explained. "I came home to an empty house and found a note saying if I ever tried to pursue her, she'd tell her brothers what I did and they would kill me. I...I always did love her. I even named a character in my first series after her. I had to use her married name, though, because Ann had found an old love letter from her, and she knew her name was Daphne Haley."

"Go on, tell us what happened after she left you," Amy said, no longer trying to hide her disgust.

"Well, I finally got the help I needed and moved on with my life," Thad said. "I met Ann and things started to go really well for me—both with my personal life and in my writing career. I got a publisher for my first book series, we had Wess, and then the Gator Haven books were a big hit. Everything was going well, and then I got that visit from one of her brothers."

Thad stopped talking and he began to tremble. "He...he told me that Daphne had gotten married, but I already knew that. I had seen the announcement in the papers way back then. What I didn't know was that she and her husband had tried having kids, but she never got pregnant. At first, they thought it was the man's fault, but he got tested and everything was normal with him. When...when they tested her, they found out she was infertile. Her husband wanted a woman who could give him kids, so he left her.

"They said she was devastated, but after a while, she got back on her feet and tried dating again. It didn't go well for her. Every man she found wanted to have kids, and they each broke up with her when they found out she was barren. They said it wrecked her, and she spiraled into a deep and dark depression. And that's when she saw me on the news with Ann and Wess. Her brother said it was more than she could bear. That's when she decided to end her own life."

Amy clenched and unclenched her fists in plain view of Thad. It was all she could do to keep her voice calm. "Was she infertile because of the beating you gave her?"

"They...they think so, because she wrote a suicide note on the first page of my book blaming me for everything." Tears were rolling freely down his face, but Amy wasn't moved by it. "Apparently, the injury she sustained had caused some internal damage and they figured it got infected. Since she hadn't gone to the doctor to get treated, it caused scarring or something. I'm not real sure what exactly happened. I just know she blamed me for everything."

"I'd blame you, too," Amy said with a snort, pausing to study her notes for a second. "Have you suspected Daphne's brothers this whole time?"

Thad nodded. "They've followed the plot to my first book like a blueprint. They ran over Ann with her own car and stole it. They kidnapped Wess. It's the third day, so...so they've already...he's already gone!"

Thad let out a scream and began bawling loudly. He banged his head on the desk several times, but Amy didn't try to stop him. She was overcome with sorrow for Wess. However, she didn't feel anything but hate for the man sitting before her. She glanced at Homer and rolled her eyes before turning back to Thad.

"If you knew they were responsible for kidnapping your son, and you knew you had three days to save him," Amy began in a deathly tone, "why in the hell didn't you tell us?"

"I...I didn't want y'all...to...to find out about Daphne...and...and what I had done," he said through choking sobs. "It...it would've ruined me, don't you see?"

"Oh, I see clearly," Amy said in unveiled contempt. What sickened her the most was that Daphne was dead, so Thad would never have to answer for his crimes.

"That's why I tried to kill myself," Thad continued. "I couldn't live with what I had done."

"No, that's not it." Amy shook her head. "You've been living just fine with what you had done. You knew we were getting close to finding out who you really were. You knew you were about to lose it all—that's what you couldn't live with."

When Thad didn't say anything more, Amy was about to ask another question, but her cell phone rang.

CHAPTER 61

Amy put the phone to her ear without looking at the screen.

"This is Amy," she said, staring daggers into Thad's eyes while she talked.

"Amy, it's Clint," came a tired voice. "We've got the boy. We found Wess Griffin."

"What?" Amy sprang to her feet. "Is he okay? Is he alive? Is he hurt? Come on, tell me already!"

"Yeah," Clint said. "He's fine. Daphne's brothers had him locked up in a house in Devil's Gap, Tennessee."

"I can't believe he's okay!" Amy felt as though a huge boulder had been lifted from her shoulders. "What happened?"

"They attempted to poison him, but he's fine. And before we got to him, the brothers shot up my truck pretty bad. It's disabled. We had to hump out of there on foot."

"Wait—there was a shootout?"

"Yeah, they ambushed Susan when she was going for help. Thankfully, we were able to get them before they got us. One of them died before he could talk, but the other fella confessed before the devil collected his soul. He admitted to murdering Ann and kidnapping Wess." Clint paused for a breath. "And Ames, we got to Wess in the nick of time. Those assholes had fed him some orange juice laced with antifreeze."

"Antifreeze?" Amy asked incredulously. "Oh, I hope they died a horrible death! Did he drink any of it?"

"He said he was about to when he heard us knock on the door." Clint let out a long sigh. "Had we been a few minutes later…"

"That would've been a bad way to go." Amy shook her head at Thad. Had he admitted what he'd done on day one, they might've found Wess much sooner. She turned her attention back to her call with Clint. "How far did you have to hump?"

"About ten miles, and through a storm," Clint said. "It seems someone heard the gunfire and called the local sheriff. Thank God the calvary showed up when they did, because the weather got even worse. At least one tree fell in the road while we were walking, and the creek overran its bank by a lot. It wasn't a place for a small boy."

"What about you and Susan?" Amy asked, her voice softening. "Are y'all okay? Any injuries?"

"We're fine. Susan has some scratches to her face, but she's okay otherwise."

Clint went on to explain in more detail what had happened, including that he had found a copy of Thad's book with Daphne's suicide note inscribed on the first page. He read it to her, and it was exactly as Thad had detailed; Daphne had rightfully blamed him for robbing her of the ability to bear children.

Clint also updated Amy on Wess' status, and he ended by saying the local sheriff had called in TBI to work the shooting, and that he and Susan would have to remain there until they'd been interviewed.

"What in the hell is the TBI?" Amy wanted to know.

"Tennessee Bureau of Investigation," Clint explained. "They're like the FBI for the state, only they're competent."

Amy laughed. "Get home safe."

"Will do."

"They found Wess," she said with a sigh after she'd ended the call. "He's fine. Child Services contacted your mom. She's en route to get him. After the State of Tennessee finds out what a piece of shit you are, I'm sure they'd hesitate to give you custody of a Vietnamese pot-bellied pig, much less your own—"

"Wait," Thad interrupted. "They found Wess? And he's okay?"

Amy nodded. "He wasn't hurt at all."

"What in the hell?" Thad's tears had suddenly dried up. "Are you telling me all of this was for nothing?"

Amy cocked her head to the side. "What do you mean?"

"What I mean is, did I just tell you all of this for nothing?" He was exasperated. "Everything I just told you—none of it had to be said!"

"Oh, but I'm glad you did." Amy leaned forward and stared him right in the eyes. "In fact, I might become a writer myself someday. However, instead of writing fiction like you do, I'll write true crime.

Yeah, I'll pen the story of a piece of shit, rat bastard author who chose fame over his family."

Coming June of 2024:

But Not Forthcoming: A Clint Wolf Novel

While waiting for the next Clint Wolf book, please consider reading the London Carter Mystery Series, also by BJ Bourg.

BJ Bourg is a former professional boxer and a lifelong martial artist who hails from the swamps of Louisiana. A thirty-year veteran of law enforcement, he has worked as a patrol cop, a detective, a detective sergeant, a police academy instructor, and the chief investigator for a district attorney's office. He has successfully investigated all types of felony cases and has trained hundreds of law enforcement officers in self-defense, firearms, criminal operations, and many other areas. He retired in October of 2020 and is now a fulltime writer.

Throughout his career, Bourg has served on many specialized units such as SWAT, Honor Guard, the Explosives Search Team, and the Homicide Response Team. He founded his agency's sniper program and served as its leader and instructor for nearly a decade. A graduate of seven basic and advanced sniper schools, he deployed as the primary sniper on dozens of call-outs, including barricaded subjects, hostage rescue operations, and fugitive apprehensions. He also served as the sniper instructor for the 2001 L.T.P.O.A. Conference.

Bourg has been the recipient of numerous awards, including Top Shooter at an FBI Sniper School, the Distinguished Service Medal, and Certificates of Commendation for his work as a homicide detective. He is a public speaker and has also written dozens of articles for law enforcement magazines, covering a wide range of topics such as defensive tactics, sniper deployment, suspect interrogation, report writing, and more. Above all else, he is a father, husband, and pépère, and the highlight of his life is spending time with his beautiful wife, wonderful children, adorable grandchildren, and German shepherds.

Bourg is originally from Galliano, Louisiana, and he lived most of his life in the Mathews area. He now proudly calls Tellico Plains, Tennessee his home.

Made in United States
Orlando, FL
01 March 2025

59049467R00152